文法重點總是記不住嗎？
連結相關文法概念✕快速釐清學習盲點
心智圖帶你輕鬆學文法！

本書使用方式

心智圖整理文法重點，預習複習都輕鬆

　　人的大腦是靠影像來記憶與思考，所以比起條列式的筆記，在編排上較多變的心智圖更容易幫助記憶。本書共17個單元，每單元的開頭都會有一張囊括本單元所有文法重點觀念的心智圖，將相關聯的重點串聯起來。不僅可以在開始學習單元內容前拿來預習，還是考前快速複習的最佳材料。

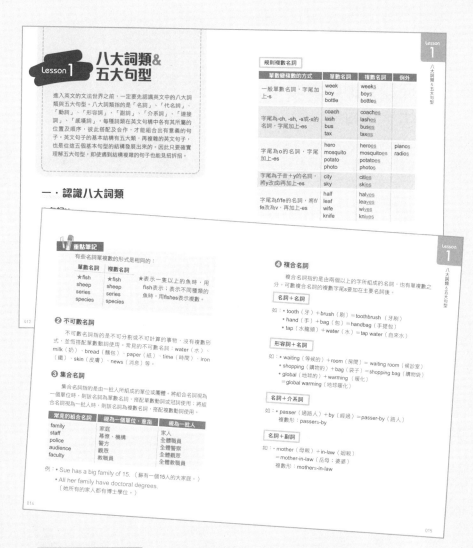

Lesson 1 八大詞類&五大句型

進入英文的文法世界之前，一定要先閱讀英文中的八大詞類與五大句型。八大詞類指的是「名詞」、「代名詞」、「動詞」、「形容詞」、「副詞」、「介系詞」、「連接詞」、「感嘆詞」，每種詞類在英文句構中各有其所屬的位置及順序，彼此搭配及合作，才能組合出有意義的句子。英文句子的基本結構有五大句型，再複雜的英文句子，也是從這五個基本句型的結構發展出來的。因此只要確實理解五大句型，即使遇到結構複雜的句子也能見招拆招。

一·認識八大詞類

規則複數名詞

單複數變複數的方式	單數名詞	複數名詞	例外
一般單數名詞，字尾加上 -s	week boy bottle	weeks boys bottles	
字尾為-ch, -sh, -s或-x的名詞，字尾加上-es	coach lash bus tax	coaches lashes buses taxes	
字尾為o的名詞，字尾加上-es	hero mosquito potato photo	heroes mosquitoes potatoes photos	pianos radios
字尾為子音+y的名詞，將y改成i再加上-es	city sky	cities skies	
字尾為f/fe的名詞，將f/fe改為v，再加上-es	half leaf wife knife	halves leaves wives knives	

重點筆記

有些名詞單複數的形式是相同的：

單數名詞	複數名詞
★fish sheep series species	★fish sheep series species

★表示一隻以上的魚時，用fish表示；表示不同種類的魚時，用fishes表示複數。

② 不可數名詞

不可數名詞指的是不可分割或不可計量的事物，沒有複數形式，並恆搭配單數動詞使用。常見的不可數名詞：water（水）、milk（奶）、bread（麵包）、paper（紙）、time（時間）、iron（鐵）、skin（皮膚）、news（消息）等。

③ 集合名詞

集合名詞指的是由一批人所組成的單位或團體。將組合名詞視為一個單位時，則該名詞為單數名詞，搭配單數動詞或冠詞使用；將組合名詞視為一批人時，則該名詞為複數名詞，搭配複數動詞使用。

常見的組合名詞	視為一個單位，意指	視為一批人
family	家庭	家人
staff	幕僚、機構	全體職員
police	警方	全體警察
audience	觀眾	全體觀眾
faculty	教職員	全體教職員

例：• Sue has a big family of 15.（蘇有一個15人的大家庭。）
• All her family have doctoral degrees.（她所有的家人都有博士學位。）

④ 複合名詞

複合名詞指的是由兩個以上的字所組成的名詞，也有單複數之分。可數複合名詞的複數字尾s要加在主要名詞後。

名詞＋名詞

如：• tooth（牙）＋brush（刷）＝toothbrush（牙刷）
• hand（手）＋bag（包）＝handbag（手提包）
• tap（水龍頭）＋water（水）＝tap water（自來水）

形容詞＋名詞

如：• waiting（等候的）＋room（房間）＝ waiting room（候診室）
• shopping（購物的）＋bag（袋子）＝shopping bag（購物袋）
• global（地球的）＋warming（暖化）＝global warming（地球暖化）

名詞＋介系詞

如：• passer（過路人）＋by（經過）＝passer-by（路人）
複數形：passers-by

名詞＋副詞

如：• mother（母親）＋in-law（姻親）
＝mother-in-law（岳母；婆婆）
複數形：mothers-in-law

★學習關鍵2

詳細解析文法，一次破解所有疑難雜症

每一單元的文法皆有詳盡又好理解的解析，再搭配大量的例句示範與比較，讓你一看就懂文法在句子中的實際用法。「重點筆記」欄位更進階提醒文法使用上，不能不注意的小細節，幫你避開常見錯誤以及易混淆觀念，學習更全面！

多元題目即時驗收，找出學習盲點

　　本書每講解完一項文法重點，就有五題的「馬上動手練一練」，多元題型依文法重點變化，讓你每學完一個重點，就可以馬上動手實際練習，將文法知識融會貫通，學習成效更顯著！此外，每一單元結束後，還有「文法總複習」馬上驗收本單元學習成果，寫完後別忘了閱讀詳解，找出學習盲點喔！

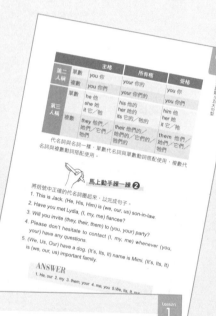

Preface 前言

　　如果說單字是英語學習的基石，那麼文法就是將單字砌成橋梁所不可或缺的水泥。沒有文法的話，單字就無法有規律的堆疊起來，也就無法形成有意義或具有完整意義的句子。所以光是背單字是無法讓我們用英文進行有效溝通的。

　　然而說起來容易，做起來難。文法是許多英語學習者的罩門，甚至有許多人因為怕文法錯誤，導致在生活中不敢開口說英文，花了許多心力學英文卻無用武之地。更何況文法不好，不只是影響口說和寫作能力，更有甚者，會讓人在閱讀及聽力上受到影響。這是因為許多英文表達方式仰賴對文法及語句結構的理解，如果對文法不求甚解的話，很可能就會產生誤解喔！

　　那麼要如何才能學好文法呢？首先，我們要先釐清不同詞性在語句中的功能，以及組成句子的基本結構。接著，再藉由學習常用的特殊用法與句型，來完善文法知識。本書編排難度循序漸進，由最基礎的「八大詞類與五大句型」開始介紹，並藉由心智圖來幫助建構完整文法體系，讓讀者能更輕易地掌握文法運用的規則與邏輯。最後再利用習題來檢視學習盲點，就萬無一失了。只要跟著本書按部就班學習，英文文法就再也難不倒你！

　　希望本書的讀者們，都能從本書獲得想要的收穫，讓文法不再是英語學習的阻礙，而是讓英文能力突飛猛進的助力。

Contents 目錄

五大句型

S＋V
→He ran.

S＋V＋O
→I hit him.

S＋V＋SC
→She is beautiful.

S＋V＋O1＋O2
→She bought me a gift.

S＋V＋O＋OC
→You made me proud.

Lesson 1

八大詞類 & 五大句型

八大詞類

名詞 Noun
- 可數名詞：cats, lashes, feet
- 不可數名詞：water, time
- 集合名詞：family, police
- 複合名詞：shopping bag

代名詞 Pronoun
- 主格：I, we, you, he, she, it, they
- 所有格：my, our, your, his, her, its, their
- 受格：me, us, you, him, her, it, them

動詞 Verb
- 及物動詞：要加受詞
- 不及物動詞：不加受詞

形容詞 Adjective
- 修飾名詞

副詞 Adverb
- 一般副詞：修飾動詞、形容詞、副詞
- 頻率副詞：always, seldom
- 時間副詞：now, today
- 地方副詞：here, home

介系詞 Preposition
- in, on, by, at

連接詞 Conjunction
- 對等連接詞：and, but, or
- 相關連接詞：either...or...
- 從屬連接詞：because, if

感嘆詞 Interjection
- oh, wow, ouch

Lesson 1 八大詞類& 五大句型

進入英文的文法世界之前，一定要先認識英文中的八大詞類與五大句型。八大詞類指的是「名詞」、「代名詞」、「動詞」、「形容詞」、「副詞」、「介系詞」、「連接詞」、「感嘆詞」，每種詞類在英文句構中各有其所屬的位置及順序，彼此搭配及合作，才能組合出有意義的句子。英文句子的基本結構有五大類，再複雜的英文句子，也是從這五個基本句型的結構發展出來的。因此只要確實理解五大句型，即使遇到結構複雜的句子也能見招拆招。

一・認識八大詞類

◆名詞Noun
→表示具體的人、事、物或抽象概念之名稱

名詞有單複數之分，在英文的使用中，我們會以單數動詞搭配單數名詞，並以複數動詞搭配複數名詞。一般而言，單數可數名詞及不可數名詞，會搭配單數動詞；複數可數名詞，會搭配複數動詞。組合名詞則可以視情況搭配單數動詞或複數動詞使用。

❶ 可數名詞

單數可數名詞前面通常會有冠詞a/an（表示一個……）或是定冠詞the（表示指定），複數可數名詞則不加冠詞a/an，其表示複數的方式有規則及不規則兩種：

八大詞類＆五大句型

規則複數名詞

單數變複數的方式	單數名詞	複數名詞	例外
一般單數名詞，字尾加上-s	week boy bottle	week<u>s</u> boy<u>s</u> bottle<u>s</u>	
字尾為-ch, -sh, -s或-x的名詞，字尾加上-es	coach lash bus tax	coach<u>es</u> lash<u>es</u> bus<u>es</u> tax<u>es</u>	
字尾為o的名詞，字尾加上-es	hero mosquito potato photo	hero<u>es</u> mosquito<u>es</u> potato<u>es</u> photo<u>s</u>	piano<u>s</u> radio<u>s</u>
字尾為子音＋y的名詞，將y改成i再加上-es	city sky	cit<u>ies</u> sk<u>ies</u>	
字尾為f/fe的名詞，將f/fe改為v，再加上-es	half leaf wife knife	hal<u>ves</u> lea<u>ves</u> wi<u>ves</u> kni<u>ves</u>	

不規則複數名詞

	單數名詞		複數名詞	
改變母音的名詞	f<u>oo</u>t t<u>oo</u>th	man woman	f<u>ee</u>t t<u>ee</u>th	m<u>e</u>n wom<u>e</u>n
字尾加上ren或en的名詞	child	ox	child<u>ren</u>	ox<u>en</u>
字尾改變的名詞	dat<u>um</u> cris<u>is</u> phenomen<u>on</u>		data cris<u>es</u> phenomen<u>a</u>	
整個字改變的名詞	person mouse		people mice	

重點筆記

有些名詞單複數的形式是相同的：

單數名詞	複數名詞
★fish	★fish
sheep	sheep
series	series
species	species

★表示一隻以上的魚時，用 fish表示；表示不同種類的魚時，用fishes表示複數。

❷ 不可數名詞

不可數名詞指的是不可分割或不可計算的事物，沒有複數形式，並恆搭配單數動詞使用。常見的不可數名詞：water（水）、milk（奶）、bread（麵包）、paper（紙）、time（時間）、iron（鐵）、skin（皮膚）、news（消息）等。

❸ 集合名詞

集合名詞指的是由一批人所組成的單位或團體。將組合名詞視為一個單位時，則該名詞為單數名詞，搭配單數動詞或冠詞使用；將組合名詞視為一批人時，則該名詞為複數名詞，搭配複數動詞使用。

常見的組合名詞	視為一個單位，意指	視為一批人
family	家庭	家人
staff	幕僚、機構	全體職員
police	警方	全體警察
audience	觀眾	全體觀眾
faculty	教職員	全體教職員

例：• Sue has a big family of 15. （蘇有一個15人的大家庭。）

　　• All her family have doctoral degrees.
　　（她所有的家人都有博士學位。）

❹ 複合名詞

複合名詞指的是由兩個以上的字所組成的名詞，也有單複數之分。可數複合名詞的複數字尾s要加在主要名詞後。

名詞＋名詞

如：• tooth（牙）＋brush（刷）＝toothbrush（牙刷）
• hand（手）＋bag（包）＝handbag（手提包）
• tap（水龍頭）＋water（水）＝tap water（自來水）

形容詞＋名詞

如：• waiting（等候的）＋room（房間）＝ waiting room（候診室）
• shopping（購物的）＋bag（袋子）＝shopping bag（購物袋）
• global（地球的）＋warming（暖化）
＝global warming（地球暖化）

名詞＋介系詞

如：• passer（過路人）＋by（經過）＝passer-by（路人）
複數形：passers-by

名詞＋副詞

如：• mother（母親）＋in-law（姻親）
＝mother-in-law（岳母；婆婆）
複數形：mothers-in-law

馬上動手練一練 ❶

將括號內的名詞改為複數，以完成句子

1. _____(mango), _____(melon), _____(peach) and_____
   (guava) are all my favorite _____(fruit).
2. We need more_____(spoon), _____ (fork) and_____(knife)
   for our guests.
3. We are a group of eight_____(person). There are three_____
   (man) and five_____(woman).
4. These_____(shoe) are too small for me. My_____(foot) can
   hardly fit in.
5. I bought some gifts for my_____(parent-in-law).

ANSWER

1. Mangos/Mangoes, melons, peaches, guavas, fruits
2. spoons, forks, knives
3. people, men, women
4. shoes, feet
5. parents-in-law

◆代名詞Pronoun
→在知道所指為何的情況下，代替名詞

代名詞有單複數的區別，並有主格、所有格及受格三種形式：

		主格	所有格	受格
第一人稱	單數	I 我	my 我的	me 我
	複數	we 我們	our 我們的	us 我們

		主格	所有格	受格
第二人稱	單數	you 你	your 你的	you 你
	複數	you 你們	your 你們的	you 你們
第三人稱	單數	he 他 she 她 it 它／牠	his 他的 her 她的 its 它的／牠的	him 他 her 她 it 它／牠
	複數	they 他們／ 她們／它們／ 牠們	their 他們的／ 她們的／它們的／ 牠們的	them 他們／ 她們／它們／ 牠們

　　代名詞與名詞一樣，單數代名詞與單數動詞搭配使用，複數代名詞與複數動詞搭配使用。

馬上動手練一練 ❷

將括號中正確的代名詞圈起來，以完成句子。

1. This is Jack. (He, His, Him) is (we, our, us) son-in-law.

2. Have you met Lydia, (I, my, me) fiancee?

3. Will you invite (they, their, them) to (you, your) party?

4. Please don't hesitate to contact (I, my, me) whenever (you, your) have any questions.

5. (We, Us, Our) have a dog. (It's, Its, It) name is Mimi. (It's, Its, It) is (we, our, us) important family.

ANSWER

1. He, our 2. my 3. them, your 4. me, you 5.We, Its, It, our

◆動詞Verb
→用來描述人、事、物的動作或行為狀態

動詞可分為「不及物動詞」與「及物動詞」。

❶ 不及物動詞表達主詞所做的動作，後面不需接受詞

　如：・She cried.（她哭了。）

　　　・The door opens.（門打開了。）

❷ 及物動詞表達主詞對受詞所做的動作，後面需接受詞，作為動作接受者。有些動詞會有兩個受詞。

　如：・He hit me.（他打我。）

　　　・They brought me some flowers.
　　　（他們帶了些花給我。）

英文句子有時態之分，藉由助動詞或動詞變化表示不同時態。

❶ 現在式時態使用動詞簡單式，第三人稱單數主詞要搭配單數動詞。

　如：・We love each other.（我們彼此相愛。）

　　　・He works hard.（他努力工作。）

❷ 過去式時態使用動詞過去式。

　如：・It rained yesterday.（昨天下雨。）

❸ 未來式時態則使用未來助動詞will表示。

　如：・She will come.（她將會來。）

❹ 進行式使用be動詞與現在分詞來表示。

　如：・They are having dinner.（他們正在吃晚餐。）

❺ 完成式時態用助動詞have/has與動詞的過去分詞來表示。

　如：・I have cleaned up the room.
　　　（我已經清理好房間了。）

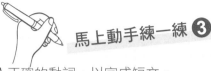

在空格中填入正確的動詞，以完成短文。

named	took	likes	take
has	wants	saw	decided

Larry [1]＿＿＿ dogs. He always [2]＿＿＿ a dog as a pet. One day, Larry's father [3]＿＿＿ him to the animal shelter. There, Larry [4]＿＿＿ a very cute puppy, and [5]＿＿＿ to [6]＿＿＿ him home. Larry [7]＿＿＿ the puppy "Hero". Now he [8]＿＿＿ a pet dog. Larry is very happy.

ANSWER

1. likes 2. wants 3. took 4. saw 5. decided 6. take 7. named 8. has

◆形容詞Adjective
→用來描述或說明名詞或代名詞

❶ 形容詞通常放在名詞前修飾名詞

如：• a happy child （一個快樂的孩子）

• my friend （我的朋友）

❷ 形容詞也可放在連綴動詞後作補語

如：• Strangers can be dangerous. （陌生人可能很危險。）

• The melon tastes sweet. （甜瓜嚐起來很甜。）

一個名詞可以有一個以上的形容詞來修飾，其格式、位置有一定的排列順序，一般來說，「表達個人主觀感覺」的形容詞會放在「描述客觀事實」的形容詞之前。

如：• a beautiful white dress （一件美麗的白色洋裝）

• a famous Japanese singer （一位有名的日本歌手）

描述客觀事實的形容詞通常按以下次序排列：

大小＞年齡＞形狀＞顏色＞血統＞材料＞用途

如：a young Indian woman 一個年輕的印度女性

　　a large white wooden house 一棟很大的白色木屋

馬上動手練一練 4

將括號中的形容詞按適當順序排列，以完成句子

1. (leather/white/small) –
   She bought a ＿＿＿＿＿＿＿ handbag.
2. (lonely/old/poor) –
   He is just a ＿＿＿＿＿＿＿ man.
3. (evening/beautiful/pink) –
   Amanda looks gorgeous in that ＿＿＿＿＿＿＿dress.
4. (math/three/difficult/these) –
   I'm trying to solve ＿＿＿＿＿＿＿ questions.
5. (cozy/Italian/small) –
   We love having dinner at that ＿＿＿＿＿＿＿ restaurant.

ANSWER

1. small white leather　2. poor lonely old　3. beautiful pink evening
4. these three difficult math　5. small cozy Italian

◆副詞Adverb
→副詞可用來修飾動詞、形容詞或其他副詞，也可說明動作發生的頻率、時間或地點

❶ 一般副詞修飾動詞、形容詞或其他副詞

副詞位置：動詞後，形容詞或副詞前。

如：• The dog runs fast. （這隻狗跑得很快。）

　　• It is very hot. （天氣非常熱。）

　　• They work extremely hard. （他們工作得極度認真。）

❷ 頻率副詞說明動作發生的頻率

副詞位置：be動詞後，一般動詞或形容詞前。

如：• She's always late for work. （她上班總是遲到。）

　　• I seldom stay up. （我很少熬夜。）

❸ 時間副詞描述動作發生的時間

副詞位置：句尾。

如：• They left yesterday. （他們昨天離開了。）

　　• Get out now. （現在就給我出去！）

❹ 地方副詞表示動作發生的地點

副詞位置：句尾。

如：• Let's sit here. （我們就坐在這裡吧。）

　　• I'm going home. （我要回家了。）

重點筆記

若一個句子中同時有時間副詞及地方副詞，先後順序為：
地方副詞＞時間副詞。

如：• We went there last week. （我們上週才去過那兒。）

　　• Could you come here immediately? （你可以立刻過來這兒嗎？）

馬上動手練一練 ❺

將括號中的副詞加入句子中

1. The boy cried. (sadly)

_____

2. The woman spoke fast, so I couldn't understand her. (too/ clearly)

_____

3. He told us a hilarious joke. (very)

_____

4. We eat Chinese food for dinner. (often)

_____

5. The man was killed. (three years ago/ right here)

_____

ANSWER

1. The boy cried sadly.
2. The woman spoke too fast, so I couldn't understand her clearly.
3. He told us a very hilarious joke.
4. We often eat Chinese food for dinner.
5. The man was killed right here three years ago.

◆介系詞Preposition
→用來表示兩者之間的關係，或說明地點、時間、方式、因果，也可動詞連用，形成片語動詞

如：• I don't want to talk about it. （我不想討論這件事。）

　　• Look at this picture. （看這張圖片。）

❶ 介系詞後面接名詞、代名詞、動名詞，以形成介系詞片語

> 表示地點的介系詞片語 ：介系詞＋地方＝地方副詞

如：• in the park （在公園裡）　• under the tree （在樹下）

　　• by the window （在窗邊）

　　• in front of the house （在屋子前面）

> 表示時間的介系詞片語 ：介系詞＋時間＝時間副詞

如：• on time （準時）　　　　• at three o'clock （在三點）

　　• on Sunday （在星期天）　• by tomorrow （明天以前）

　　• within three days （在三天之內）

> 表示方式的介系詞片語 ：介系詞＋工具

如：• by bus （搭公車）

　　• with chopsticks （用筷子）• on foot （步行）

> 表示因果的介系詞片語 ：

如：• for some reason （為了某個原因）

> 描述服裝的介系詞片語 ：

如：• in white （穿著白衣的）

❷ 介系詞與動詞連用，形成片語動詞。

如：• turn down 拒絕　　• pick up 撿起來　　• take off 脫掉
　　• take care of 照顧　　• look after 看顧　　• laugh at 嘲笑

馬上動手練一練 ❻

選出適當的介系詞填入空格中

at	into	by	behind	for

1. Traveling around the city _____ MRT is rather cheap and convenient.
2. Please do not park your car _____ the gate of the hotel.
3. We plan to move _____ our new apartment next week.
4. The concert has been cancelled _____ some unknown reason.
5. The money was hidden _____ the picture.

ANSWER

1. by　2. at　3. into　4. for　5. behind

◆連接詞Conjunction
→用來連接單字、片語或子句

　　連接詞依功能可分為對等連接詞、相關連接詞及從屬連接詞，連接詞所連接的前後詞性須保持一致。

❶ 對等連接詞

如：and, but, for, or, yet, so等。

- The new secretary can speak fluent Chinese, English and Spanish. （新秘書會説流利的中文、英文及西班牙文。）
- Would you like to pay by credit card or by cash? （你想用信用卡或現金付費？）

❷ 相關連接詞

如：either...or..., neither...nor..., both...and..., whether...or..., not only...but also...等。

- Either Sam or James will be appointed the director of the Finance Department. （不是山姆就是詹姆士會被任命為財務部主任。）
- Both Tokyo and London are cosmopolitan cities. （東京與倫敦都是國際大都會。）

❸ 從屬連接詞

如：if, before, because, when, although等。

- You can contact me if you have any questions. （如果你有任何問題，可以與我聯絡。）

- I won't be able to attend the meeting because I have prior arrangement. （因為我有事先安排活動了，沒辦法出席會議。）

◎關係代名詞也是連接詞的一種，用來引導子句，修飾前面的先行詞。

如：which, who, whose, that等。

- The man who was accused of murder claimed that he was innocent. （被控謀殺的男子聲稱自己是無辜的。）
- Peter declined the job offer that requires heavy business travel.（彼得拒絕那個需要大量出差的工作機會。）

馬上動手練一練 ❼

選出適當的連接詞，填入空格中

| although | and | because | both | so | neither |

1. The new office assistant was fired _____ she was not adequate to the job.
2. _____ he is the richest man in town, he is extremely stingy.
3. David's father is American and his mother is Chinese, _____ he can speak _____ English and Chinese.
4. _____ of you know him better than I do.
5. I have been to many European countries, such as Germany, Holland, Belgium _____ Italy.

ANSWER

1. because 2. Although 3. so, both 4. Neither 5. and

◆感嘆詞Interjection
→用來表達各種情緒

感嘆詞可以用來表示驚訝、哀傷、生氣、興奮等情緒。

如：•oh, ouch, wow, ah等。

• Ouch! My back hurts！（噢，我的背好痛！）

• Wow! You look gorgeous！（哇，你看起來好美！）

二・認識五大基本句型

英文的基本句型有五大類，五大基本句型乃所有英文複雜句型的骨架。

◆第一大句型S+V

主詞(Subject)與動詞(Verb)為句子的兩大最基本元素。

當動詞是不及物動詞，如 lie, leave, dance, sing 等時，後面不接受詞也能表達完整意義。任何具有名詞性質，無論是單字名詞、複合名詞或片語，都可以作為句子的主詞；同樣地，任何具有動詞性質，無論是單字動詞、片語動詞或動詞片語，都可以作為句子的動詞。

如：• The man died.（那男人死了。）

　　• Skipping breakfast won't help.（不吃早餐也沒用。）

◆第二大句型S+V+O

主詞(S)＋及物動詞(V)如tell, watch, hear等後面一定要接受詞(Object)，作為動作的接受者，才能使整個句子意義完整。只要具有名詞性質的單字或片語，都可以放在動詞後面作受詞。

如：• I can't hear you.（我聽不到你說話。）

　　• We missed our train.（我們錯過我們的火車了。）

◆第三大句型S+V+SC

當動詞為連綴動詞（如be動詞或感官動詞）時，後面可接主詞補語(S.C.)來修飾主詞。主詞補語可以是名詞（包括代名詞和各種具名詞性質的片語），也可以是形容詞（包括形容詞片語）。

如：・This is my father.（這是我父親。）
　　・That woman is beautiful.（那女子很美麗。）
　　・The meat smells bad.（這肉聞起來壞了。）

◆第四大句型S+V+O1+O2
主詞(S)＋動詞(V)＋受詞1(O1)＋受詞2(O2)

　　當動詞(V)為授與動詞，如buy, give, make等時，動詞後面可接直接受詞(the Direct Object/Object 1)與間接受詞(the Indirect Object/Object 2)。

如：・We bought a bread machine for Melissa.
　　（我們買了一台麵包機給梅莉莎。）
　　・Can you give me some money?
　　（你可以給我一點錢嗎？）

◆第五大句型S+V+O+OC
主詞(S)＋動詞(V)＋受詞(O)＋受詞補語(O.C.)

　　只要是名詞或形容詞，無論是單字、片語或子句，都可以接在受詞後面作為受詞補語（Object Complement），使受詞的意義更完整。

如：・They named their first daughter Eva.
　　（他們將他們的長女取名為伊娃。）
　　・The police found the woman dead.
　　（警察發現女子已經死亡。）
　　・You made me proud.
　　（你讓我感到很驕傲。）

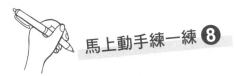

馬上動手練一練 ❽

閱讀下列句子，並將句子中的「主詞、動詞及受詞」挑出來並分類，填入空格中。

1. The lawyer proved the man guilty.
2. Lillian bought a bracelet for her mother.
3. All my friends call me Nini.
4. The idea sounds practical.
5. Time flies.

	S主詞	V動詞	O受詞
1.			
2.			
3.			
4.			
5.			

ANSWER

S主詞	V動詞	O受詞
1. the lawyer	proved	the man
2. Lillian	bought	a bracelet, her mother
3. all my friends	call	me, Nini
4. the idea	sounds	××
5. time	flies	××

文法總複習
快來試試自己的實力吧！

A. 選出正確的字

1. (　) The dentist checked his ___ and found a decayed _____.
   A. teeth; tooth　　B. tooth; teeth
   C. teeth; teeth　　D. tooth; tooth

2. (　) It is important to prepare yourself for opportunities, because opportunity waits for no _____.
   A. people　　　　B. women
   C. man　　　　　D. child

3. (　) The _____ actor is going to play the lead role in a high-budget Hollywood movie.
   A. good-looking popular Asian
   B. popular good-looking Asian
   C. Asian good-looking popular
   D. Asian popular good-looking

4. (　) The whole team tried _____ to get the job done by the deadline.
   A. very difficult　　B. tired enough
   C. quite happy　　D. so hard

5. (　) The interview is scheduled ___ the 26th of June __ 10 am.
   A. on; at　　　　B. in; by
   C. about; for　　D. for; of

6. (　) The _____ of this company are all excellent scientists.

　　A. boss　　　　B. staff

　　C. founder　　　D. manager

7. (　) The story he _____ _____ is not entirely true.

　　A. us; told　　　B. tells; they

　　C. tell; her　　　D. told; you

8. (　) You can contact me _____ you have any questions.

　　A. because　　　B. if

　　C. that　　　　D. so

9. (　) I can't buy that bag _____ I have no money.

　　A. because　　　B. so

　　C. that　　　　D. but

10. (　) She _____ a cake for her friend yesterday.

　　A. dropped　　　B. threw

　　C. made　　　　D. sent

B. 寫出下列名詞的複數，

若是不可數名詞，則在空格內打X

1. cash（　　　　　）

2. bridge（　　　　　）

3. flower（　　　　　）

4. problem（　　　　　）

5. water（　　　　　）

6. country（　　　　　）

7. housewife（　　　　　）

8. understanding（　　　　　）

9. wolf（　　　　　）

10. king（　　　　　）

ANSWER

A. 選出正確的字

1.**A** 2.**C** 3.**B** 4.**D** 5.**A**
6.**B** 7.**D** 8.**B** 9.**A** 10.**C**

1. 不規則複數名詞單數tooth→teeth複數

2. "Opportunity waits for no man." 為西方諺語，指機會不等人

3. 多個形容詞修飾同一名詞時的順序是固定的，其順序為：①冠詞、指示代詞、不定代詞、物主代詞＋②序數詞＋基數詞＋③一般性描繪形容詞＋④大小、長短、形狀＋年齡、新舊＋⑥顏色＋⑦國籍、出處＋⑧材料＋⑨用途、類別＋⑩最終修飾的名詞或動名詞

4. 副詞修飾動詞hard修飾tried，努力地嘗試

5. on使用於特定日子 on Christmas/on June first，at用於時間點at noon/at night

6. staff為集合名詞，由一批人所組成的單位或團體，組合名詞視為一批人時，則該名詞為複數名詞，搭配複數動詞使用

7. 受詞補語當主格

8. A. 因為   B. 如果   D. 所以

9. A. 因為

10. A. 掉下   B. 丟擲   C. 製作   D. 寄，僅made後面可加for

B. 寫出下列名詞的複數，若是不可數名詞，則在空格內打X

1. x   2. bridges   3. flowers   4. problems   5. x
6. countries   7. housewives   8. x
9. wolves   10. kings

NOTE

Lesson 2

名詞
作為主詞

名詞

專有名詞　Canada, Google

抽象名詞　love, time

物質名詞　air, metal

名詞子句

that子句
- **that子句+V+O**
  - →That he never loved me breaks my heart.

whether子句
- 「是否」疑問句當主詞
- 疑問句改為直述句
- 子句末尾or not可不加
- → Whether he was injured was not mentioned in the news.

疑問詞子句
- what, how, where, why, when
- 疑問句改為直述句
- →Why she is here confused me.

名詞片語
- **疑問詞+to V**
  - → What to eat for dinner is always a tough decision.

虛主詞it
- 代替不定詞片語
- →It is hard to perform in front of an audience.
- 代替that子句
- →It is hard to believe that the café is closing down.

Lesson 2　名詞作為主詞

「主詞」與「動詞」是五大句型的最基本元素。句構中的主詞，最常見的是「名詞」，除此之外，「代名詞」、「動名詞」、「不定詞」、「名詞子句」以及「名詞片語」都可以被歸類在「名詞」範疇，並在句子中作為主詞用。

另外，有些句子會用it或there來作主詞，但it或there 並不是句子的真正主詞，只是被借來作為假主詞的「虛主詞」。

一‧名詞

以名詞作為句子的主詞時，必須先知道該名詞是「單數名詞」還是「複數名詞」。名詞的「單複數」會直接決定後面的動詞，是要用「單數動詞」或是「複數動詞」。

例：• A handsome boy comes toward me and asks me to dance.
（一位英俊的男孩朝我走來，並邀我跳舞。）

• All women need to be treated with more respect, whether at home or at work.
（所有女人都必須得到更多尊重的對待，無論是在家庭或是在職場。）

有些名詞沒有單複數之分，恆以單數名詞視之，因此後面永遠都是接單數動詞。

◆ **專有名詞：**
→ **表示特定人、事、物、品牌、地點、國家或概念的名稱，通常沒有複數形。**

例：• Spinosaurus is the largest carnivorous dinosaur known so far. （棘龍是目前所知最大的肉食性恐龍。）

• Singapore is a multicultural and multiracial country in South East Asia.
（新加坡是一個東南亞的多元文化及多種族國家。）

• Nausea can be a warning sign of cancer as well as a symptom of pregnancy.
（噁心可能是癌症的警訊，也可能是懷孕的症狀。）

◆ **抽象名詞：**
→ **無法以五官感受的抽象概念，亦無複數形。**

例：• Love doesn't end with death. （愛不會隨著死亡而消逝。）

• Time flies so quickly, especially when you are having fun.
（時間過得好快，尤其是當你過得很開心時。）

◆ **物質名詞：**
→ **表示天然資源、食物與化學元素等物質的名稱，沒有複數形。**

例：• Air primarily contains 78% nitrogen, 21% oxygen, and other components. （空氣主要包含78%的氮，21%的氧及其他物質。）

• Metal is a perfect conductor of both heat and electricity.
（金屬是熱與電的良導體。）

馬上動手練一練 ❶

根據主詞，將句子中的動詞或助動詞做適當的變化

1. Opportunity _____(wait) for no man.
2. Red _____(be) considered a lucky color in Chinese culture.
3. Cheetahs _____(run) faster than any other animals in the world.
4. Fish _____(breathe) through gills while whales _____(breathe) through lungs.
5. Water _____(freeze) at 0 degrees Celsius and _____(boil) at 100 degrees Celsius.

ANSWER
1. waits 2. is 3. run 4. breathe, breathe 5. freezes, boils

二‧名詞子句

　　在英文的句構中，句子不能作為另一個句子的主詞，必須要先變成名詞子句，才能作主詞用。將句子變成子句的方式，就是在句子前面加上that、whether或疑問詞。

　　不論是哪一種名詞子句作為主詞時，恆以單數名詞視之，故句子的動詞也必須使用單數動詞。

◆that子句

　　凡是在以主詞為首的句子前面加上that，即為that子句。

例：• An old woman was killed in her home.
（一位老婦人在自宅中遇害。）
→ That an old woman was killed in her home shocked
the whole country.
（一名老婦人在自宅中遇害的消息，震驚了全國。）
• He never loved me.（他從未愛過我。）
→ That he never loved me breaks my heart.
（他從未愛過我，這讓我傷透了心。）

◆whether子句

　　Whether為表示「是否」的連接詞，可以用yes/no回答的疑問句，都可以在前面加上whether，並將問句中倒裝的主詞與動詞（或助動詞）位置還原，則可變成whether子句，作為句子的主詞。Whether子句的句尾也可以加上or not，表示「是否」。

❶ 疑問句中有be動詞時，主詞與be動詞位置還原為直述句

　　例：• Is he rich?（他富有嗎？）
→ Whether he is rich (or not) makes no difference to me.
（他是否富有對我來說並沒有差別。）
• Were they injured?（他們有受傷嗎？）
→ Whether they were injured (or not) was not mentioned
in the letter.
（他們是否有受傷，在信中並未被提及。）

❷ 疑問句中有do/does/did等助動詞時，主詞與助動詞位置還原後，去掉助動詞，後面動詞根據主詞及時態做變化

　　例：• Do you have leadership qualities?
（你具有領導特質嗎？）

→ Whether you have leadership qualities will affect your chances of promotion.

（你是否具備領導特質，將影響你升遷的機會。）

- Did you turn off the gas? （你有關瓦斯嗎？）

→ Whether you turned off the gas (or not) is a matter of life and death. （你有關瓦斯還是沒有關瓦斯，可是一件攸關生死的事啊。）

❸ 疑問句中有一般助動詞，如can/will/should/must/have等時，主詞與助動詞位置還原為直述句

例：• Can you quit smoking? （你可以戒煙嗎？）

→ Whether you can quit smoking (or not) depends on your willpower.

（你是否能夠戒煙，取決於你的意志力。）

- Will he pass the finals? （他會通過期末考嗎？）

→ Whether he will pass the finals (or not) really worries me. （他是否能通過期末考，還真是讓我擔心。）

◆疑問詞子句

疑問詞what/how/where/why/when也可以作連接詞用。要將疑問詞如what/how/where/why/when等所引導的疑問句變成主詞時，只要將問句中倒裝的主詞與動詞（或助動詞）位置還原，則可變成疑問詞子句，作為句子的主詞。

❶ 疑問句中有be動詞時，主詞與be動詞位置還原為直述句

例：• Why is she here? （她為何在這裡？）

→ Why she is here confuses me.

（她為何會在這裡，讓我感到很困惑。）

- What was his secret? （他的秘密是什麼？）
- → <u>What his secret was</u> remains unknown.

（他的秘密是什麼，仍然不為人所知。）

❷ 疑問句中有do/does/did等助動詞時，主詞與助動詞位置還原後，去掉助動詞，後面動詞根據主詞及時態變化

例：• How did the dinosaurs become extinct?

（恐龍是怎麼滅絕的？）

→ <u>How the dinosaurs became extinct</u> is still a mystery today. （恐龍是如何滅絕的，至今仍是個謎。）

- What did he do to me? （他對我做了什麼？）
- → <u>What he did to me</u> has changed my life forever.

（他對我所做的事永遠地改變了我的人生。）

❸ 疑問句中有一般助動詞，如can/will/should/must/ have等時，主詞與助動詞位置還原為直述句

例：When can we go home? （我們何時能回家？）

→ • <u>When we can go home</u> depends on the weather.

（我們何時能回家，得視天氣情況而定。）

- How will he solve the problem?

（他將如何解決問題？）

→ <u>How he will solve the problem</u> makes me very curious.

（他將如何解決問題，讓我感到非常好奇。）

將下列句子變成另一個句子的主詞

1. Can I keep a dog in the apartment?

_____ is very important to me.

2. He didn't come to the meeting.

_____ made his boss very angry.

3. What was the man's intention?

_____ was to be verified.

4. She didn't tell me the truth.

_____ makes me really sad.

5. I wasn't invited to his wedding.

_____ doesn't bother me at all.

ANSWER

1. Whether I can keep a dog in the apartment
2. That he didn't come to the meeting
3. What the man's intention
4. That she didn't tell me the truth
5. That I wasn't invited to his wedding

三‧名詞片語

　　名詞片語是由名詞子句簡化而來的，指的是由「疑問詞＋不定詞片語」所組合而成，具有名詞性質的片語，如where to live（要住哪裡）、what to say（該說什麼）、when to leave（何時要離開）、how to deal with it（該如何處理）等等。

當名詞子句（原本是問句）中的主詞與主要子句的主詞相同時，就可以將問句中的助動詞與主詞省略，以「疑問詞＋不定詞片語」來表示。

例：• Where shall we live?（我們將要住哪裡？）

→ <u>Where to live</u> is the first thing that we should consider.
（要住哪裡是我們應該考慮的第一件事。）

• How can we deal with difficult customers?
（我們能如何應付難纏的顧客？）

→ <u>How to deal with difficult customers</u> is no easy task.
（如何應付難纏的顧客可不是一件簡單的事。）

四‧虛主詞it

主詞為不定詞片語或that子句時，為了避免句子因為主詞太長而顯得頭重腳輕，常以it作為句子的虛主詞，將it放在主詞的位置，而將句子真正的主詞放在句尾。

◆代替不定詞片語

例：• <u>To participate in the Olympic Games</u> is many athletes' ultimate
不定詞片語為主詞

goal.

= <u>It</u> is many athletes' ultimate goal <u>to participate in the Olympic</u>
虛主詞　　　　　　　　　　　　　不定詞片語為真正主詞

Games.
（參加奧運是許多運動員的終極目標。）

- To completely avoid genetically modified food is almost

  不定詞片語為主詞

  impossible.
= It is almost impossible to completely avoid genetically modified

  虛主詞   不定詞片語為真正主詞

  food.

  （要完全避免基因改造食品幾乎是不可能的事。）

◆代替that子句

例：
- That his dog has been missing for days worries him.

  that子句為主詞

= It worries him that his dog has been missing for days.

  虛主詞   that子句為真正主詞

  （他的狗兒已經失蹤好幾天讓他很擔心。）

- That she finally found a decent job is worth celebrating.

  that子句為主詞

= It is worth celebrating that she finally found a decent job.

  虛主詞   that子句為真正主詞

  （她終於找到一個像樣的工作，實在值得慶祝。）

重點筆記

表示天氣狀態、時間時，也常用it作為主詞，取代the weather及
the time。

例：
- It is pretty warm today. （今天天氣頗暖和。）
- It is half past ten now. （現在時間是十點半。）

馬上動手練一練 ❸

以虛主詞it改寫句子

1. That she has never talked to me since then makes me sad.

_____

2. To admit a mistake is nothing to be ashamed of.

_____

3. That he is happy with his life matters most.

_____

4. To commute to work takes me two hours every day.

_____

5. That you don't believe me is really disappointing.

_____

ANSWER

1. It makes me sad that she has never talked to me since then.
2. It is nothing to be ashamed of to admit a mistake.
3. It matters most that he is happy with his life.
4. It takes me two hours to commute to work every day.
5. It is really disappointing that you don't believe me.

文法總復習
快來試試自己的實力吧！

A. 選出正確的主詞

1. (　) _____ in the past stays in the past.
   A. What happened　　　　　　　B. What has happened
   C. It happened　　　　　　　　D. To happen

2. (　) _____ is never too late to learn new things.
   A. What　　　　B. It　　　　C. When　　　D. There

3. (　) _____ was never really part of my plan. It just happened.
   A. Be an actor　　　　　　　　B. Been an actor
   C. Was an actor　　　　　　　D. Being an actor

4. (　) _____ the finals is the goal that you should stay focused on.
   A. Pass　　　　　　B. To pass　　　C. Passed　　　D. Passes

5. (　) _____ really frustrates me.
   A. That he never listens to me　　B. He seldom listens to me
   C. Why doesn't he listen to me　　D. He won't listen to me

6. (　) _____ is not easy, but definitely worth trying.
   A. Love what you do　　　　　　B. Loves what you do
   C. Loved what you do　　　　　D. To love what you do

7. (　) _____ is that he doesn't help with any housework at all.
   A. To bother me most　　　　　B. Bothering me most
   C. What bothers me most　　　　D. What to bother me

8. (　) _____ food with friends is wonderful.

　　A. Enjoying　　　B. enjoyed　　C. Kissed　　D. Threw

9. (　) _____ weight, she exercises every day.

　　A. To lose　　　B. Gain　　　C. Lost　　　D. Get

10. (　) _____ of the girls is an anime lover.

　　A. One　　　　B. Two　　　C. All　　　D. Most

B. 依括號中的提示寫出句子的主詞

1. (What has he done to me?)

　_____ is unforgettable.

2. (Does he like me?)

　_____ makes no difference to me.

3. (My son talked back to me this morning.)

　_____ really pissed me off.

4. (What should we eat for dinner?)

　_____ is up to you.

5. (Speak English like a native speaker)

　_____ is a dream for many English learners.

6. (Protect the earth from global warming)

　_____ is everyone's responsibility.

7. (Be a full-time mother)

　_____ might be the toughest job in the world.

8. (He didn't spend much time studying for the test.)

　_____ is definitely why he failed.

9. (Stay up late)

　_____ is unhealthy.

10. (Go against the rules)

　_____ will be punished.

ANSWER

A. 選出正確的主詞

1. **A**　2. **B**　3. **D**　4. **B**　5. **A**

6. **D**　7. **C**　8. **A**　9. **A**　10. **A**

1. 當疑問詞本身就是疑問句的主詞（如who/what/which）時，變成名詞子句時，主詞與動詞的位置結構不變：
→ What happened this morning was an accident.

2. 虛主詞It當主格時, 後面to+原形動詞補上真正主詞It is not easy to raise a lot of children. 畫底線為真主詞

3. 動名詞當主格，動詞與其他組成的名詞片語，如：
Staying safe is the most important.

4. 當To後面接動詞片語或片語動詞＋受詞時，即為不定詞片語

5. 句子不能作為另一個句子的主詞，必須要先變成名詞子句，才能作主詞用。將句子變成子句的方式，就是在句子前面加上that、whether或疑問詞
He cheated me.
→That he cheated me breaks my heart.

6. 不定詞片語，to後面接動詞片語，如：
To sleep early is one of the steps to stay healthy.

7. What本身為疑問詞，當疑問詞本身為疑問句主詞時，主詞動詞順序不變

8. 動名詞當主格用法，Enjoying food with friends成為句子的主詞

9. To+原形動詞用法為不定詞，不定詞片語為主詞的句子

10. is 為單數，girl又是可數名詞，故one為正解

B. 依括號中的提示寫出句子的主詞

1. What he has done to me
2. Whether he likes me (or not)
3. That my son talked back to me this morning
4. What to eat for dinner
5. To speak English like a native speaker/
   Speaking English like a native speaker
6. To protect the earth from global warming/
   Protecting the earth from global warming
7. To be a full-time mother/ Being a full-time mother
8. That he didn't spend much time studying for the test
9. Staying up late/ To stay up late
10. Going against the rules/ To go against the rules

代名形容詞

指示形容詞
指示代名詞當形容詞：
this, that, these, the other, another

不定形容詞
不定代名詞當形容詞
some, many, all, much, more

所有形容詞
所有格代名詞當形容詞
my, your, their, our, his, her

疑問形容詞
疑問代名詞當形容詞
what, which, whose

關係形容詞
關係代名詞當形容詞
who, whom, whose, which, that

Lesson 3

一般名詞前的詞語

單位量詞

用容器、重量來計量
a cup of, a piece of, a kilo of

用形態來計量
a bunch of

冠詞

定冠詞the
- 特定的人、事、物：the woman
- 獨一無二的自然事物：the earth
- 特定的方向或方位：the left
- 專屬名稱：the Alps
- 序數：the first
- 形容詞最高級：the best
- very或only：the only
- 姓氏（表示一家）：the Obamas
- 形容詞（表示群體）：the poor
- 年代：the 1920s

不定冠詞a/an
- 首字母非母音a：a cat
- 首字母為母音an：an elephant

數量形容詞

不定數量
- few, a few, several, many＋可數複數名詞
- much, little, a little＋不可數名詞
- some, all, any, more, less, enough＋可數複數名詞／不可數名詞

定量
- 數詞：one, two
- 序數詞：first, second
- 倍數詞：half, double

一般名詞前的詞語

這一個單元主要介紹可以放在一般名詞之前的語詞。除了描述外觀及特性的形容詞之外，在一般名詞之前，通常會加上冠詞。若沒有特別指定，加上不定冠詞a或an，表示「一個」；有特別指定名詞時，則加上不定冠詞the，表示「該（人、事物）」。

但是一般名詞之前如果有以下形容詞，就可以不加冠詞：
1. 代名形容詞：包含指示形容詞如this/that、不定形容詞如some/any、所有形容詞如my/your及疑問形容詞如what/which。
2. 數量形容詞：包含定量形容詞如one/half/double及不定數量形容詞如many/some/enough。
3. 單位量詞：如a loaf of/a box of/a cup of等。

一‧冠詞

冠詞是一種限定詞，可分為「定冠詞」和「不定冠詞」兩種。

◆定冠詞the

the沒有單複數之分，後面可以接單複數可數名詞，也可以接不可數名詞。在名詞前加上定冠詞the，目的在表示「指定」，而非泛指任何一個或隨便一個。使用定冠詞the的時機如下：

① 「特定的」人、事、物之前

當有特定指稱的對象時，前面加定冠詞the以表示「指定」。

例：• She is the woman that I want to spend the rest of my life with.

（她就是我想要共度餘生的女子。）

• I just bought two tickets to the concert.
（我剛買了兩張那場演唱會的門票。）

② 獨一無二的自然事物之前

在自然界中獨一無二的事物之前必須加定冠詞，以表示「唯一」。

例：• The moon orbits around the earth once every 28 days.
（月亮每二十八天繞著地球運行一週。）

• The sun shines so brightly in the sky.
（太陽在天空中如此明亮地閃耀著。）

③ 特定的方向或方位之前

在方向或方位的名詞前要加定冠詞，以表示「特定」方向，

例：• When you turn to the right, you will see the bookstore on the left.
（當你向右轉，就會在左側看到書店了。）

• I was born in the North, but both of my parents are from the South.
（我是在北方出生的，但我的父母都是南方人。）

❹ 專有名稱之前

有「專屬名稱」的自然景觀，如河流、山脈、群島、海洋，或建築物等，前面會加上定冠詞，以表示「特定」。

例：• Gertrude Ederle swam across the English Channel at the age of 19.
（傑楚德‧伊德在十九歲時泳渡英吉利海峽。）

• The Alps situates in south-central Europe.
（阿爾卑斯山坐落於中南歐。）

❺ 序數之前

在表示「第……」的序數之前要加定冠詞。

例：• Doing anything for the first time can be exciting.
（第一次嘗試新事物可能是令人興奮的。）

• You are the last person that I want to see in the world.
（你是這個世界上我最不想看到的人。）

❻ 形容詞最高級之前

在表示「最……」的形容詞最高級之前要加定冠詞。

例：• Family is the most important thing to me in the world.
（家庭是我在這世界上最重要的東西。）

• Steven Hawking was one of the most influential physicists of the time.
（史蒂芬‧霍金是當代最具影響力的物理學家之一。）

❼ very或only之前

在表示「強調」的very或表示「唯一」的only之前要加定冠詞。

例：• A man had plastic surgery two weeks ago, and the very next day, he died.
（有個男子兩週前做了整形手術，隔天就死了。）

• This is the only request I have for you.
（這是我對你唯一的請求。）

❽ 姓氏前

在姓氏前加上the，表示「某氏」一家。由於一家人是由一群人組成的，因此姓氏後面要加上s，表示複數。

例：• The Obamas and the Clintons used to be the focus of the media.
（歐巴馬家與柯林頓家曾經是媒體的焦點。）

❾ 形容詞前

定冠詞可以加在形容詞前表示整個群體。

例：• We are taught to respect the elderly and help the weak.
（我們被教導要尊敬長者，幫助弱者。）

• It is a sad but true fact that the rich get richer, and the poor get poorer.
（富者越富，貧者越貧，是可悲又千真萬確的事實。）

❿ 年代前

年代前加上the，則可以指稱某一個年代。因為不只一年，因此表示年份的數字後要加上s。

例：• Jazz used to be very popular in the 1950s.
（爵士樂在50年代曾經很很受歡迎。）

- Computers are one of the most essential technological innovations of the 90s.
（電腦是九〇年代最主要的創新科技產物之一。）

重點筆記

以下名詞之前不加定冠詞：
1. 加了有所有格、指示形容詞及不定形容詞的名詞，如my husband（我的丈夫）、this movie（這部電影）、some money（一些錢）
2. 物質名詞，如iron（鐵）、gold（金）、copper（銅）
3. 抽象名詞，如honesty（誠實）、sadness（悲傷）
4. 學科，如geometry（幾何學）、geography（地理學）
5. 運動項目，如volleyball（排球）、pole vault（撐竿跳）
6. 顏色，如pink（粉）、blue（藍）
7. 語言，如German（德語）、Spanish（西班牙語）

◆不定冠詞a/an

「未指定」的單數名詞前通常會放「不定冠詞」a或an。

❶ 名詞首字母非母音用不定冠詞a：
例：• I want to open a restaurant of my own.
（我想要開一間我自己的餐廳。）

• Would you like a cup of tea?
（你想要來一杯茶嗎？）

② 名詞首字母為母音，用不定冠詞an：

例：• Can I borrow <u>an evening gown</u> from you?
（我可以跟你借一件晚禮服嗎？）

• She refused to ride <u>an elephant</u> when she was in Thailand.
（在泰國時，她拒絕騎大象。）

 重點筆記

1. 首字母的母音字母不發母音，而是發子音時，冠詞用a

例：• My roommate is <u>a European</u>. She's from Hungary.
（我的室友是個歐洲人。她來自匈牙利。）

• This is just <u>a one-hour meeting</u>. It won't take you too much time.
（這只是個一小時的會議，不會花你太多時間的。）

2. 首字母的子音不發音，而以母音為首字母發音時，冠詞用an

例：• It took me <u>an hour</u> to clean up the room.
（我花了一個小時才把房間清理好。）

• It's <u>an honor</u> to be invited to participate in this symposium.
（受邀參加這次座談會實在是很榮幸。）

 馬上動手練一練 ①

在空格中填入a, an 或the，若不需冠詞，則在空格內打X

1. Earth is ____ third planet from ____ Sun and ____ only known planet with ____ atmosphere.

2. Instead of returning good for _____ evil, I personally believe in ___eye for ___ eye and ___ tooth for ___ tooth.

3. _____ Great Wall of _____ China is _____ only man-made construction visible from ___ space.

4. You can't teach ___ old dog ___ new tricks.

5. ___ Marilyn Monroe was one of ___ most popular sex symbols of _____ 1950s.

二・代名形容詞

代名形容詞指的是可以轉作形容詞用的代名詞，不與冠詞同時使用。

◆指示形容詞：

指示代名詞也可以做形容詞。常用的有：this/that/these/that/the other/another等。

例：• I've always wanted to see that movie.
（我一直都很想看那部電影。）

• Could you please move these chairs to the other room?
（能麻煩你把這些椅子搬到另一個房間去嗎？）

◆**不定形容詞：**

不定代名詞可以放在名詞前作形容詞，如some/many/all/ much/most/more等。

例：• Would you please give me <u>some advice</u>？
（可以請你給我一些建議嗎？）

• Please hurry up. We don't have <u>much time</u> to waste.
（請快一點。我們沒有太多時間可以浪費。）

① **some與any**

同：some（一些）與any（任何、任一）後面可接複數名詞及不可數名詞。

異：some一般用在肯定句及預期對方回答yes的疑問句，any一般用在否定句及沒有預期特定答案的疑問句。

例：• I've got <u>some money</u> with me.（我身上有一些錢。）

• I haven't got <u>any money</u> with me.
（我身上完全沒有錢。）

• Don't you have <u>any money</u> with you?
（你身上一點錢都沒有嗎？）
→ 只想知道對方身上有沒有錢

• Can I borrow <u>some money</u> from you?
（我可以跟你借一點錢嗎？）
→ 期望對方能給予肯定答覆

any經常與含否定意義的字彙合用。

例：• She arrived at the hotel <u>without any trouble</u>.
（她很順利地抵達了飯店。）

• You never do <u>any housework</u> at home.
（你在家從不做任何家事。）

any用在肯定直述句，表示「任何……也無妨」。

例：• You can collect your train ticket from <u>any train station</u>.
（你在任何一個火車站都能取票。）

• Feel free to call me if you need <u>any help</u>.
（如果你需要任何幫助，儘管打電話給我。）

no= not a（沒有一個）/ not any（沒有任何），但是no的語氣更強烈。
後面可接單數可數名詞，複數可數名詞以及不可數名詞。
例：There is <u>not a bathtub</u> in my bathroom.
＝There is <u>no bathtub</u> in my bathroom.
（我的浴室裡沒有浴缸。）
There <u>aren't any calls</u> for you today.
＝There <u>are no calls</u> for you today.
（今天沒有找你的電話。）
We <u>don't have any time</u> for a slow lunch.
＝We <u>have no time</u> for a slow lunch.
（我們沒有時間慢慢吃午餐。）

❷ all、whole與every

同：all、whole與every都可以表示「所有」。

異：all可用於複數可數名詞及不可數名詞；whole通常用於單數可數名詞；every後面只能接單數可數名詞。

例：• <u>All the students</u> in this school participate in after-school activities.（這學校所有的學生都會參加課後活動。）

• I always do <u>all the housework</u> by myself.
（我總是獨自做完所有家事。）

- The whole situation is getting out of control.
（整個情況都失控了。）

- Every child in this country deserves an education.
（這個國家的每一個孩子都應該受教育。）

❸ both、either 與neither

同：都是用來討論「兩者」。

異：both用在肯定句，表示「兩者都……」，後面接複數可數名詞，動詞為複數動詞；either表示「兩者之一」，neither表示「兩者都不」，後面接單數可數名詞。

例：• Both my grandparents are still alive and healthy.
（我的祖父母都仍健在。）

- We can meet at 10 am or 2 pm. Either time works for me.
（我們可以上午十點或下午兩點碰面。這兩個時間我都可以。）

- Neither train is bound for Taipei.
（這兩班火車都不是開往臺北的。）

◆所有形容詞

人稱代名詞所有格可以放在名詞前作所有形容詞用，如my/your/their/our/his/her等。

例：• I'm looking forward to receiving your feedback.
（我很期待得到您的回應。）

- Their children are adorable little angels.
（他們的孩子是可愛的小天使。）

◆疑問形容詞

疑問代名詞可放在名詞前，作疑問形容詞，如what/which/whose等。

例：• What kind of movies do you like?
（你喜歡哪一種電影？）

• Whose handbag is that on the table?
（桌上那個是誰的手提包？）

◆關係形容詞——由關係代名詞轉形容詞用

例：• You can decide which day we should meet.
（你可以決定我們應該在哪一天碰面。）

• I don't know whose idea is this.
（我不知道這是誰的點子。）

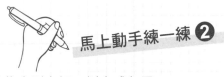

馬上動手練一練 ❷

圈出正確的代名形容詞，以完成句子

1. (All/Every/Whole) children deserve to grow up in a loving and caring home.

2. I can't believe that you spent the (every/some/whole) day doing nothing at all!

3. (Which/Whose/What) hotel do you prefer, the Hilton or the Ritz?

4. The poor girl experienced the death of (both/neither/either) parents in less than six months.

5. Thanks to (either/this/your) warm hospitality. We really had a wonderful time there.

ANSWER
1. All   2. whole   3. Which   4. both   5. your

三‧數量形容詞

數量形容詞是用來表示名詞的數或量有多少的形容詞，這些形容詞分別與單複數的名詞搭配使用。

◆不定數量形容詞：用來修飾沒有一定數量的名詞

$$\left.\begin{array}{l} \text{few} \\ \text{a few} \\ \text{several} \\ \text{many} \end{array}\right\} + 可數複數名詞$$

例：• I received so <u>many gifts</u> on my birthday.
（我生日那天收到好多禮物。）

• There are <u>several theories</u> for dinosaur extinction.
（有幾個解釋恐龍滅絕的理論。）

$$\left.\begin{array}{l} \text{much} \\ \text{little} \\ \text{a little} \end{array}\right\} + 不可數名詞$$

例：• I don't have <u>much time</u>, so let's get this done quickly.
（我沒有太多時間，所以我們趕快把這件事做完。）

• Let's take <u>a little break</u>.
（讓我們稍作休息吧。）

$$\left.\begin{array}{l} \text{some} \\ \text{all} \\ \text{any} \\ \text{more} \\ \text{less} \\ \text{enough} \end{array}\right\} + 可數複數名詞／不可數名詞$$

例：• Would you like <u>some more soup</u>?
（你想要更多湯嗎？）

• <u>Some people</u> believe students should wear uniforms, while others don't. （有些人認為學生就是應該穿制服，而其他人並不這麼認為。）

• Do you take credit card? I don't have <u>enough cash</u> with me. （你們接受信用卡嗎？我身上沒有足夠的現金。）

• You need to make sure we have <u>enough chairs</u> for all our guests.
（你需要確定我們有足夠的椅子讓所有的賓客用。）

 **重點筆記**

1. few與a few用法差異：

few表示「很少，少到幾乎沒有」，具否定意義。

例：• <u>Few people</u> understand what Carbon reduction really means.
（很少人明白減碳真正代表什麼意義。）

a few 表示「幾個，數量約2～3個」，用在肯定句。

例：• I invited <u>a few friends</u> over for dinner tonight.
（我邀請了幾個朋友今晚過來吃晚餐。）

2. little與a little用法差異：

little表示「很少，少到幾乎沒有」，具否定意義。

例：• I got little information about the new school regulation.（我沒有得到什麼關於新校規的資訊。）

a little 表示「有一點，少許」。

例：• You are not supposed to drive even you only had a little alcohol.

（即使你只喝了一點酒，也不應該開車。）

◆定量形容詞：用來表示名詞的數量或分量、表示名詞的順序的形容詞

❶ 數詞—— 如one/two等

例：• My school is only two blocks away from my home.
（我的學校離我家僅兩個路口的距離。）

• This tree is estimated to be three thousand years old.
（這棵樹據估計已經三千歲了。）

❷ 序數詞——如first/second/last等

序數詞加在名詞前面，以表示順序。如前所述，序數詞前面必須要加上定冠詞，或是其它可以取代冠詞的形容詞（如代名形容詞）。

例：• It's normal to be nervous on your first day of school.
（第一天上學會緊張，是很正常的。）

- Why am I always <u>the last one</u> to be informed?
  （我為何總是最後一個被通知的人？）

❸ 倍數詞——如half/double/triple等

例：• We waited <u>half an hour</u> to get our table.
（我們等了半小時才能入座。）

- You can get <u>double pay</u> if you work on the weekend.
  （如果你在週末工作，可以得到兩倍工資。）

馬上動手練一練 ❸

圈出正確的數量形容詞，以完成句子

1. I have (a little/a few/few) questions for you. Do you have time?

2. We are not allowed to reveal (any/some/neither) personal information about our customers.

3. Marie divorced her husband after (first/double/four) years of marriage.

4. I would be very appreciated if you could kindly give me a (double/second/few) chance.

5. The boy accomplished the task with (a few/a little/less) help from his parents.

ANSWER

1. a few 2. any 3. four 4. second 5. a little

四・單位量詞

單位量詞是用來形容沒有一定形體而無法計數，或是數量太多而無法計量之名詞的形容詞。

單位量詞的形成包含三部分，即：①冠詞／數詞／序數詞＋②名詞＋③of。

◆無法計數的名詞

不可數名詞因為無法計數，因此常以盛放的容器、呈現的形態或是重量單位作為計量單位。

常用的單位量詞如下：

以容器計量	以形態計量	以重量計量
a cup of 一杯	a piece of 一片／塊／張	a ton of 一噸
a box of 一盒	a loaf of 一條	a pound of 一磅
a can of 一罐	a bite of 一口	a kilo of 一公斤
a bottle of 一瓶	a drop of 一滴	an ounce of 一盎司

另外，還有以數量計量的單位量詞，如：a dozen of（一打）。

例：• She drank up a whole bottle of wine by herself.
（她自己喝光一整瓶酒。）

• Please write down your contact information on a piece of paper.（請在一張紙上寫下你的聯絡資訊。）

• I would like 500 grams of ground pork.
（我想要五百公克的豬絞肉。）

◆無法計量的名詞

有些可數名詞，當以龐大數量狀態存在，而無法確實計算時，常以單位量詞來做描述。除了跟不可數名詞一樣，可以用容器來計量之外，也可用呈現的形態來形容。

例：• She brought <u>a bunch of</u> roses as a gift.
（她帶來一束玫瑰花作為禮物。）

• The police arrested <u>a gang of robbers</u> in the city center last night.
（警方昨夜在市中心逮捕了一幫搶匪。）

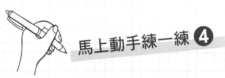

馬上動手練一練 ❹

填入正確的單位量詞，以完成句子

a cup of   a bunch of   a spoon of   a piece of   half dozen of

1. We need _____ egg yolks to make this cake.

2. _____ hot chocolate can quickly warm you up in the cold winter.

3. If you don't know what to bring to a friend's party, _____ beautiful flowers may be a good idea.

4. The lady added _____ sugar into her coffee and took a gulp.

5. He took out _____ paper and wrote down his name and contact information.

ANSWER

1. half dozen of 2. A cup of 3. a bunch of 4. a spoon of
5. a piece of

A. 為空格選出正確的形容詞，可以重複

A. piece	E. her
B. the	F. a bowl of
C. four	G. two
D. a little	H. both(Both)

1. That's a very useful _____ of information. Thanks a lot.

2. Sarah is celebrating her birthday with _____ family and friends tonight.

3. Hi, I'd like to book a table for _____ adults and _____ children, 4 and 2, at seven tonight.

4. For dinner, she only ate _____ fried rice and _____ soup.

5. I have _____ good news and bad news for you. Which would you like to hear first?

6. _____ young should respect _____ old.

7. _____ of the girls are teachers.

8. I'd like to have _____ rice, please.

9. Don't take Anna's pen. It's _____ pen.

10. It's enjoyable to have a cup of milk tea and a _____ of cake together.

B. 翻譯填空

1. 我需要一杯水才能吃藥。

   I need _____ water to take the medicine.

2. 他的父親死後，他繼承了一大筆錢。

   He inherited _____ large _____ money after his father died.

3. 她的小公寓裡只有幾件傢俱。

   There are only _____ of furniture in _____ tiny apartment.

4. 我不餓，所以我只要點一杯咖啡就好。

   I'm not hungry, so I'll just order _____ coffee.

5. 別擔心。我的朋友沒有幾個知道我的真實身份。

   Don't worry. _____ friends of mine know _____ real identity.

6. 我不能吃乳製品和海鮮。我對這兩種食物都會過敏。

   I can't eat dairy products and seafood. I am allergic to _____

   kinds of food.

7. 對我來說，兩性都不比對方具優勢。

   For me, _____ gender is superior.

8. 可以請你給我一些建議嗎？

   Would you please give me _____ advice?

9. 你在家從不做任何家事。

   You never do _____ housework at home.

10. 今天是我第一天上學。

   Today is my _____ day to school.

ANSWER

A. 為空格選出正確的形容詞，可以重複

1. **A**
2. **E**
3. **C、G**
4. **D、F**
5. **H**
6. **B、B**
7. **H**
8. **F**
9. **E**
10. **A**

1. information 單位量詞用piece

2. her family=Sarah's family her為代名詞代替Sarah's

3. 四位大人和兩位小孩

4. fried rice為不可數故搭配a little
   a bowl of soup一碗湯

5. good news及bad news為兩項both搭配兩者用在肯定句

6. 定冠詞the可以加在形容詞前表示整個群體

7. Both搭配兩者用於可數及肯定句

8. a bowl of rice一碗白飯

9. 所有形容詞人稱代名詞所有格可以放在名詞前做所有形容詞用，如my/your/their/our/his/her等。
   Ann's pen=her pen

10. a piece of cake一塊蛋糕

B. 翻譯填空
1. a glass of
2. a, sum of
3. a few pieces, her
4. a cup of
5. Few, my
6. both
7. neither
8. some
9. any
10. first

NOTE

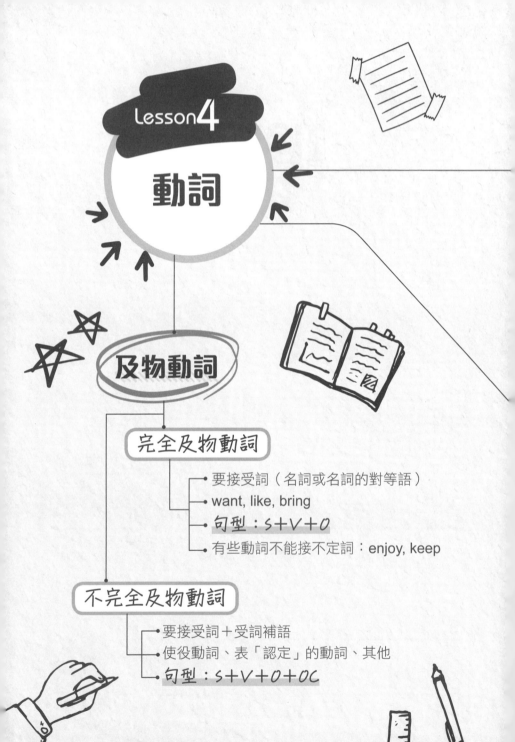

Lesson **4**

動詞

及物動詞

完全及物動詞

- 要接受詞（名詞或名詞的對等語）
- want, like, bring
- **句型：S＋V＋O**
- 有些動詞不能接不定詞：enjoy, keep

不完全及物動詞

- 要接受詞＋受詞補語
- 使役動詞、表「認定」的動詞、其他
- **句型：S＋V＋O＋OC**

不及物動詞

完全不及物動詞

- 不用受詞
- run, sleep
- 句型：S+V

不完全不及物動詞

- 要接主詞補語
- 連綴動詞：be動詞、感官動詞
  - am, is, are, sound, seem
  - 見Lesson 6
- 其他：fall, run, come

授與動詞

- 要接直接受詞和間接受詞
- ask…of…/ give…to…/buy…for…
- 句型：S+V+I.O.+D.O.

Lesson4 動詞

動詞的種類與用法，決定動詞與受詞的關係，並影響整個句子的結構。認識一個動詞時，要先知道這個動詞是屬於哪一種動詞，才能知道要怎麼將這個動詞運用在句子中。

英文的動詞可分為三大類：不及物動詞、及物動詞以及授與動詞。不及物動詞又可以分為完全不及物動詞及不完全不及物動詞，及物動詞也可以分為完全及物動詞及不完全及物動詞。這些文法名詞乍聽之下讓人甚感混亂，但是千萬別被這些看似複雜的名詞給嚇倒了。其實所謂的及物或不及物，說穿了不過就是動詞與受詞之間的關係罷了。花點耐心弄清楚，就會知道這很簡單。

一‧不及物動詞

「物」代表「受詞」。不及物動詞，指的就是「不需要受詞的動詞」。

當一個動詞在<u>沒有受詞</u>的情況下，即能完整表達句意，就是不及物動詞。

例：• He <u>died</u>. （他死了。）

    → 動詞die後面不需要受詞，句意完整，die為不及物動詞。

• Birds <u>fly</u>. （鳥兒會飛。）

    → 動詞fly後面不需要受詞，句意完整，fly亦為不及物動詞。

不及物動詞可以分為以下兩種：

◆完全不及物動詞

意指<u>不需要受詞</u>，就可以讓<u>句意完全</u>的動詞。

完全不及物動詞使用在五大句型中的第一大句型：S＋V。
例：• She <u>cried</u>.（她哭了。）
　　• Everyone <u>laughed</u>.（大家都笑了。）

以下列出幾個常用的完全不及物動詞：

sing（唱歌）	scream（尖叫）	sigh（歎氣）
dance（跳舞）	murmur（低語）	sleep（睡覺）
run（跑）	whistle（吹口哨）	giggle（咯咯笑）
leave（離開）	whisper（耳語）	weep（哭泣）

馬上動手練一練 ①

將括號中的完全不及物動詞做適當變化，以完成句子

1. The little girl heard the joke and _____ (giggle)

2. They _____ (sing) and _____ (dance) until midnight last night.

3. When we finally _____ (arrive), he had already _____ (leave).

4. The woman read the letter and started to _____ (weep).

5. Stop _____ (scream)! You're waking everybody up!

ANSWER

1. giggled　　　2. sang, danced　　　3. arrived, left
4. weep　　　5. screaming

◆不完全不及物動詞

　　意指不需要受詞，但是需要接主詞補語來修飾主詞，才能讓句意完全的動詞。之後會講的連綴動詞，就是不完全不及物動詞（請見Lesson6三‧連綴動詞）。

　　例：
- Good medicine tastes bitter. （良藥苦口。）
- Good advice is harsh to the ear. （忠言逆耳。）
- We became very close. （我們變得非常親近。）

(1) 不完全不及物動詞使用在五大句型中的第三大句型：
S＋V＋SC

(2) 不完全不及物動詞後面需要有主詞補語。主詞補語可以是「名詞」、「形容詞」、「名詞或形容詞的對等語」、「地方副詞」或「地方副詞片語」。

　　名詞對等語有：代名詞、名詞片語、動名詞、不定詞、名詞子句、名詞片語。

　　形容詞對等語則有：現在分詞、過去分詞、介系詞片語。

❶ 不完全不及物動詞接各種主詞補語：

(1) 名詞
例：
- We are sisters. （我們是姐妹。）

(2) 代名詞
例：
- It's me. （是我。）

(3) 動名詞／動名詞片語
例：
- Teaching is learning. （教學相長。）

- My job is <u>teaching teachers how to teach</u>.
（我的工作是教老師們如何教學。）

(4) 不定詞／不定詞片語

例：• To give is <u>to take</u>.（給予就是獲得。）

- Her goal is <u>to get rid of 10 kilos</u>.
（她的目標是減去十公斤。）

(5) 名詞子句

例：• I didn't notice <u>that you had a haircut</u>.
（我沒注意到你有剪頭髮。）

(6) 名詞片語

例：• The problem is <u>how to convince the employer to hire you</u>.
（問題是如何說服僱主僱用你。）

(7) 形容詞

例：• The whole performance was <u>amazing</u>.
（整場表演都很精彩。）

- My wife gets <u>emotional</u> easily.
（我的太太很容易情緒激動。）

(8) 現在分詞作形容詞用

例：• Your idea sounds <u>interesting</u>.
（你的點子聽起來很有意思。）

- You seem very <u>confusing</u>.（你看起來非常困惑。）

(9) 過去分詞作形容詞用

例：• You'd better give your mother a call. She sounded very
<u>worried</u>.
（你最好打個電話給你媽媽。她聽起來非常憂心。）

(10) 介系詞片語與作形容詞用

例：• I am <u>afraid of ghosts</u>. （我很怕鬼。）

(11) 地方副詞

例：• She is <u>downstairs</u>. （她在樓下。）

(12) 地方副詞片語

例：• Mr. Robinson is <u>in his office</u>.
　　（羅賓森先生在他的辦公室裡。）

 **重點筆記**

感官動詞後面必須直接接形容詞作補語：

例：• I feel exhausted. （我感到筋疲力盡。）

　　• It sounds terrific. （這聽起來真是棒極了。）

感官動詞接名詞時，要有介系詞like：

例：• It sounds like a fantastic trip.
　　（聽起來像是個超棒的旅行。）

　　• The fabric feels like linen.
　　（這布料摸起來像是亞麻。）

★ feel like 後面如果接動名詞，表示「想要做某事」＝would like＋不定詞

例：• I feel like going home. （我想要回家了。）
　　＝ I would like to go home.

　　除了連綴動詞之外，還有一些動詞也可作不完全不及物動詞用，較常用的有：

(1) fall，表「變成」，fall＋形容詞＝變成某種狀態

例：• Jerry <u>fell asleep</u> as soon as the concert started.
（音樂會一開始，傑瑞就睡著了。）

　　• Mary <u>fell in love</u> with Tom at first sight.
（瑪麗對湯姆一見鍾情。）

(2) run，表「成為，變得」，run＋形容詞＝成為某種狀態

例：• The lake <u>ran dry</u>.（湖水開始乾涸起來。）

　　• Let your imagination <u>run wild</u>.（盡情放縱你的想像力。）

(3) come，表「變成」，come＋形容詞＝達到某種狀態

例：• Your shoes <u>came untied</u>.（你的鞋帶沒綁好。）

馬上動手練一練 ❷

將句子中的主詞補語圈起來

1. It hasn't rained for a long time. The river has nearly run dry.

2. I felt uncomfortable when he said that to me.

3. The problem is that it's way beyond our budget.

4. It is my dream to visit all the three Bridges of Sighs in the world.

5. We fell in love with each other when we first met.

ANSWER

1. It hasn't rained for a long time. The river has nearly run dry .
2. I felt uncomfortable when he said that to me.
3. The problem is that it's way beyond our budget .
4. It is my dream to visit all the three Bridges of Sighs in the world .
5. We fell in love with each other when we first met.

二 · 及物動詞

當一個動詞在有<u>受詞</u>的情況下，才能完整表達句意，就是及物動詞。

例：• I have（我有）
　　→動詞have後面沒有受詞，讓人不知道主詞到底「有」什麼，句意不完整。

• I have a dream.（我有一個夢想。）
　　→動詞have後面有了受詞a dream，句意完整了。have為及物動詞。

• He makes （他做）
　　→動詞 make後面沒有受詞，讓人不知道主詞到底「做」了什麼，句意不完整。

• He makes films.（他製作電影。）
　　→動詞make後面有了受詞 films，句意完整了。make為及物動詞。

及物動詞也可以分為以下兩種：

◆完全及物動詞

意指後面接了受詞，<u>句意才算完全</u>的動詞。

例：• He <u>hit</u> me.（他揍我。）
　　• She <u>wrote</u> a book.（她寫了一本書。）

以下列出幾個常用的完全及物動詞：

eat（吃）	do（做）	bring（運送）
want（想要）	like（喜歡）	purchase（購買）
avoid（避免）	enjoy（喜歡）	hire （僱用）
kill（殺害）	produce（生產）	support（支持）

完全及物動詞使用在五大句型中的第二大句型：S＋V＋O。

可以作為及物動詞的受詞，為「名詞」或名詞的對等語，如「代名詞」、「動名詞」、「不定詞」、「名詞片語」、「名詞子句」等具有名詞特性的詞類。

❶ 完全及物動詞接各種形式的受詞

(1) 名詞

例：• I bought milk.（我買了牛奶。）

(2) 代名詞

例：• He doesn't like it.（他不喜歡。）

(3) 動名詞或動名詞片語

例：• She enjoys mountain climbing.（她喜歡登山。）

　　• Most people avoid talking about death.
　　（大部份的人避免談論死亡。）

(4) 不定詞或不定詞片語

例：• I love to travel.（我熱愛旅遊。）

　　• They hope to see each other again.
　　（他們希望能再次見到對方。）

(5) 名詞子句

例：• He wonders whether she is telling the truth.
　　（他不知道她是否說真話。）

　　• The jury believed that the man was guilty.
　　（陪審團認為那男子是有罪的。）

(6) 名詞片語

例：• No one knows how to make contact with him.
（沒人知道如何跟他取得聯繫。）

有些及物動詞後面接不定詞與動名詞當受詞，意義是一樣的，常見的有：

like（喜歡） love（喜愛）	hate（討厭） continue（繼續）	start（開始） begin（開始）

例：• She likes to read mystery fiction.
＝She likes reading mystery fiction.
（她喜歡讀懸疑小說。）

　　• The man continued to criticize the boy's parents.
＝The man continued criticizing the boy's parents.
（男子繼續抨擊男孩的父母。）

但是有些及物動詞後面接不定詞與接動名詞，表示的意義是不同的：

(1) stop
stop＋不定詞，表「停下來做某事」。

例：• She stopped (what she was doing) to speak to the little girl.（她停下來跟小女孩說話。）

stop＋動名詞，表「停止做某事」。

例：• She stopped talking to the little girl when the man came in.
（男子進來時，她便停止跟小女孩說話。）

(2) remember
remember＋不定詞，表「記得（要）做某事」。

例：• I hope Dad remember to buy souvenirs for me.
（我希望爸爸記得要買紀念品給我。）

remember＋動名詞，表「記得做過某事」。

例：• I remember buying a souvenir for you, but I can't find it.
（我記得我有買個紀念品給你，但我找不到。）

(3) forget

forget＋不定詞，表「忘記（要）做某事」。

例：• Oops! I forgot to buy you a souvenir.
（糟糕！我忘記買紀念品給你了。）

forget＋動名詞，表「忘記做過某事」。

例：• He forgot buying a souvenir, so he didn't give it to her.
（他忘記自己有買紀念品，所以沒有拿給她。）

有些及物動詞後面只能接動名詞或名詞當受詞，不能接不定詞，常見的有：

enjoy（喜愛，享受）	risk（冒險）	anticipate（預期）
imagine（想像）	avoid（避免）	recommend（建議）
quit（戒除）	resist（抗拒）	suggest（建議）
keep（繼續不斷）	practice（練習）	mind（介意）

例：• We enjoyed the view. （我們很享受這片景觀。）

• She doesn't enjoy dancing ballet at all.
（她一點也不喜歡跳芭蕾舞。）

• I can't imagine life without a smartphone.
（我無法想像沒有智慧手機的生活。）

• I can't imagine living on a desert island by myself.
（我無法想像一個人生活在荒島上。）

• Peter recommended cycling around the island.
（彼德建議騎單車環島。）

• No one can resist <u>having some ice cream</u> on a hot summer day.（沒有人在炎熱的夏日能夠抗拒吃冰淇淋。）

馬上動手練一練 ❸

圈出正確的字，以完成句子

1. I really enjoyed (camp/to camp/camping) by the lake.

2. I remember (bring/to bring/bringing) it with me, but I forgot (where/whether/to where) I put it.

3. The man risked (lose/to lose/losing) his job by refusing to work overtime.

4. Can you (imagine/purchase/stop) life without the Internet?

5. The woman (continued/avoid/resist) to complain about the food.

ANSWER

1. camping   2. bringing, where   3. losing   4. imagine   5. continued

◆不完全及物動詞

有些及物動詞，雖然加了受詞，意思也並不完全，必須加上受詞補語，補充受詞不足的意思，才能讓句子意思完全。

不完全及物動詞使用在五大句型中的第五句型：S＋V＋O＋OC。

「使役動詞」（make/have/let）就是不完全及物動詞，接了受詞之後，必須接原形動詞作為受詞補語。

例：• Mom <u>made me run</u> errands for her.
（媽媽叫我幫她跑腿。）

• I'll <u>have him apologize</u> to you.（我會叫他跟你道歉。）

• Steve Jobs never <u>let his kids use</u> an iPad.
（賈伯斯從不讓他的孩子使用平板電腦。）

let的受詞後，也可接副詞作為受詞補語。
例：Don't <u>let me down</u>. （不要讓我失望。）

make的受詞後，也可接形容詞或名詞作為受詞補語。

(1) make表「使……變成某狀態」，受詞後接形容詞
例：• The man <u>made her life miserable</u>.
（那男人讓她的人生很悲慘。）

(2) make表「使……成為……」，受詞後接名詞
例：• My wife <u>made me a better man</u>.
（我的妻子讓我成為一個更好的人。）

• They <u>made it a rule</u> to do the dishes by turns.
（他們説好輪流洗碗。）

有些表示「要求」、「催促」、「鼓勵」的動詞，受詞後接不
定詞作為受詞補語，這類動詞常用的有：

tell（告訴）	force（強迫）	encourage（鼓勵）
ask（要求）	compel（迫使）	expect（期望）
want（希望）	push（催促）	entice（慫恿）

例：• Mom <u>told me to come home</u> early today.
（媽媽告訴我今天要早點回家。）

• Don't <u>force your teenagers to talk</u> to you.
（不要強迫你的青少年孩子跟你談話。）

- My teacher <u>encouraged me to take part in</u> the speech contest. （我的老師鼓勵我參加演説比賽。）

有些動詞可以作完全及物動詞，也可以作不完全及物動詞。

(1) 感官動詞

| see（看到） | observe（觀察） | hear（聽到） | feel（覺得） |
| watch（看） | look at（看） | listen to（聽） | notice（注意到） |

作完全及物動詞時，受詞後不需補語，句意也完全。

例：
- Listen to <u>me</u>. （聽我説。）
- Look at <u>that</u>. （你看那個。）
- I can feel <u>it</u>. （我可以感覺到。）

作不完全及物動詞時，受詞後需要受詞補語，句意才算完全。

例：
- The students observed a caterpillar <u>transform into a butterfly</u>.
  （學生們觀察一隻毛毛蟲轉變成一隻蝴蝶。）
  →以原形動詞作受詞補語，表「事實」。

- The judge found his testimony <u>very suspicious</u>.
  （法官發現他的證詞非常可疑。）→以形容詞作受詞補語

- They saw the couple <u>fighting</u> in front of a restaurant.
  （他們看到那對夫妻在一家餐廳前爭吵。）
  →以現在分詞作受詞補語，表「進行狀態」。

- I heard the door <u>opened</u>. （我聽到門被打開的聲音。）
  →以過去分詞作受詞補語，表「被動狀態」。

(2) 表「認定」的動詞

see（認為）	think（認為）	believe（認為，相信）
view（看待）	consider（認為）	deem（認為）
regard（認為）	find（發覺、認為）	take（以為、看作）
look upon（看待）		mistake（誤認）

　　這類動詞都有「將……視為……」之意，受詞後面接形容詞或名詞作受詞補語。

a. 接名詞作受詞補語時：

　　find後面可直接接名詞。

　　例：• You will <u>find</u> him <u>a trustworthy person</u>.
　　　　（你將發現他是個值得信賴的人。）

　　think/consider/deem 的受詞後面以to be接名詞，但是to be可省略。

　　例：• He never <u>considered</u> his son <u>(to be) his successor</u>.
　　　　（他從未將他的兒子視作接班人。）

　　　　• I <u>think</u> myself <u>(to be) an actor</u>, not a movie star.
　　　　（我將自己視為一名演員，而不是電影明星。）

　　see/view/regard/look upon，受詞後面以介系詞as接名詞。

　　例：• We <u>see</u> John <u>as our class leader</u>.
　　　　（我們將John視為我們的班長。）

　　　　• Everyone <u>regarded</u> Mozart <u>as a musical genius</u>.
　　　　（所有人都認為莫札特是為音樂天才。）

　　mistake的受詞後面以介系詞for接名詞。

　　例：Most people <u>mistake</u> the long-haired man <u>for a woman</u>.
　　　　（大部分的人都會把那長髮男子誤認為女人。）

b. 接形容詞作受詞補語時：

find的受詞後面直接接形容詞。

例：• I <u>find</u> our new neighbor <u>very mysterious</u>.
（我發現我們的新鄰居很神秘。）

think/consider/deem 的受詞後面以to be接形容詞，但是to be 可省略。

例：• We all <u>consider</u> this design <u>(to be) unpractical</u>.
（我們都認為這項設計不實用。）

• They <u>deem</u> their performance <u>(to be) unsatisfactory</u>.
（他們認為自己的表現差強人意。）

regard的受詞後面以介系詞as接形容詞。

例：• We <u>regard</u> this kind of behavior <u>as unacceptable</u>.
（我們認為這種行為是令人無法接受的。）

take的受詞後面以介系詞for接形容詞。

例：• Don't <u>take</u> everything <u>for granted</u>.
（不要將一切視為理所當然。）

c. 表示「認為做某事是……」時，受詞用虛受詞it，真受詞（不定詞）放在作受詞補語的形容詞後，句型結構為：

think believe consider find deem	＋it＋	受詞補語 （形容詞） （名詞）	＋to V

例：• Many people find it <u>interesting</u> to learn Spanish.
（很多人都發現學西班牙文很有趣。）

- I believe it <u>necessary to clarify</u> my stand on this issue.
（我認為澄清我在這個議題的立場是有必要的。）

- I deem it <u>an honor to be</u> nominated.
（我認為能獲得提名是一件榮耀的事。）

- Most moms find it <u>a great challenge to balance</u> their work and family.（大部分的媽媽發現，要在工作與家庭間取得平衡，是個很大的挑戰。）

重點筆記

think/believe/consider/find/deem也可作完全及物動詞，接that引導的名詞子句作為受詞：

例：
- They believe that the suspect planned this murder beforehand.
（他們認為嫌犯事先計劃好這次謀殺行動。）

- He found that his biological parents were still alive.
（他發現他的親生父母仍然還活著。）

- She considered that bitcoin is worth-investing.
（她認為比特幣是值得投資的。）

d. 表示「任命、指派」的動詞，受詞後面接表「職位名稱」的名詞作受詞補語，表「作為」的介系詞**as**，可省略不用。表示職位名稱的定冠詞**the**在這類句型中亦不需要。

這類動詞常用的有：

elect （選舉）	designate （指定）	nominate （提名）	appoint （任命）

例：• We elected Jack (as) the class representative.
（我們選傑克作為班代表。）

• They have designated this area (as) a nature reserve.
（他們已經將這個地區指定為自然保育區。）

• The President nominated Paul Dylan (as) Foreign Minister.
（總統任命鮑伯‧迪倫為外交部長。）

(3) 其他不完全及物動詞（建議記下動詞，並熟讀例句，以做類似應用。）

a. name（命名）

例：• They name their first child Juliet.
（他們將第一個寶寶取名為茱麗葉。）

b. set（使處於特定狀態）

例：• Let's set the little bird free. （我們把這隻小鳥給放了吧。）

c. paint（塗以顏色）

例：• I'm thinking to paint the baby's room light blue.
（我打算把寶寶的房間漆成淡藍色。）

d. call（稱呼）

例：• My name is Jacqueline, but you can just call me Jackie.
（我的名字是賈桂琳，但你可以叫我潔姬就好。）

e. drive（迫使成為某種狀態）

例：• The loud noise is driving me crazy.
（巨大的噪音快要把我逼瘋了。）

f. leave（使成為某種狀態）

例：• Turn off the tap. Don't leave it <u>running</u>.
（把水龍頭關起來。不要讓水一直流。）

　• Leave him <u>alone</u>.（不要煩他。）

馬上動手練一練 ❹

圈出正確的動詞

1. Jerry looks after these children with all his heart. No wonder these children (call/see/let) him as their father.

2. It is very easy to (see/view/mistake) Emily for Emma, her twin sister.

3. Most people (deem/observe/regard) another nuclear power plant unnecessary.

4. We have an unexpected visitor. I can hear someone (to walk/walk/walking) downstairs.

5. Could you (tell/have/want) a plumber fix our leaking faucet as soon as possible?

ANSWER

1. see　　2. mistake　　3. deem　　4. walking　　5. have

三‧授與動詞

　　授與動詞屬於及物動詞，與其他及物動詞不同的地方在於，授與動詞有兩個受詞。接受動作的受詞為直接受詞（Direct Object/ D.O.），動作授與的對象則為間接受詞（Indirect Object/I.O.）。

授與動詞使用在句子中，為五大句型中的第四句型：S＋V＋I.O.＋D.O.。

1. 授與動詞後面的兩個受詞在句子結構中的位置可以互調，但若是直接受詞放前面，則需要有介系詞才能接間接受詞：

> 主詞＋V＋I.O.（間接受詞）＋D.O.（直接受詞）
> ＝主詞＋V＋直接受詞(D.O.)＋介系詞＋間接受詞(I.O.)

> 例：• She wrote me a letter. = She wrote a letter to me.
> （她寫了一封信給我。）
> 間接受詞＋直接受詞　　　直接受詞＋介系詞＋間接受詞

2. 常用的授與動詞及搭配的介系詞：

ask（問）	of（對）

> 例：The reporter asked the actress several awkward questions.
> ＝The reporter asked several awkward questions of the actress.
> （記者問了女星幾個尷尬的問題。）

give（給）　offer（提供）　write（寫） show（展示）　tell（告訴）　lend（借出） send（寄送）　leave（留下）　teach（教） owe（欠）	to（給；向）

> 例：• I would like to give you some advice.
> ＝I would like to give some advice to you.
> （我想給你一些建議。）

• Never lend <u>your friends</u> <u>money</u>.
＝Never lend <u>money</u> to <u>your friends</u>.
（絕不要借錢給你的朋友。）

• The billionaire didn't leave <u>his children</u> <u>his fortunes</u>.
＝The billionaire didn't leave <u>his fortunes</u> to <u>his children</u>.
（該億萬富翁沒有將他的財產留給他的孩子。）

bring （帶來） read （讀）	to （給；對） for （為）

例：• The cold front is expected to bring <u>the island</u> <u>the needed</u>
<u>rain</u>.
＝The cold front is expected to bring <u>the needed rain</u> to
<u>the island</u>.（這道冷鋒可望能夠為島嶼帶來所需的雨
水。）

• I don't have my glasses with me. Could you read me <u>this</u>
<u>letter</u>?
＝I don't have my glasses with me. Could you read <u>this</u>
<u>letter</u> for <u>me</u>? （我沒有把眼鏡帶在身上。你可以幫我
讀這封信嗎？）

buy（買）　　find（找） make（做）　leave（留）	for （為；給）

例：• I bought <u>you</u> <u>a souvenir</u>. ＝ I bought <u>a souvenir</u> for <u>you</u>.
（我買了一個紀念品給你。）

• Let me find <u>you</u> <u>an umbrella</u>. ＝ Let me find <u>an umbrella</u>
for <u>you</u>.
（讓我來幫你找把傘吧。）

- Don't eat everything. Leave me some food.
= Don't eat everything. Leave some food for me.
（別把所有東西都吃掉。留點食物給我。）

3. 特別注意：

　　相較於上述授與動詞，在I.O.（間接受詞）後就可以直接接D.O.（直接受詞），以下授與動詞的間接受詞後，需要介系詞with才能接直接受詞：

provide（提供）　supply（供應）　present（呈獻）	for（為）

例：
- They provided us with comfortable accommodations during our stay.
  = They provided comfortable accommodations for us during our stay.
  （他們在我們停留期間提供我們舒適的住宿。）

- The dairy farm supplies our restaurant with fresh dairy products.
  = The dairy farm supplies fresh dairy products for/to our restaurant.
  （該酪農場供應我們餐廳新鮮的乳製品。）

- They presented their mother with a bunch of carnations.
  = They presented a bunch of carnations for their mother.
  （他們獻給他們的母親一束康乃馨。）

 重點筆記

直接受詞（物）在間接受詞後時，不可以用代名詞表示。

例：• I owe Mary an apology.

= I owe an apology to Mary.

（我欠瑪麗一個道歉。）

在這個句子中，owe為授與動詞，an apology（物）為直接受詞，Mary（人）為間接受詞。要將兩個受詞換成代名詞時：

（○）I owe it to her.

（X）I owe her it.（直接受詞在後面時，不用代名詞。）

 馬上動手練一練 ❺

在空格中填入正確的介系詞，以完成句子

1. I'm going to the supermarket. Do you want me to buy anything ＿＿＿ you?

2. Make sure you won't tell this secret ＿＿＿ anyone else.

3. The company not only offered a job ＿＿＿＿ Jack, but also provided him ＿＿＿ accommodations.

4. The students asked many questions ＿＿＿＿ their teacher after class.

5. We would like to present a song ＿＿＿ our beloved mother.

ANSWER

1. for   2. to   3. to, with   4. of   5. for

文法總複習
快來試試自己的實力吧！

A. 選出正確的答案，以完成句子

1. (　) The unforeseen misfortune _____ him into an eccentric old man.

   A. made　　　B. let　　　C. turned　　　D. became

2. (　) If you don't get enough sleep tonight, you may ___ asleep in class tomorrow.

   A. fall　　　B. get　　　C. run　　　D. come

3. (　) The committee nominated Steven Jones _____ their representative.

   A. to be　　　B. for　　　C. with　　　D. as

4. (　) I ___ you to apologize to Judy, because you owe her one.

   A. let　　　B. want　　　C. have　　　D. make

5. (　) People ___ Warren Edward Buffett as the god of stocks.

   A. watch　　　B. view　　　C. look　　　D. wonder

6. (　) They find it unnecessary ___ another office assistant.

   A. hire　　　B. hires　　　C. to hire　　　D. hiring

7. (　) The new policy ___ undesirable at first, but it turned out to be beneficial for the people.

   A. seemed　　　B. felt　　　C. noticed　　　D. considered

8. (　) The man ___ her life miserable.

   A. made　　　B. liked　　　C. loved　　　D. forced

9. (　) My father asked me ___ my homework.
   A. doing   B. to do   C. do   D. did

10. (　) She made a cake ___me yesterday.
   A. to   B. as   C. for   D. be

B. 選擇正確的動詞，並做適當變化後填入空格中

make	smell	taste	suggest	sound	find
provide	hear	live	explain	scream	crazy

1. The government's intervention _____ the whole situation more complicated.

2. Durians _____ awful, but _____ great.

3. I _____ a woman talking, and her voice _____ very familiar to me. So I turned around to look at her, and _____ that she was my high school teacher.

4. Can you imagine _____ together with the dinosaurs?

5. The store doesn't _____ customers with enough information about their return policy.

6. The restaurant manager had a waitress _____ the menu for us.

7. My mother _____ that we take a trip to Singapore in summer.

8. I'm going _____ if the kids don't stop _____.

ANSWER

A. 選出正確的答案，以完成句子
1. C   2. A   3. D   4. B   5. B
6. C   7. A   8. A   9. B   10. C

1. make表「使……成為……」，受詞後接名詞

2. fall asleep睡著

3. 表示「任命、指派」的動詞如：elect（選舉）、
   designate（指定）、nominate（提名）、appoint
   （任命），受詞後面接表「職位名稱」的名詞作受詞
   補語，表「作為」的介系詞as，可省略不用

4. 完全及物動詞意指後面接了受詞，句意才算完全的動
   詞，want（想要）+to v

5. see/view/regard/look upon，受詞後面以介系詞as接
   名詞

6. 表示「認為做某事是……」時，受詞用虛受詞it，
   真受詞（不定詞）放在作受詞補語的形容詞後，句
   型結構為：Many people find it interesting to learn
   Spanish.（很多人都發現學西班牙文很有趣。）

7. seem似乎+形容詞

8. make表「使……變成某狀態」，受詞後接形容詞

9. ask要求+to原形動詞

10. 授與動詞make+受詞+for

B. 選擇正確的動詞，並做適當變化後填入空格中

1. made

2. smell, taste

3. heard, sounded, found

4. living

5. provide

6. explain

7. suggested

8. crazy, screaming

現在完成式

使用時機
- 從過去持續到現在的動作
- 已存在一段時間的狀態
- 剛剛完成的動作
- 至今的經驗

have/has＋過去分詞（V-p.p.）

Lesson 5

動詞
的時態

現在完成進行式

使用時機
└ 從過去持續到現在，
仍然進行中的動作

have/has＋been＋現在分詞（V-ing）

過去完成式

使用時機
- 發生在過去時間已經結束的動作
- 在過去特定時間前已經發生的事

had＋過去分詞（V-p.p.）

過去完成進行式

使用時機
└ 過去某時間前已經持續一段時間的事

had been＋現在分詞（V-ing）

完成式

未來完成式

使用時機——預期未來某時間已經完成的事

willhave＋過去分詞（V-p.p.）

未來完成進行式

使用時機——持續到未來某一刻的動作

will have been＋現在分詞（V-ing）

簡單式

現在簡單式
- **使用時機**
  - 習慣性動作
  - 知覺或狀態
  - 恆常不變的事實
  - 不會改變的將來
- 用原形動詞
- 第三人稱單數動詞＋s
- 疑問句／否定句用do/does

過去簡單式
- **使用時機**
  - 過去的習慣或狀態
  - 過去的動作或經驗
- 過去式動詞
- 疑問句／否定句用did

未來簡單式
- **使用時機**
  - 未來會發生的動作或狀態
  - 條件成立時會發生的事
- will＋原形動詞

進行式

現在進行式
- **使用時機**
  - 正在進行的動作
  - 即將發生的動作
  - 頻繁發生的動作
  - 逐漸變成某種狀態
- be動詞＋現在分詞（V-ing）

過去進行式
- **使用時機**
  - 過去正在進行的動作
  - 在過去時間即將發生的事
- was/were＋現在分詞（V-ing）

未來進行式
- **使用時機** — 未來某時間進行的動作
- will＋be＋現在分詞（V-ing）

Lesson 5　動詞的時態

英文的句子有時態的區別，而區別時態的方式，主要是仰賴句子中動詞的變化。從時間上來説，英文的句子時態有「現在」、「過去」、「未來」之分；描述發生在這三個時間區塊時，還有「簡單式」、「進行式」及「完成式」這三種句型。

英文的動詞時態非常重要，只要能徹底理解清楚，並正確使用，英文文法就算是搞定七成了。

一‧簡單式

◆現在簡單式：
→動詞使用原形動詞，並根據主詞做適當變化。

例：• I am a college student. I study Computer Engineering.
（我是個大學生。我讀的是電腦工程。）

• You are my best friend. You always give me good advice.
（你是我最好的朋友。總是給我好建議。）

• Puffy is my dog. It does various tricks, and snores like a pig.
（帕妮是我的狗。牠會做很多把戲，而且打起鼾來就像一隻豬。）

使用助動詞do/does搭配原形動詞於疑問句與否定句中。助動詞do/does用於肯定句時旨在「強調語氣」。

例：• <u>Do</u> you <u>play</u> tennis?（你打網球嗎？）

　　• They <u>do not/don't wear</u> uniforms to school.
　　（他們上學不穿制服。）

　　• He <u>does not/doesn't have</u> any brothers or sisters.
　　（他沒有任何兄弟姐妹。）

　　• I <u>do speak</u> a little English.（我的確會說一點英文。）

❶ 使用現在簡單式的時機

①表習慣性動作（常與時間副詞或頻率副詞搭配）

例：• He <u>commutes</u> to school by bus every day.
　　（他每天搭公車通勤上學。）

　　• We seldom <u>eat</u> out.（我們很少在外面吃飯。）

②表知覺或狀態

例：• I <u>hear</u> someone crying.（我聽到有人在哭。）

　　• You <u>don't look</u> well.（你看起來不太舒服。）

③表恆常不變的事實

例：• The earth <u>rotates</u> on its axis once a day and <u>orbits</u> the
　　sun once a year.
　　（地球每天自轉一圈，每年繞著太陽公轉一圈。）

　　• God <u>helps</u> those who <u>help</u> themselves.
　　（天助自助者。）

④以現在式表未來式

當將來的事情是不會改變的事實，或是不太可能改變的安排或計劃，則以現在簡單式來表示未來式。以下即常用於現在式表示未來發生的事的動詞。

begin/start 開始	arrive 到達	leave 離開
end/finish 結束	come 來	go 去

例：
- The concert begins at 7:30.
（音樂會七點半開始。）

- The exhibition ends tomorrow.
（展覽明天結束。）

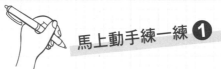

馬上動手練一練 ❶

將括號內的提示字做適當變化填入空格中，以完成句子

1. When _____(do) the next train _____(leave) for Birmingham?

2. I _____(take) a shower every morning.

3. Most weekends my parents _____(go) to the hypermarket for grocery and food shopping.

4. What time _____ you usually _____(finish) your work?

5. Traditionally, the President of the USA _____(live) in the White House.

ANSWER
1. does, leave   2. take   3. go   4. do, finish   5. lives

◆ 過去簡單式：
→ 無論主詞為何，動詞都使用過去式。

例：• I received a spam phone call, asking for my bank account information.

（我接到一通垃圾來電問我的銀行帳戶資訊。）

• I lived with my grandparents until I was six.
（我六歲之前都是跟我爺爺奶奶住在一起。）

使用助動詞did搭配原形動詞於疑問句與否定句中。助動詞did用於肯定句時旨在「強調語氣」。

❶ 使用過去簡單式的時機

過去簡單式常與表示過去時間的副詞或副詞子句搭配。

①表過去的習慣或狀態

例：• We used to be very close to each other.
（我們過去曾經很要好。）

• He always stayed up late before he got sick.
（他在生病之前總是熬夜熬得很晚。）

②表過去的動作或經驗

例：• I watched the movie last weekend.
（我上週末看了那部電影。）

• They lived next to us before they moved to Japan.
（他們在搬到日本之前，住在我們隔壁。）

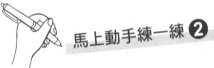

馬上動手練一練 ❷

將括號內的提示字做適當變化填入空格中，以完成句子

1. I ____(do) tell you not to touch anything on my desk.
2. It ____ (rain) a lot yesterday, so we ____(not/go) out and ____ (stay) at home all day.
3. Helen Keller ____(lose) her sight and hearing after she ____(recover) from an illness.
4. Marie and Pierre Curie ____(discover) radium as well as penicillin.
5. Before Jane ____(become) a famous singer, she ____(earn) her living as a waitress in her hometown.

ANSWER

1. did   2. rained, didn't go, stayed   3. lost, recovered
4. discovered   5. became, earned

◆未來簡單式

在未來簡單式的句子中，無論主詞為何，都是使用助動詞will搭配原形動詞。

例：• We will get the job done on schedule.
（我們會如期將工作完成。）

• Everything will be OK. （所有一切都會沒事的。）

• Will your parents come to your graduation ceremony?
（你的爸媽會來參加你的畢業典禮嗎？）

① 使用未來簡單式的時機

①表未來時間會發生的動作或狀態（常與未來時間副詞搭配）

例：• It will snow tomorrow. （明天會下雪。）

　　• They will build a hypermarket in this area.
　　（他們將會在這地區蓋一個大規模超市。）

②表條件成立時會發生的事（常與when/unless/if/once
　引導的副詞子句搭配）

例：• If you invite him, he will probably come.
　　（如果你邀請他，他就可能會來。）

　　• The students won't understand unless you explain it
　　clearly. （除非你解釋得很清楚，否則學生們不會了解。）

馬上動手練一練 ❸

將括號內的提示字做適當變化填入空格中，以完成句子

1. Don't sit on the wall! You ＿＿＿(fall) and ＿＿＿(hurt) yourself.

2. If you don't clean your bedroom, Mom ＿＿＿(be) very angry.

3. I don't have any plans for the weekend. Maybe I ＿＿＿(go) to
   the supermarket with my parents, or just ＿＿＿＿(look after) my
   cousins at home.

4. Your secret is safe with me. I ＿＿＿＿(not/tell) anyone about it.

5. Dinner ＿＿＿(be) ready in a minute. Go wash your hands before
   you eat.

ANSWER

1. will fall, hurt	2. will be	3. will go, look after
4. will not/won't tell	5. will be	

二・進行式

　　進行式是用來表示正在進行中或正在發生的動作,由「be動詞＋現在分詞」組成。be動詞視主詞及時態做變化。

原形動詞變成現在分詞的方式

1. 直接加ing

例: • explain → explaining　　• pray → praying
　　• build → building

2. 字尾字母為e的動詞,去字尾e再加ing

例: • use → using　　• urge → urging
　　• participate → participating

3. 重複字尾加ing

a. 單母音＋單子音的單音節動詞,要重複字尾字母,再加ing

例: • step → stepping　　• swim → swimming
　　• run → running

b. 重音在第二音節,且第二音節為單母音＋單子音的雙音節動詞,要重複字尾字母,再加ing

例: • admit → admitting　　• transfer → transferring
　　• prefer → preferring

4. 去ie加ying

字尾為ie動詞,要把ie改成y之後,再加ing

例: • die → dying　　• tie → tying

字尾為e，但e為字母發音，如e/ee/oe/ye的動詞，不去e直接加ing

例：
- be→being
- flee→fleeing
- hoe→hoeing
- dye→dyeing

◆現在進行式：
→be動詞（am/is/are）＋現在分詞（V-ing）

例：
- What are they doing in the basement?
（他們正在地下室做什麼？）

- He is repairing the broken vase.
（他正在修復破掉的花瓶。）

- I am reading an article about global warming.
（我正在讀一篇有關地球暖化的文章。）

❶ 使用現在進行式的時機

①表正在進行的動作

例：
- He is preparing for his oral presentation.
（他正在為口頭報告作準備。）

- The firefighters are trying to put out the fire.
（消防員正試著將火撲滅。）

②表即將發生的動作

現在進行式可用來表示不久的將來即將發生的事

例：
- We are leaving tomorrow. （我們明天就要離開了。）
- Christmas is coming in a week.
（聖誕節再過一星期就到了。）

③表頻繁發生的動作

當某個動作或事件出現次數十分頻繁時，經常用現在進行式取代現在簡單式，並與always/constantly/forever等副詞連用。使用現在進行式取代現在簡單式時，通常帶有一點無奈或不耐煩的意味。

例：• The baby <u>is forever crying</u>. （寶寶永遠都在哭。）

　　• My boss <u>is constantly changing his mind</u> at the last minute. （我老闆總是在最後一刻改變主意。）

④表示逐漸變成某個狀態

當某種狀態是採漸進的方式出現時，可以用現在進行式來表示。

例：• It's getting dark. I think it's going to rain.
　　（天色越來越暗了。我想就快要下雨了。）

　　• The economy in this country <u>is improving</u>.
　　（這個國家的經濟逐漸好轉中。）

---

be going to的用法

1. be going to 可以表示「正要去某處」

例：• I <u>am going to</u> the movies. （我正要去看電影。）

　　• They <u>are going to</u> school. （他們正要去上學。）

2. be going to 也可取代助動詞will，用來表示「即將發生的動作」

一般來說：be going to＋V ＝will＋V

例：• I am going to tell her the truth. （我要告訴她實情。）

　　＝ I will tell her the truth. （我將會告訴她實情。）

　　雖然可以互用，但兩者之間仍有語用上的差異： be going to＋V用來表示「動作即將發生」，用在已經知道發生機率很高，並且幾乎已經確定何時會發生的情況下。will＋V則用來表示「動作會在未來時間發生，但不確定何時」，用在有計劃發生，但是仍有變數的情況下。

例：• The patient is very sick. He <u>is going to die</u> soon.
（病人病得很重。他很快就會死了。）
→此人在不久的將來就會死亡

• No matter how long you live, you will die eventually.
（無論你會活多久，最終你都是會死的。）
→不確定將來何時會發生

◆過去進行式：
→be動詞過去式（was/were）＋現在分詞（V-ing）

經常搭配表過去某一特定時間的時間副詞。

例：• I <u>was talking</u> on the phone then. （我那時正在講電話。）

• He <u>was taking</u> a shower when the phone rang.
（電話響時，他正在淋浴。）

❶ 使用過去進行式的時機

①表過去某時間正在進行的動作

例：• Everyone <u>was sleeping</u> when I came home.
（我回到家時，所有人都在睡覺。）

• All students <u>were paying</u> attention when the teacher explained the assignment. （當老師解釋作業時，所有學生都非常注意聽。）

過去進行式可用來表示在過去時間，<u>不久的將來</u>即將發生的事。

例：• He was very sad because his father <u>was dying</u>.
（他非常難過，因為他的父親就快死了。）

• She knew the baby <u>was coming</u> when the labor pains occurred.（當陣痛發生時，她知道寶寶就快要出生了。）

◆未來進行式

未來進行式以助動詞will搭配be動詞原形＋現在分詞（V-ing）來表示。未來進行式是用來表示在未來某個特定時間將會進行的動作。

例：• We <u>will be flying</u> to New York this time tomorrow.
（我們明天此時將正飛往紐約。）

• Take your time. I <u>will be waiting</u> at the arrival lounge.
（你慢慢來。我到時候將會在入境大廳等。）

❶ 不使用進行式的動詞

有些動詞通常只用於簡單式，不能用於進行式。

①表示瞬間動作的動詞

find（找到）　　discover（發現）　　admit（承認）

例：(O) Columbus discovered the New World in 1492.
（哥倫布在1492年發現新大陸。）

(X) Columbus ~~was discovering~~ the New World in 1492.

②描述事實或狀態，而非動作發生的動詞

have（有）	belong to（屬於）	contain（包含）	need（需要）
weigh（重）	own（擁有）	include（包含）	
cost（花費）	deserve（值得）	owe（欠）	

例：(O) She owns three apartments in the city center.
（她在市中心擁有三間公寓。）

(X) She ~~is owning~~ three apartments in the city center.

③表示感官、感覺的動詞

smell（聞到）	see（看見）	hear（聽到）	feel（摸起來）
sound（聽起來）	seem（看起來）	taste（嘗起來）	need（需要）
cost（花費）	deserve（值得）	owe（欠）	

例：(O) Your idea doesn't sound very practical to me.
（你的主意在我聽來不是非常實際。）

(X) Your idea ~~is not sounding~~ very practical to me.

④表示腦部思想的動詞

think（認為，相信）	believe（相信）	understand（明白）
know（認識）	see（明白）	recognize（認得）
suppose（想）	remember（記得）	imagine（想像）
forget（忘記）	mean（意指）	realize（理解）

例：(O) I don't believe a word the woman said.
（那女子所說的話，我一個字都不相信。）

(X) I ~~am not believing~~ a word the woman said.

馬上動手練一練 ❹

依句意填入正確的進行式

1. I didn't answer the phone. Because when it rang, I _____(take) a shower.

2. You can visit me around 10 AM tomorrow. I _____(not work) at that time.

3. Don't go in right now. Mr. Barrymore _____(have) a meeting with some very important clients.

4. Could you please stop talking right now? I _____ (watch) the Korean drama.

5. Julie _____(argue) with her brother when Mom came home.

ANSWER

1. was taking   2. will not/won't be working   3. is having
4. am watching   5. was arguing

特別收錄
動詞的三態變化

動詞的三態指的是「原形動詞」、「過去式動詞」與「過去分詞」。

1. 原形動詞：

在現在式的句子中,動詞要用「原形動詞」。當主詞為第三人稱單數時,動詞要變成「單數動詞」。

例：• The players practice hard in order to win the game.
（選手們為了贏得比賽,練習得很辛苦。）

• She practices the piano two hours a day.
（她一天練兩小時鋼琴。）

句子中有助動詞時,助動詞後面的動詞保持原形動詞。

例：• I won't go home until I finish my work.
（直到我完成工作之前,我是不會回家的。）

• She didn't know the answer to the question.
（她不知道問題的答案。）

2. 過去式動詞：

句子時態為「過去式」時,動詞要改成「過去式」。無論主詞為何,動詞過去式的形式都相同。

例：• The customers complained that our after-sale service was unsatisfactory.
（顧客們抱怨我們的售後服務令人不滿。）

- The suspect <u>denied</u> all allegations of murder.
（嫌犯否認所有殺人的指控。）

3. 過去分詞：

　　句子時態為「完成式」時，動詞要改成「過去分詞」，並與助動詞have/has搭配使用。（有關完成式將在P124介紹。）

　　例：• I <u>have been</u> an elementary school teacher for twenty years.（我已經擔任小學老師二十年了。）

　　　　• She <u>hasn't seen</u> her biological parents since she was abandoned.
（她自從被拋棄之後，就沒有再見過親生父母。）

動詞三態變化方式

　　英文中的動詞變化，有「規則變化動詞」及「不規則變化動詞」兩種。

　　動詞的過去式、過去分詞之變化有一定規則的動詞，稱為「規則變化動詞」；反之，則稱為不規則變化動詞。

1. 規則變化動詞

　　規則變化動詞的過去式及過去分詞，通常是字尾加上d或ed：

(1) 直接在動詞字尾加ed。常見的動詞有：

現在式	過去式／過去分詞	現在式	過去式／過去分詞
clean	cleaned	stay	stayed
wash	washed	visit	visited
happen	happened	work	worked
watch	watched	look	looked
play	played	rain	rained
pick	picked	talk	talked

(2) 動詞字尾為e者，字尾加d。常見的動詞有：

現在式	過去式／過去分詞	現在式	過去式／過去分詞
like	liked	love	loved
dance	danced	invite	invited
close	closed	agree	agreed
wipe	wiped	live	lived
hope	hoped	decide	decided
arrive	arrived	smile	smiled

(3) 單音節動詞，其母音為短音、字尾為單子音的動詞，需**重複字尾字母**再加ed。常見的動詞有：

現在式	過去式／過去分詞	現在式	過去式／過去分詞
jog	jogged	stop	stopped
mop	mopped	drop	dropped
plan	planned	clap	clapped

(4) 字尾為y且前一個字母為子音的動詞，需**去掉y**再加ied。常見的動詞有：

現在式	過去式／過去分詞	現在式	過去式／過去分詞
cry	cr**ied**	apply	appl**ied**
try	tr**ied**	marry	marr**ied**
study	stud**ied**	carry	carr**ied**
spy	sp**ied**	comply	compl**ied**

(5) 兩音節以上的音節，重音落在第二音節，且字尾為子音時，需重複字尾再加ed。常見的動詞有：

現在式	過去式／過去分詞	現在式	過去式／過去分詞
occur	occur**red**	admit	admi**tted**
prefer	prefer**red**	commit	commi**tted**

2. 不規則變化動詞

不規則變化動詞的過去式及過去分詞之變化沒有一定規則，但依然可以分為以下四種：

(1) A-B-C型——動詞三態皆不同。常見的動詞有：

現在式	過去式	過去分詞	現在式	過去式	過去分詞
begin	began	begun	grow	grew	grown
blow	blew	blown	hide	hid	hidden
break	broke	broken	know	knew	known
choose	chose	chosen	ring	rang	rung
do	did	done	ride	rode	ridden

draw	drew	drawn	see	saw	seen
drink	drank	drunk	sing	sang	sung
drive	drove	driven	speak	spoke	spoken
eat	ate	eaten	steal	stole	stolen
fall	fell	fallen	swim	swam	swum
fly	flew	flown	take	took	taken
forget	forgot	forgot/ forgotten	throw	threw	thrown
give	gave	given	wear	wore	worn
go	went	gone	write	wrote	written

(2) A-B-B型——過去式與過去分詞相同。常見的動詞有：

現在式	過去式	過去分詞	現在式	過去式	過去分詞
catch	caught	caught	lose	lost	lost
bring	brought	brought	make	made	made
build	built	built	meet	met	met
buy	bought	bought	pay	paid	paid
feel	felt	felt	say	said	said
find	found	found	sell	sold	sold
get	got	got	sit	sat	sat
have	had	had	spend	spent	spent
hear	heard	heard	sleep	slept	slept
hold	held	held	tell	told	told
keep	kept	kept	think	thought	thought
leave	left	left	understand	understood	understood
lend	lent	lent	win	won	won

(3) A-B-A型──現在式與過去分詞形式相同。常見的動詞有：

現在式	過去式	過去分詞
come	came	come
become	became	become
run	ran	run

(4) A-A-A型──動詞三態形式皆不變。常見的動詞有：

現在式	過去式	過去分詞	現在式	過去式	過去分詞
cost	cost	cost	let	let	let
cut	cut	cut	put	put	put
hit	hit	hit	read	read	read
hurt	hurt	hurt			

馬上動手練一練 **5**

依提示做變化，完成句子

1. We _____(have) a lot of snow last winter. I _____(hope) it _____(not/snow) that much this year.

2. _____ you _____(know) Bill, the tall boy living next to us? He _____(go) to the same school as you.

3. Teacher: Why _____ you _____(hit) James?

   Mike: He _____ (hit) me first.

4. I _____(have) enough money to take a taxi. So

   I _____(walk) home last night.

5. We _____(be going to/spend) our summer vacation in Honolulu.

ANSWER

1. had, hope, won't snow
2. Do, know, goes
3. did, hit, hit
4. didn't have, walked
5. are going to spend

三‧完成式

完成式的時態,是用來描述自某一時間開始並持續到某一個時間的動作或事件。完成式時態主要由「助動詞have/has＋過去分詞」組合而成。

現在完成式,用來表示發生在過去某時間,並持續到現在的動作或事件;過去完成式,用來表示發生在過去某時間,並持續到過去某一時間的動作或事件;未來完成式,則用來表示未來某個時間將已完成的動作或事件。

只要時態觀念清楚,並且熟記動詞三態,僅僅一天就能輕鬆駕馭完成式囉!

◆現在完成式:

現在完成式的主要句型結構為: | have/has＋過去分詞(V-p.p.) |

關於過去分詞的變化方式,請複習特別收錄的動詞三態變化!而現在完成式是一個將過去與現在串聯在一起的句型:

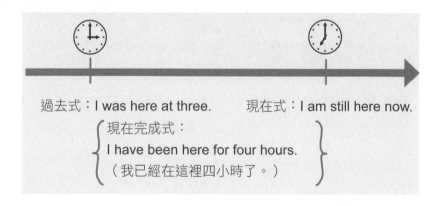

過去式:I was here at three.　現在式:I am still here now.

現在完成式:
I have been here for four hours.
(我已經在這裡四小時了。)

從前面框框中，三個時態的比較如下：

1. 過去式：描述發生在過去時間的動作或狀態。
   - I was here at three o'clock. （我三點時在這裡。）
2. 現在式：描述發生在現在時間的動作或狀態。
   - It is seven o'clock. I am still here.
   （現在是七點。我仍在這裡。）
3. 現在完成式：描述發生於過去，並持續到現在的動作或狀態。
   - I have been here since three o'clock.
   （我從三點就一直在這裡。）

表示完成式的助動詞have/has視主詞不同而做變化。

例：• I have made up my mind. （我已經下定決心了。）
   • She has left for work. （她已經去上班了。）

若為be動詞句型，則be動詞使用過去分詞been，後面接補語。

例：• My parents have been married for fifteen years.
   （我爸媽已經結婚十五年了。）
   • Mr. Freeman has been single for a long time.
   （費里曼先生已經單身很長一段時間了。）

現在完成式的否定句：助動詞have/has＋not即表否定。

have not＝haven't		has not＝hasn't

例：• This poor boy hasn't eaten anything for two days.
   （這可憐的男孩已經兩天沒有吃任何東西了。）
   • We haven't seen each other since we graduated from high
   school.
   （我們自從高中畢業之後就沒有再見過彼此了。）

現在完成式的疑問句：將助動詞have/has移到句首，即為疑問句。

例：• Have you heard anything about the new teacher?
（你有聽過任何有關新老師的事嗎？）

• Has Jason changed his phone number? I can't reach him. （傑森改了電話號碼嗎？我聯絡不上他。）

① 使用現在完成式的時機

①描述發生在過去時間，並持續到現在的動作

例：• I have worked in this company for more than ten years.
（我已經在這間公司工作超過十年了。）

• Anna has decided to quit her job and pursue further studies. （安娜已經決定辭掉工作去進修學業了。）

②描述到目前為止已存在一段時間的狀態

例：• The dinner has been ready. （晚餐已經準備好了。）

• The rooms haven't been so clean for a long time.
（這些房間已經很長一段時間沒有這麼乾淨了。）

③描述剛剛完成的動作

例：• He has sold his apartment.
（他已經賣掉了他的公寓。）

• I have just booked an appointment with my dentist.
（我剛剛已經跟牙醫預約看診時間了。）

④描述過去完成的動作，其後果持續至今

例：• The pickup shuttle from the hotel <u>has arrived</u>.
（飯店的接駁專車已經到了。）

• The earthquake <u>has destroyed</u> most part of the village.
（地震摧毀了大部分的村落。）

⑤描述至今曾經發生過的經驗

例：• I <u>have never seen</u> a ghost. （我從來沒有看過鬼。）

• She <u>has been to</u> London many times.
（她去過倫敦許多次。）

現在完成式與過去簡單式之比較

1. **現在完成式將過去與現在串聯在一起，過去簡單式只單純描述發生在過去的動作或事情。**

例：• I <u>have lived</u> in the city center for ten years.
（我已經住在市中心十年了。）→ 現在仍住在市中心

• I <u>lived</u> in the city center for ten years.
（我在市中心住過十年。）→ 現在已不住市中心

2. **過去發生的動作，結果持續至今，則用現在完成式；過去發生的動作，與現在已無關係，則用過去簡單式。**

例：• She <u>has lost</u> her passport.
（她弄丟了她的護照。）→ 護照現在還沒找回來

• She <u>lost</u> her passport.
（她把護照弄丟了。）
→ 單純描述這則發生在過去的事情，提供消息

馬上動手練一練 6

將括號內的動詞改成現在完成式，以完成句子

1. This village _____ (change) a lot.

2. I _____ (call) 119. The ambulance will be here soon.

3. The police _____ (not/find) any evidence yet.

4. She _____ (do) everything she could to help me.

5. We _____ (hear) a lot about the Italian restaurant, but _____ (not/get) time to eat there.

ANSWER

1. has changed   2. have called   3. haven't found
4. has done   5. have heard, haven't got

❷ just、already與yet用在現在完成式

just、already與yet是三個常用在現在完成式的副詞。

①just 表「剛；才；只」

放在助動詞have/has之後，在完成式中表示「剛發生」的動作或事情。

例：• The train has just left. （火車才剛開走。）

　　• We have just arrived at the train station.
　　（我們才剛抵達火車站。）

②already表「已經」

放在助動詞have/has 之後，或放在句尾加強語氣，在完成式中表示「比預期時間還要早發生或完成」的動作或事情。

例：• I have already completed the payment online.
（我已經在線上完成繳款了。）

• She has returned the defective goods to the store already. （她早就已經將瑕疵品退回商店了。）

③yet 表「還（沒）；已經」

放在句尾，用在期待某事發生的情況，通常只出現在疑問句或否定句。

例：• Have you cancelled the appointment with your dentist yet? （你取消跟牙醫的預約了沒？）

• I haven't received any response from the school yet. （我還沒有收到學校的回覆。）

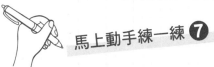

馬上動手練一練 ❼

在空格中填入just、already或yet

1. The plane has ＿＿ landed at the Haneda Airport.

2. I have ＿＿＿＿ been to Japan many times, but I am still very excited to be here.

3. I have booked a pickup shuttle ＿＿＿, so I will take the shuttle directly to the hotel from the airport.

4. I haven't called my mom ＿＿＿. I will do that as soon as I get to the hotel.

5. Finally, I got my luggage. I guess I'll have to wait for a while because my shuttle hasn't arrived ＿＿＿.

ANSWER
1. just　2. already　3. already　4. yet　5. yet

❸ for與since用在現在完成式

現在完成式句型用來表示「某個動作所進行或持續的時間」之時間副詞的方式：

①for＋一段時間

介系詞for後面接表示「一段時間」的名詞，形成時間副詞。

例：• I have known this man for twenty years.
　　（我已經認識這個男子二十年了。）

　　• She has locked herself in the room for hours.
　　（她已經把自己鎖在房間裡好幾個小時了。）

②since＋過去時間點／過去簡單式子句

since意指「自從」，後面接表「過去某一特定時間」的名詞，或是說明過去某時間點的過去簡單式子句，形成時間副詞，表示「自從（何時）起」。

例：• Mr. Ronald has been a taxi driver since 1990.
　　（羅納德先生從1990年起就是個計程車司機。）

　　• He has remained single since his wife died.
　　（自妻子過世後，他就一直維持單身狀態。）

❹ It has been＋一段時間＋since＋過去簡單式

是用來表示「距離某事」已經過多久時間的完成式句型。

例：• It has been two weeks since I left home.
　　（我離家至今已兩星期了。）

　　• It has been a long time since we last saw each other.
　　（自我們上次見面至今已經過了好長一段時間了。）

在空格中填入for或since

1. My grandparents have been in love with each other _____ the first time they met, and have been married ____ sixty years now.

2. I have had diarrhea _____ three days, and haven't eaten anything _____ yesterday.

3. This house has been vacant _____ 1978. No one has lived here _____ the past 40 years.

4. I have lost contact with Jack _____ months. I haven't heard from him _____ June.

5. Mr. Green hasn't been well _____ he came back from his business trip. He has been absent from work _____ three weeks. I'm really worried.

ANSWER

1. since, for   2. for, since   3. since, for
4. for, since   5. since, for

❺ gone與been用在現在完成式

①have been to＋地點

用來表示「曾去過某地」，意在描述過去的經驗。說明某人曾經去過某地，但目前人並一定不在該處。主詞可以是任何人。

例：• I have been to Canada once.（我去過加拿大一次。）

    • None of us has been to the USA.

    （我們之中沒有人去過美國。）

②have gone to＋地點

用來表示「曾去過某地」，意在描述動作的完成。說明某人已經前往或到達某地，且目前人正在該處。因為第一人稱是說話者，第二人稱是聽話者，因此這個句型的主詞必是第三人稱。

例：• She has gone to Shanghai already.
（她早就已經到上海去了。）

• They have already gone home.（他們已經離開了。）

★使用have been to或have gone to句型時，代名詞here/there或home前不需要加to。

馬上動手練一練 ❾

在空格中填入gone或been

1. Jessie is not home at the moment. She has _____ to the hair salon.

2. Mom and Dad have already _____ to the airport. Their flight departs at six.

3. I have never _____ to the city before. I can't wait!

4. As a flight attendant, I have _____ to most of the countries in Asia.

5. Why are you so late? Leslie and Mike have already _____ home.

ANSWER
1. gone   2. gone   3. been   4. been   5. gone

❻ 現在完成進行式

現在完成進行式的句型結構為have/has＋been＋現在分詞
（V-ing）。

用來描述在過去時間開始，並一直進行或持續至現在，而且目前正在仍然持續進行中的動作或事情。

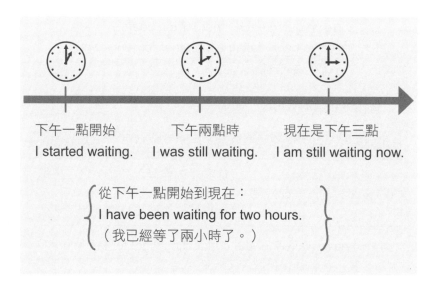

下午一點開始　　　下午兩點時　　　現在是下午三點
I started waiting.　I was still waiting.　I am still waiting now.

從下午一點開始到現在：
I have been waiting for two hours.
（我已經等了兩小時了。）

例：• Dr. Yang has been doing cancer research for decades.
（楊博士已經從事癌症研究好幾十年了。）
→目前仍持續進行研究中

• We have been planning for a family trip for the past few
months.（我們過去幾個月一直在計劃一次家庭旅行。）
→目前仍持續計劃中

現在完成式與現在完成進行式之比較

很多時候，現在完成式與現在完成進行式幾乎沒有太大的差別。

例：• I've worked in this company since I was 22.
　　＝I've been working in this company since I was 22.
　　（我從二十歲開始就一直在這家公司上班。）

　　• We've dated each other for ten years.
　　＝We've been dating each other for ten years.
　　（我們已經交往十年了。）

但兩個句型仍有用法差異：

現在完成式	現在完成進行式
(1) 表示動作已經完成 (2) 截至目前的完成進度	(1) 表示動作尚未完成，仍在持續進行 (2) 描述一個動作持續進行了多久

例：• I have waited for the connecting flight for ten hours.
　　（我已經等轉接班機等了十個小時了。）
　　　→可能已經即將上機，等待動作即將結束
　　• I have been waiting for the connecting flight for ten hours.
　　（我已經等轉接班機等了十個小時了。）
　　　→ 轉接班機仍無影蹤，等待動作仍要持續進行
　　• I've baked 10 apple pies so far this morning.
　　（這個上午到目前為止我已經烤了十個蘋果派。）
　　　→ 說明目前完成進度，但動作還會繼續進行

　　• I've been baking apple pies all day long.
　　（我一整天一直在烤蘋果派。）
　　　→ 說明動作持續進行一整天，目前還沒結束

以現在完成進行式將兩個句子合併

1. It started raining a week ago. It is still raining now.

_____

2. I tried to get in touch with her. I am still trying now.

_____

3. They began working on the project since June. They are still working on it.

_____

4. Dad started to look for his glasses days ago. He is still looking for them.

_____

5. We started to clean the house at two. We are still cleaning the house.

_____

ANSWER

1. It has been raining for a week.
2. I have been trying to get in touch with her.
3. They have been working on the project since June.
4. Dad has been looking for his glasses for days.
5. We have been cleaning the house since two.

◆ 過去完成式

描述發生在過去時間,並且在過去時間已經結束,與現在時間無關的動作或事情。句型結構為:had + 過去分詞(V-p.p.)

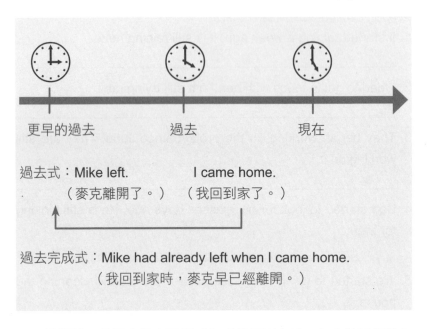

更早的過去　　　　　　過去　　　　　　現在

過去式:Mike left.　　　I came home.
　　　　(麥克離開了。)　(我回到家了。)

過去完成式:Mike had already left when I came home.
　　　　　　(我回到家時,麥克早已經離開。)

當描述一件過去特定時間(如「我回到家時」)之前已經發生(如「他已離開」)的事時,就要使用過去完成式。

例:• The plane <u>had</u> already <u>taken off</u> when they finally arrived at the airport.
(當他們終於到達機場時,飛機早就已經起飛了。)

• The post office <u>had closed</u> when I got there.
(當我到的時候,郵局已經關了。)

❶ 過去完成進行式

過去完成進行式的句型結構為: | had been + 現在分詞(V-ing) |

用來描述在過去某時間之前，已經持續進行一段時間的事。

例：• I <u>had been running</u> for half an hour before I started to sweat.

（在我開始流汗之前，我已經跑了半個小時了。）

• Dad <u>had been working</u> for 40 years when he retired at the age of 65.

（爸爸在六十五歲退休時，已經工作了四十年。）

馬上動手練一練 ⑪

將括號中的動詞依句意改為過去完成式或過去完成進行式，以完成句子

1. Henry _____(search) for his glasses for an hour when he finally saw them on his head.

2. My grandpa _____ (live) in the nursing home for five years when he passed away in 2015.

3. Lillian _____ (study) in college for six years before she finally graduated.

4. The boys _____ (wait) for the train for nearly an hour when they realized they were at the wrong platform.

5. The patient _____ (was) in a coma for weeks before he started to show signs of being aware.

ANSWER

1. had been searching   2. had lived   3. had studied
4. had been waiting   5. had been

◆未來完成式

未來完成是用在描述未來某特定時間將已經完成的動作或事情，或表示某活動的進行不會超過未來某特定時間。

未來完成式句型結構：$\boxed{\text{will＋have＋過去分詞（V-p.p.）}}$

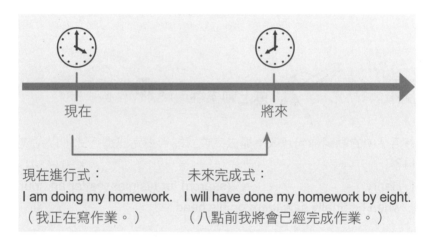

現在進行式：
I am doing my homework.
（我正在寫作業。）

未來完成式：
I will have done my homework by eight.
（八點前我將會已經完成作業。）

當描述一個「預期在未來某時間將已經完成」的動作時，就要使用未來完成式。

例：• I will have arrived in New York this time tomorrow.
（明天此時，我將已經抵達紐約。）

• Mom and Dad will have been married for 20 years next month. （爸爸媽媽下個月時將已經結婚二十年。）

重點筆記

未來完成式句子中的時間副詞，必須是可以表示未來時間的時間副詞，如：

1. by＋時間點

by表「在……之前」，如by tomorrow（明天以前）、by next week（下週前）、by the time he came back（在他回來之前）等。

2. in＋一段時間

in表「在……之後」，如in two weeks（兩星期後）、in six months（六個月後）。

3. next＋表時間之名詞

next表「下一個」，如next summer（明年夏天）、next Christmas（明年聖誕節）。

4. 其他常用在未來完成式的時間副詞，還有this time next year（明年此時）等。

① 未來完成進行式

未來完成進行式是用來描述過去發生的動作，持續進行到現在，並將繼續進行以至未來某一時刻的句型。

未來完成進行式的基本句型結構為：

will have been＋現在分詞（V-ing）

例：• By the end of this month, we will have been dating each other for one year.

（到這個月底，我們將已經交往一年。）

• He will have been waiting to see the doctor for three hours in five minutes.

（再過五分鐘，他等著看醫生就將等三小時了。）

馬上動手練一練 ⑫

將括號中的動詞依句意改為未來完成式或未來完成進行式，以完成句子

1. You can come pick me up at eight. I will _____ (finish) my work by then.

2. We will _____ (travel) in Europe for exactly three months in three days.

3. Kitty _____ (miss) for a week by Sunday. I'm so worried and I really hope to find it as soon as possible.

4. Julia and I met in 2013. We _____ (know) each other for a decade next September.

5. The man _____ (eat) three kilos of food when he finishes this giant burger.

ANSWER

1. have finished
2. have been travelling
3. will have been missing
4. will have known
5. will have eaten

Lesson 5

文法總複習
快來試試自己的實力吧！

A. 選出正確的動詞時態

1. (　) My brother is very untidy. He always _____ his stuff lying on the bedroom floor.
   A. is leaving   B. left
   C. leaves   D. leave

2. (　) When we were little, my cousin, Nick, often _____ me.
   A. hit   B. hits
   C. is hitting   D. will hit

3. (　) Grandma's memory _____ very bad lately. She _____ things.
   A. get; forgets
   B. got; forgot
   C. will get; forgotten
   D. is getting; is forgetting

4. (　) The bus _____ every twenty minutes during rush hour.
   A. is running   B. runs
   C. ran   D. run

5. (　) My roommate is very annoying. She always _____ my stuff without telling me.
   A. uses   B. used
   C. is using   D. will use

6. (　) Everyone _____ when the earthquake _____.
   A. panics; was occurring
   B. was panicking; will occur
   C. will panic; occurs
   D. panicked; occurred

7. (　) Give me a call as soon as you _____ safely in London.
   A. arrived   B. arrives
   C. arrive   D. will arrive

8. (　) _____ twelve years since the destructive tsunami hit the Southeast Asia.
   A. It has been
   B. There has been
   C. We have been
   D. It will be

9. (　) When I wake up at nine, Mom and Dad _____ to work. So I had to make breakfast for myself.
   A. have gone
   B. had already gone
   C. will have gone
   D. will have been going

10. (　) My hometown _____ a lot since I left in 1990. My elementary school is not there anymore.
   A. have been changing
   B. has changed
   C. had been changing
   D. will have changed

B. 將括號中的動詞改成適當的完成式時態

1. I _____ (have) a stomachache for days. I think I need to go to the doctor and find out the problem.

2. Leonardo DiCaprio _____ always _____ (be) my favorite actor.

   I _____ (watch) every movie he acted in.

3. It _____ (rain) all week. I wonder when the rain is going to stop.

4. The elevator of this building _____ (be) out of order for nearly a month before they finally got someone to repair it.

5. My daughter _____ (live) in Vancouver since she found a job there in 2003. She _____ (leave) Calgary, her hometown, for fifteen years by the end of this year.

6. Jack _____ (work) three jobs for five years. He has no option because he has a big family to support.

7. I _____ just _____ (finish) a huge meal. I am so full right now that I can't even move.

8. When she realized that the man was a thief, he _____ already _____ (go) with her money.

9. I _____ (learn) English since I was six.

10. I _____ (plan) the family trip for almost ten month.

ANSWER

A. 選出正確的動詞時態
1. **C**   2. **A**   3. **D**   4. **B**   5. **A**
6. **D**   7. **C**   8. **A**   9. **B**   10. **B**

1. 現在式第三人稱動詞加s/es，leave→leaves

2. were為are過去式，hit→hit（過去式）

3. 現在進行式 get old→is getting old、forget→is forgetting

4. 現在簡單式用於常態bus=it、run→runs

5. 現在簡單式用於常態第三人稱加s/es，use→uses

6. 敘述過去發生的事用過去簡單式，panic→panicked、occur→occurred

7. as soon as 一……就……，you非第三人稱故使用原形

8. It has been＋一段時間＋since＋過去簡單式用來表示「距離某事」已經過多久時間的完成式句型。如：
It has been two weeks since I left home.
（我離家至今已兩星期了。）

9. 當描述一件過去特定時間前已發生的事時，就要使用過去完成式

10. 現在完成式句型用來表示「某個動作所進行或持續的時間」之時間副詞的方式since意指「自從」，後面接表「過去某一特定時間」的名詞，或是說明過去某時間點的過去簡單式子句，形成時間副詞，表示「自從（何時）起」。如：
He has remained single since his wife died.
（自妻子過世後，他就一直維持單身狀態。）

B. 將括號中的動詞改成適當的完成式時態

1. have had

2. has been, have watched

3. has been raining

4. had been

5. has lived, will have left

6. has been working

7. have finished

8. had gone

9. have learned

10. have been planning

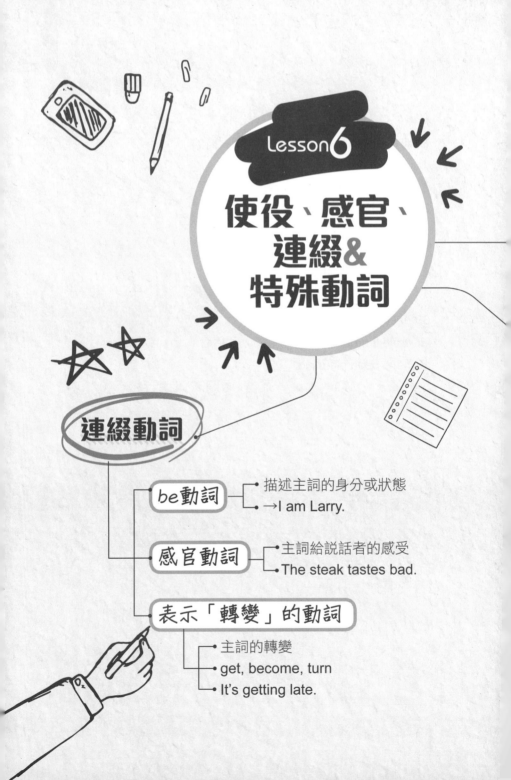

Lesson 6

使役、感官、連綴 & 特殊動詞

連綴動詞

- **be動詞**
  - 描述主詞的身分或狀態
  - →I am Larry.

- **感官動詞**
  - 主詞給說話者的感受
  - The steak tastes bad.

- **表示「轉變」的動詞**
  - 主詞的轉變
  - get, become, turn
  - It's getting late.

使役動詞

- 指使他人做某事
- make, have, let
- 使役動詞＋受詞＋原形動詞
  →He made me wait outside.

感官動詞

- see, watch, hear, notice, feel
- 感官動詞＋受詞＋原形動詞
  - I saw the boy hit the girl.
  - 已發生
- 感官動詞＋受詞＋現在分詞（V-ing）
  - I saw the boy hitting the girl.
  - 正在發生

使役、感官、連綴動詞&特殊動詞

本單元將介紹相對於一般動詞，有特殊用法的動詞。一般而言，英文句子中只能有一個動詞，當同一個句子中出現兩個以上的動詞時，第二個動詞必須以「變裝」，以「不定詞」或「動名詞」的方式出現。但是有一些動詞比較特別，能在不要求其他動詞變裝的情況下與之和平共處。有這類性質的動詞，除了「使役動詞、「感官動詞」之外，還有help這個動詞。

另外，英文中還有一類動詞，不是用來表示動作，而是用來當做主詞與補語間的橋樑，這類動詞稱為「連綴動詞」。

一・使役動詞

用來表示「指使」他人做某事的動詞，即使役動詞。

常用的使役動詞有：

(1) make（使）：表示「迫使某人做某事」，語氣最強烈。

例：• He made me wait outside.（他叫我在外面等。）

(2) have（要；叫）：表示「叫；使」某人去做某事，口氣較委婉。

例：• I'll have him return your call as soon as he comes back.（他一回來，我就叫他回你電話。）

(3) let（允許；讓）：表示「讓」某人去做某事，有「允許」的含義。

例：• The gentleman let me use his umbrella.
（那位紳士讓我用他的傘。）

❶ 使役動詞的基本句型結構： 使役動詞＋受詞＋原形動詞

使役動詞須隨主詞及時態做變化，受詞後的動詞，則不受主詞或時態影響，保持原形動詞。

例：• Cinderella's stepmother made her do all the house chores.
（仙杜瑞拉的後母要她做所有的家務事。）

• The kitchen faucet is leaking. The landlord will have someone fix it today.
（廚房水龍頭在漏水。房東今天將會請人來修。）

• That man stole my money! Don't let him get away.
（那男人偷了我的錢！別讓他逃了。）

❷ 使役動詞句型的否定句與疑問句

使役動詞為句子的主要動詞，因此由使役動詞加上助動詞及not來表示否定句。疑問句的助動詞亦以使役動詞的主詞、時態及語氣來做變化。

例：• My boss won't make me do anything illegal.
（我的老闆不會叫我做任何違法的事。）

• You mustn't let him take you for granted.
（你絕不能讓他把你視為理所當然。）

• Did the security officer have you wait here?
（警衛叫你在這裡等嗎？）

◆let的其他用法：let us與let's的比較

let的受詞為us時，可以縮寫成let's，但是let us與let's表達的是不同的意思。let us的受詞us（我們）指不包含對方的「我與其他人」時，let us＋V表示「允許我們做某事」，let us不能縮寫；受詞us（我們）指包含對方的「你與我（們）」，經常縮寫為let's，let's ＋V表示「讓我們（一起）去做某事」。

試比較下列兩個句子：

* Will you let us take a look at the newborn puppies?
（你能讓我們看一眼剛出生的小狗寶寶嗎？）
→向對方請求允許

* Let's take a look at the newborn puppies.
（我們來看一下剛出生的小狗寶寶吧！）
→向對方提出邀請或建議

例：• The parking officer didn't let us park our car here.
（停車場管理員不讓我們把車停在這兒。）

* The police won't let us leave if we don't tell the truth.
（如果我們不説實話，警方是不會讓我們離開的。）

* Let's just tell them everything.
（我們就將所有事情告訴他們吧。）

* Let's not make it complicated.
（我們別把事情弄得複雜了。）

◆have 的其他用法

have受詞後的動詞，若為受詞本身去身體力行的動作，則接原形動詞（V），表示「叫某人做某事」；若為受詞被動完成的動作，則接過去分詞（V-p.p.），表示「要……被……」。

試比較下列兩個句子：

- Mom <u>had me wash</u> my hands. （媽媽要我去洗手。）
  →受詞me必須「主動」洗手

- I <u>had my hands washed</u>. （我把手洗好了。）
  →受詞my hands是「被動」被洗好

例：• My professor <u>had me submit</u> my assignment by September 8th.
（我的教授要我在九月八日前繳交作業。）
→「繳交作業」是要受詞me身體力行，主動完成的動作，故受詞後的動詞使用原形動詞

- Can you <u>have</u> someone <u>come</u> here to help me?
（你可以找一個人過來這裡幫我嗎？）

- I will try my best to <u>have the work done</u> on schedule.
（我會盡力讓工作如期完成。）
→「工作完成」是受詞the work被動完成的動作，故受詞後的動詞使用過去分詞

- Can you <u>have it fixed</u> as soon as possible?
（你可以盡快讓它被修好嗎？）

馬上動手練一練 ❶

將正確的動詞用法圈起來

1. You should stop feeding him, and let him (eat/to eat) by himself.

2. Mr. Sullivan had all of us (work/to work) overtime.

3. The man hasn't had his hair (wash/to wash/washed) for a long time.

ANSWER
1. eat   2. work   3. washed

◆make 的其他用法

❶ 與have一樣，make的受詞後面的動作，若是由受詞主動做的，接原形動詞，表示「迫使某人做某事」；若是受詞被動完成的動作，則接過去分詞，表示「使……被……」。

試比較下列兩個句子：

- She tried to <u>make me understand</u> her question.
  （她試著使我了解她的問題。）

  → 受詞me必須主動去了解問題，故受詞後的動詞為原形動詞

- She tried to <u>make herself understood</u>.
  （她試著讓別人了解她的意思。）

  → 受詞herself是指被他人所了解，是被動完成的動作，故動詞要改為過去分詞

例：
- The traffic police <u>made the car stop</u>.
  （交通警察迫使那輛車停下來。）

- The police <u>made the driver get</u> out of the car.
  （警察叫駕駛下車。）

- We had to shout to <u>make ourselves heard</u>.
  （我們得大叫才能讓別人聽到我們的聲音。）

- You can use body language or gestures to <u>make yourself understood</u>.
  （你可以用肢體語言讓他人了解你的意思。）

❷ make受詞後面可接形容詞，表示「使……成為某種狀態」

例：
- The ending of the story <u>makes me sad</u>.
  （故事的結局讓我感到很悲傷。）

- The announcement <u>made everyone irritable</u>.
  （這項宣布讓所有人感到煩躁不安。）

◆其他可以用來表示「命令；指使」的動詞

❶ get

get的受詞後的動作，若是由受詞主動做的，接不定詞（to＋原形動詞），表示「要某人做某事」；若是受詞被動完成的動作，則接過去分詞，表示「使……被……；使……成為某種狀態」。

例：• Can you get someone to pick up our client at the airport?
（你可以找個人去機場接我們的客戶嗎？）

• You must get the job done as you promised.
（你必須如你所承諾的將工作完成。）

❷ ask/tell/want

ask表「要求」，受詞後面接不定詞，表示「要求某人做某事」。
tell表「告訴」，受詞後面接不定詞，表示「告訴某人做某事」。
want表「想要」，受詞後面接不定詞，表示「希望某人做某事」。

例：• It's unfair to ask women to balance home and work.
（要求女人在家庭與工作中取得平衡，是一件不公平的事。）

• We always tell our children to listen to the teachers.
（我們總是告訴孩子們要聽老師的話。）

• The teacher wanted the students to try their best to pass the exam.
（老師希望學生們盡全力通過考試。）

馬上動手練一練 ❷

將正確的動詞用法圈起來

1. I want you (finish/to finish) your homework before dinner.

2. My parents told me (be/to be) honest, but Peter made me (lie/ to lie) to them.

3. Pleace get a place (to hold/held) the party.

ANSWER

1. to finish　2. to be, lie　3. to hold

◆祈使句

　　除了使役動詞之外，也可以用祈使句向對方下達「指令」，或是提出「要求」、給予「提議」或「勸告」。祈使句的主詞一定是you（你或你們），因此這類句型的主詞經常省略不用，直接用原形動詞作句首，使語氣更堅定或強烈。

　　祈使句的句型結構： (You)＋原形動詞（包括單字動詞及片語動詞）

　　祈使句中的動詞必為「原形動詞」，若是及物動詞，則必須加上受詞。

　　例：• Hurry!（快！）　　　• Take it off!（把它脫掉！）

　　　　• Get out!（出去！）　• Give it to me.（把它給我。）

❶ 否定祈使句

　　表示命令、勸告、建議對方「不要做某事」時，在祈使句前加上Do not/Don't或Never，即為否定祈使句。

　　例：• <u>Do not/Don't</u> do that again!.（不要再那麼做了！）

　　　　• <u>Never</u> share your personal information on the Internet.
　　　　（絕不要在網路上分享你的個人資料。）

❷ be與get的祈使句

be動詞與一般動詞get後面接形容詞，表示「督促要對方進入某種狀態」。

例：• Be patient to your young children. （對小小孩要有耐心。）

　　• Get dressed for school right now!
　　（馬上去穿衣服準備上學！）

 **重點筆記**

加強語氣的祈使句

1. 保留主詞you

　例：• You shut up! （你給我閉嘴！）

　　　• Don't you come here again! （不准你再到這裡來！）

2. 動詞前加上助動詞do

　例：• Do keep in touch with me. （一定要跟我保持聯絡。）

　　　• Do give me a call when you arrive.
　　　（到那裡一定要打電話給我。）

 **重點筆記**

口氣委婉的祈使句

1. 用let 表「建議；請求」

　例：• Let me have a bite of your sandwich.
　　　（讓我吃一口你的三明治。）

2. 用please表示「委婉請求」

　例：• Leave me alone, please. ＝ Please leave me
　　　alone. （請讓我靜一靜。）

馬上動手練一練 ❸

圈出正確的動詞

1. (Be/Being/Been) quiet, please. I am trying to concentrate.

2. (Can't/Don't/Won't) mention anything about the accident in the letter. I don't want Mom to be worried.

3. Always (tell/to tell) the truth, whether others believe you or not.

4. (Stay/To stay) here until I tell you to make your next move.

5. (Do/Will) listen to your mother when I am away from home.

ANSWER

1. Be　　2. Don't　3. tell　　4. Stay　5. Do

二‧感官動詞

　　由身體感官如眼、耳、心等做出的動詞，如「看」、「聽」、「知覺」等，即感官動詞。

常用的感官動詞：

視覺感官	聽覺感官	知覺感官
see（看到；看見） watch（看著）	hear（聽到；聽見） listen to（聽）	notice（注意到） feel（感到）

　　感官動詞的受詞後可以直接加第二個動詞，以表示感官所知覺到的外界動作或狀態。

◆感官動詞的結構

其句型結構有兩種：

❶ 感官動詞＋受詞＋原形動詞

描述「刻意、主動地」全程或持續很長一段時間地觀看或聆聽受詞進行某個活動或做某件事時，後面多接原形動詞來表示。

例：• The man watched his wife give birth to their first child.
（男子看著妻子生下他們的第一個孩子。）

• The students listened carefully to the teacher explain the assignment instructions.
（學生們仔細聽老師解釋作業的做法。）

❷ 感官動詞＋受詞＋現在分詞（V-ing）

表示「非刻意、不經意地」看到或聽到受詞進行某個活動或做某件事時，後面多接現在分詞來表示。

例：• I was watching TV and suddenly heard a woman screaming from the next door.
（我正在看電視，然後突然聽到隔壁一個女人在尖叫。）

• It wasn't the driver's fault. We both saw the man running the red light.
（這不是駕駛的錯。我們都看到那男人闖紅燈。）

雖然文法上，感官動詞的受詞後面可以接原形動詞或現在分詞，但是判斷兩者間語法上的差異，最簡單的方式，就是原形動詞表示「已發生的事實」，現在分詞表示「正在發生的事情」。

例：• I saw the boy hit the girl.（我看到男孩打女孩。）

• I saw the boy hitting the girl.（我看到男孩正在打女孩。）

重點筆記

知覺感官動詞notice（注意到、發現）及feel（感覺到）都是描述當下瞬間感覺，故受詞後面接現在分詞，或是that子句。

例：• The lifeguard noticed a boy struggling in the water and rushed to save him.
（救生員發現有個男孩在水裡掙扎，立刻衝過去救他。）

• No one noticed that a boy was struggling in the water except the lifeguard.
（除了那個救生員之外，沒有人發現有個男孩在水中掙扎。）

• I put my hand on my chest and felt my heart beating so fast.
（我將手放在胸口，感覺到我的心臟跳得好快。）

• I feel that my heart is going to jump out of my chest.
（我感覺我的心臟就要從胸口跳出來了。）

◆動詞help的用法

help（幫助）不是使役動詞，也不是感官動詞，但是這個動詞後面的受詞也可以直接接原形動詞。

help＋受詞＋原形動詞表示「幫……做……」。

例：• A kind young man helped the old lady find her way home.
（一個好心的年輕人幫老太太找到了回家的路。）

• People donated a large sum of money to help the villagers reconstruct their homeland.
（人們捐了一大筆錢，好幫助村民重建他們的家園。）

help的其他用法

1. can't help but＋原形動詞＝can't help 現在分詞（V-ing）

表示「忍不住……」。

例：• I can't help but smile when I think of my daughter.
＝I can't help smiling when I think of my daughter.
（當我想起我女兒時，我就忍不住想微笑。）

2. help＋人＋with＋事

表示「在某事上給予某人協助」。

例：• Can you help me with my math homework?
（你可以幫我看看我的數學作業嗎？）

• I would love to help you with the house chores.
（我很樂意幫你分擔家務。）

馬上動手練一練 ❹

將括號中的動詞做適當變化填入空格中，完成句子

1. It always makes me happy when I hear children _____ (laugh).
2. Don't make our guests _____(watch) you two _____(fight).
   It's embarrassing.
3. The woman didn't notice a stranger _____(sneak) into the
   house.
4. Do you smell something _____ (burn)? I think it's from the
   basement.
5. They can't help but _____(frown) when they listen to him ____
   (complain) about his work.

ANSWER

1. laughing　　2. watch, fight　　3. sneaking
4. burning　　5. frown, complaining

三‧連綴動詞

連綴動詞不是用來表現動作，而是作為主詞與主詞補語之間的橋樑，後面接「名詞」或「形容詞」來作為主詞補語，以補充說明、描述或點綴主詞。

◆be動詞──
→後面接名詞（或名詞相等語）及形容詞，以描述主詞的身份或狀態。

例：• I am Larry Kim. Nice to meet you, everyone.
（我叫賴瑞‧金很高興認識各位。）

• Your feedback is very constructive. Thanks.
（您的反饋意見非常有建設性。謝謝。）

◆描述當下感覺的感官動詞──
→sound, look, smell, feel, taste

(1) 感官動詞後面直接接「形容詞」，描述主詞當下的狀態或是主詞給說話者當下的感覺。

例：• Her story sounds unreal, but it really happened.
（她的故事聽起來很不真實，但它的確發生了。）

• You should take a day off if you don't feel well.
（如果你覺得不舒服，就應該休一天假。）

(2) 感官動詞後面接 like ＋名詞，表示主詞「讓人感覺像……」。

例：• I don't want to be rude, but the steak tastes like rubber.
（我不想無禮，但這牛排吃起來跟橡膠一樣。）

• Every girl <u>looks like a princess</u> tonight.
（每個女孩子今晚看起來都像個公主一樣。）

◆表示「轉變或轉換」的動詞──
→get, become, turn

這類動詞是用來表示主詞的轉變。

(1) get/become/turn後面可接形容詞，描述主詞轉變後的狀態。

例：• It's <u>getting late</u>. We'd better leave now.
（天色越來越晚了。我們最好現在就離開。）

• The atmosphere of the party suddenly <u>became tense</u> when Jack started quarreling with Tom.
（當傑克開始跟湯姆起爭執，派對的氣氛突然變得很緊張。）

• Extreme stress can <u>turn a person's hair gray</u> overnight.
（極度的壓力很可能讓一個人的頭髮在一夜之間變白。）

(2) become後面接名詞或代名詞，說明主詞從某種身份轉變為另一種身份。

turn要接名詞前，必須有介系詞into。

例：• At the end of the story, the ugly duckling <u>became a beautiful swan</u>.
（故事最後，醜小鴨變成了美麗的天鵝。）

• Thanks to their efforts, the abandoned bank has <u>turned into a modern restaurant</u>.
（多虧他們的努力，被廢棄的銀行已經轉變成一間現代化的餐廳。）

馬上動手練一練 ⑤

根據句意在空格中填入適當的連綴動詞

turn	look	become	get	taste

1. Be careful with the scissors if you don't want to _____ hurt.

2. The fish fillet doesn't _____ as good as I expected.

3. Lisa _____ embarrassed when the teacher told her to be quiet.

4. We'd better hurry home before the sky _____ extremely dark.

5. It costs them thirty million dollars to _____ a wasteland into a modern theme park.

ANSWER

1. get   2. taste   3. looked   4. becomes   5. turn

Lesson6

文法總複習
快來試試自己的實力吧！

A. 圈出正確的字，以完成句子

1. Sophia looks like (a real princess/very beautiful) in the pink dress and the crown.

2. The ceremony doesn't (seem/like/become) real to me. I still can't believe that I am graduating today.

3. I can't help (cry/to cry/crying) whenever I hear this story. It's really sad.

4. (Never/Seldom/Can't) trust anyone you don't know in person on the Internet.

5. The rain finally stopped. I'm so glad to see the sky (turned/turning/to turn) blue again.

6. (Let us/Let's) do something to save this man. We can't just (watch/sound/feel) him die in front of us.

7. The mother was swiping her phone and didn't (notice/look/find) her 2-year-old daughter running across the street.

8. I had an argument with my mom since she (made/let/buy) me do all the housework.

9. I told my teacher when I saw a boy (hitting/to hit/dance) a girl.

10. Please get your things (done/do/doing) first!

B. 克漏字填空

a. drink	e. feel	i. felt
b. to get	f. to stay	j. see
c. sick	g. have	k. coughing
d. let	h. told	

I didn't ___ very well when I got up yesterday morning. My wife was worried, so she asked me ___ at home. I didn't listen to her, because I had so much work to do, and I really want to ___ things done on schedule.

I became very ___ in the afternoon. My assistant, Amy, gave me a glass of warm water and made me ___ it. My boss, Julian, saw me ___ badly when he passed by my office. He walked in, ___ me go home early, and told me ___ enough water and enough rest. So I did.

I went to bed as soon as I came home. I had slept for fourteen hours when I got up at six this morning. I ___ fresh. Everyone was happy to ___ me get my energy back.

ANSWER

A. 圈出正確的字，以完成句子

1. a real princess　　2. seem　　　　3. crying
4. Never　　　　　　5. turning　　　 6. Let's, watch
7. notice　　　　　　8. made　　　　 9. hitting
10. done

1. look like看起來像like為介系詞+Ving/名詞

2. seem似乎+形容詞

3. I can't help+Ving 忍不住卻……

4. Never 永遠不

5. see 感官動詞+Ving/原形動詞

6. let's+V表示「讓我們（一起）去做某事」，watch 觀看

7. notice注意到

8. make要有命令意味，接原形動詞

9. see感官動詞+Ving/原形動詞

10. get使役動詞和things為被動，故此用do過去分詞done

B. 克漏字填空

I didn't **e** very well when I got up yesterday morning. My wife was worried, so she asked me **f** at home. I didn't listen to her, because I had so much work to do, and I really want to **g** things done on schedule.

I became very **c** in the afternoon. My assistant, Amy, gave me a glass of warm water and made me **a** it. My boss, Julian, saw me **k** badly when he passed by my office. He walked in, **d** me go home early, and told me **b** enough water and enough rest. So I did.

I went to bed as soon as I came home. I had slept for fourteen hours when I got up at six this morning. I **i** fresh. Everyone was happy to **j** me get my energy back.

授與動詞

可以用直接受詞或間接受詞當主詞
- 主動：Grandpa told us a ghost story.
- 被動1：We were told a ghost story by Grandpa.
- 被動2：A ghost story was told to us by Grandpa.

以虛主詞為首

表示普遍的說法

It is＋過去分詞＋that子句

Lesson 7

動詞語態

感官動詞

被動態感官動詞接不定詞
- 主動：主詞＋感官動詞＋受詞＋V/V-ing
  →We saw the man running the red light.
- 被動：主詞＋be＋感官動詞V-p.p.
  ＋受詞＋to V
  →The man was seen to run the red light.

使役動詞

- 主動：主詞＋使役動詞＋受詞＋V
  →Dad made Ken stay at home.
- 被動：主詞＋be動詞
  ＋使役動詞V-p.p.＋to V
  →Ken was made to stay at home.

主動語態 主詞為動詞的執行者
└─→ She took out the garbage.

被動語態 主詞為動詞的接受者
└─→ The garbage was taken out by her.

使用時機
- 強調動作的接受者
- 動作執行者不重要
- 動作執行者眾所皆知
- 不知道動作執行者是誰
- 委婉語氣

be動詞＋過去分詞（V-p.p.）

將主動語態改為被動語態
- 受詞、主詞位置對調
- 動詞改成be動詞＋過去分詞
- 動作執行者前＋by

片語動詞
- 動詞＋介系詞
- 視為一個動詞，不分開

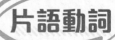

動詞語態

英文句子中的動詞有的主動與被動之分。在主動語態的句子中，主詞即為動作的「執行者」；在被動語態的句子中，主詞為動作的「承受者」。當「接受動作者」，比執行動作者更值得被強調時，我們就會用「被動語態」來突顯「被執行動作」的人或物。

一‧主動語態與被動語態

主動語態的主詞即該句動詞的執行者。

例：• Susan switched off her cellphone before the movie started.（蘇珊在電影開始前將手機關掉。）

→ Susan為「關掉手機」動作的執行者

• I will have the dinner ready in five minutes.
（我將在五分鐘內把晚餐準備好。）

→ I為「將晚餐準備好」動作的執行者

• Keep your hands off the exhibitions.
（不要用手摸展覽品。）

→ you為祈使句「不要摸」動作的執行者

被動語態的主詞即該句動詞的接受者，也就是說，被動語態的主詞原本應該是動詞的「受詞」。因此可以形成被動語態的動詞，必定是「及物動詞」。

◆ 被動語態的句型結構： be動詞＋過去分詞（V-p.p.）

被動語態的be動詞需隨主詞（即承受動作者）及時態作變化：

❶ 現在簡單式：am/is/are＋過去分詞

例：• The little girl is loved by everyone.
（小女孩受大家所喜愛。）

• We are taught to respect the elderly.
（我們被教導要尊重長者。）

❷ 過去簡單式：was/were＋過去分詞

例：• The window was opened.（窗戶被打開了。）

• Many victims were buried alive in the landslide.
（許多罹難者在這次山崩遭到活埋。）

❸ 未來簡單式：will be＋過去分詞

例：• This chair will be moved to another room.
（這椅子將被移到另一個房間。）

• Paper books will not be replaced with e-books completely.
（紙本書籍並不會全面被電子書籍取代。）

❹ 現在進行式：am/is/are＋being＋過去分詞

例：• The father doesn't know that his son is being bullied at school.
（這位父親並不知道他的兒子在學校被霸凌。）

• Many women are being treated unfairly at work.
（許多婦女在職場上受到不公平的對待。）

❺ 過去進行式：was/were＋being＋過去分詞

例：• My car was being towed when I returned.
（我回去的時候，我的車正被拖吊。）

- They didn't know that they were being watched.
（他們不知道自己被監視了。）

❻ 現在完成式：have/has＋been＋過去分詞

例：• The meeting has been cancelled.
（會議已經被取消了。）

- All the suspects have been arrested.
（所有的嫌犯都已經被逮捕了。）

❼ 過去完成式：had＋been＋過去分詞

例：• The laundry had been done when I came home.
（我回到家的時候，衣服已經被洗好了。）

- The hostages had been released before the police arrived.
（警方到達之前，人質已經被釋放了。）

❽ 未來完成式：will have＋been＋過去分詞

例：• Everything will have been done by the time you come home.
（當你回到家的時候，所有事情都將已完成。）

- The old bookshelf will have been removed by this weekend.
（這個舊書櫃會在這週末之前被搬走。）

◆使用被動語態的時機

❶ 強調動作的接受者

例：• A police officer was killed in the gun fight.
（在槍戰中有一名警察殉職。）

- No one will be left behind.（沒有人會被棄之不顧。）
→用被動語態來突顯接受動作者

❷ 動作執行者不重要

例：• These tables have been reserved.
（這些桌子有人預約了。）

• The error is being fixed.（錯誤正在被修正中。）
→重要的是動作被執行，而不是誰來執行動作

❸ 動作執行者眾所皆知時

例：• English is spoken all around the world.
（世界各地都有人説英文。）

• This song has been sung for decades.
（這首歌已經被傳唱好幾十年了。）
→語言一定是被「人」説，歌曲一定是被「人」唱，不需
贅述

❹ 不知動作執行者是誰

例：• My passport has been stolen.（我的護照被偷了。）

• More than 50 children were kidnapped last year.
（去年有超過五十個兒童被綁架。）
→ 只知道事情發生了，但是不知道是誰做了這些事

重點筆記

當主動語態中的主詞為someone（某人）時，在不確定執行
動作者為何人的情況下，在被動語態中就會被省略不提。

如：• The window was broken (by someone).
（窗戶被（某人）打破了。）

• I was being spied (by someone).
（我當時被（某人）監視著。）

❺ 使口氣較委婉

例：• My application has been rejected.
（我的申請被否決了。）

• His proposal has been turned down.
（他的求婚被拒絕了。）

→ 以被動語態使「否定」的動作顯得不那麼直接

◆被動語態的疑問句

簡單式被動語態可視為be動詞句型，將be動詞移到句首即為疑問句；有助動詞的被動語態，則將助動詞移到句首，變成疑問句。

例：• Is the letter written in English?
（這封信是以英文寫的嗎？）

• Will the party be cancelled if it rains?
（如果下雨的話，派對會被取消嗎？）

• Has the dog been fed yet? （狗兒被餵過了嗎？）

◆被動語態的否定句

表否定的not接在be動詞或助動詞後。

例：• The children are not being taken good care of.
（孩子們並沒有被好好地照顧著。）

• The final decision has not been made yet.
（最後的決定還沒有做出來。）

馬上動手練一練 ❶

將括號中的動詞做適當變化，以完成下列被動句

1. The assignment must _____(submit) to the teacher by October 12th.

2. I won't be able to go home today. All flights _____(cancel) due to the heavy rain.

3. French _____(speak) in Quebec while English is spoken in Toronto.

4. Don't worry. I'm sure your kitten _____ (take care of) at the moment.

5. I promise you that the printer _____ (fix) by the time you come back.

ANSWER

1. be submitted   2. have been cancelled
3. is spoken   4. is being taken good care of
5. will be fixed

二·將主動語態改為被動語態

◆將主動語態的句子改為被動語態的三個步驟：

(1) 受詞與主詞位置對調
(2) 動詞變成be動詞＋過去分詞（時態要一致）
(3) 執行動作者前要加上介系詞by

例：<u>Jeff</u>　　<u>stole</u>　　<u>Marie's laptop.</u>
　　主詞　　動詞steal過去式　　受詞

（傑夫偷了瑪麗的筆電。）

<u>Marie's laptop</u>　<u>was stolen</u>　<u>by Jeff</u>
　　　　　　　be動詞過去式＋steal過去分詞

（瑪麗的筆電被傑夫偷了。）

 馬上動手練一練 ❷

將下列主動句改為被動句

1. The security found the man's body in the basement.

_____

2. Hundreds of companies had rejected Tom before he finally got an offer.

_____

3. The housekeeper had cleaned the room before we returned.

_____

4. We sold the old chair on the first day of the garage sale.

_____

5. Nick and Sarah will give a housewarming party this Saturday.

_____

ANSWER

1. The man's body was found in the basement by the security.
2. Tom had been rejected by hundreds of companies before he finally got an offer.
3. The room had been cleaned by the housekeeper before we returned.
4. The old chair was sold on the first day of the garage sale.
5. A housewarming party will be given by Nick and Sarah this Saturday.

◆片語動詞的被動語態

片語動詞（動詞＋介系詞）應視為一個動詞單位，在被動語態中整個片語動詞都要緊緊黏在一起，不能被分開。

例：• Judy　　is taking care of　　the baby.
　　　主詞　　片語動詞take care of現在進行式　　受詞
　　　　　　　　　　　　　　　　　　　　　　　（茱蒂正在照
　　　　　　　　　　　　　　　　　　　　　　　　顧寶寶。）

The baby　　is being taken care of　　by Judy.
　　　be動詞現在進行式＋片語動詞take care of過去分詞

（寶寶正被茱蒂照顧。）

例：• The nurse will look after the patient.
　　（護理師會看顧病患。）

　→The patient will be looked after by the nurse.
　　（病患將被護理師看顧。）

　• His friends laughed at him behind his back.
　　（他的朋友在他背後嘲笑他。）

　→He was laughed at behind his back by his friends.
　　（他被朋友們在背後嘲笑。）

馬上動手練一練 ❸

將下列主動句改為被動句

1. Steven is cleaning up the living room for tonight's party.

_____

2. She took out of the garbage after dinner.

_____

3. We had to put off the meeting for some unexpected reason.

_____

4. The police are looking into the fraud case.

_____

5. The boy picked up the trash and threw it into the bin.

_____

ANSWER

1. The living room is being cleaned up for tonight's party by Steven.
2. The garbage was taken out by her after dinner.
3. The meeting had to be put off for some unexpected reason.
4. The fraud case is being looked into by the police.
5. The trash was picked up and thrown into the bin by the boy.

◆授與動詞的被動語態

授與動詞有兩個受詞，因此被動語態也有兩種表示方法。

例：

❶ 主動：• Grandpa told　　us　　a ghost story.
　　　　　　　　　　　間接受詞　　直接受詞
　　　　　（爺爺對我們説了一個鬼故事。）

• **被動1：間接受詞當主詞**
→We were told a ghost story by Grandpa.

• **被動2：直接受詞當主詞**
→ A ghost story was told to us by Grandpa.

❷ 主動：The little boy gave his father a hug.
　　　　　　（小男孩給了他爸爸一個擁抱。）

• **被動1：間接受詞當主詞**
→ His father was given a hug by the little boy.

• 被動2：直接受詞當主詞

→<u>A hug</u> was given <u>to the father</u> by his boy.

馬上動手練一練 ❹

依提示完成句子改寫

1. Grandma baked me a chocolate cake on my birthday.

   A chocolate cake _____ on my birthday.

2. My boss sent everyone an email this morning.

   An email _____ this morning.

3. Henry will bring us a bottle of wine when he comes.

   A bottle of wine _____ when he comes.

4. Vicky bought Jerry an expensive watch as a birthday gift.

   Jerry _____ by Vicky.

5. My wife told us a secret last night.

   A secret _____ by my wife last night.

ANSWER

1. was baked for me by Grandma
2. was sent to everyone by my boss
3. will be brought to us by Henry
4. was bought an expensive watch as a birthday gift
5. was told to me

◆以虛主詞為首的被動語態

有些動詞常以被動語態使用在虛主詞「It is＋過去分詞＋that
子句」的句型中，以表示「普遍大眾的想法或說法」，這類動詞常
用的有：

say（說）	know（知道）	hope（希望）
believe（相信，認為）	consider（認為）	understand（理解）
suppose（認為）	claim（聲稱）	expect（預期）
report（報導）	allege（宣稱）	acknowledge（承認）

以虛主詞為首時，被動語態接that子句，改為以一般主詞為首
時，被動語態後的動詞以「不定詞」表示，例如：

- 虛主詞為首的被動語態：It is said that Mr. Hamilton is a royal member.

- 一般主詞為首的被動語態：Mr. Hamilton is said to be a royal member.
（漢米爾頓先生據說是個皇家成員。）

- It is believed that the Maldives will disappear by the end of the century.

＝The Maldives are believed to disappear by the end of the century.
（據信，馬爾地夫將會在本世紀結束之前消失。）

- It is reported that the Prince is going to marry a divorced woman.

＝The prince is reported to marry a divorced woman.
（據報導，王子將要娶一名離過婚的女人。）

• It is hoped that the missing flight can be found as soon as possible.

= The missing flight is hoped to be found as soon as possible.
（希望那班失蹤的班機能儘快被找到。）

馬上動手練一練 ❺

將下列句子以虛主詞為句首改寫

1. We hope that the police can find the robbers and arrest them soon.

_____

2. The single actor is known to have more than one illegitimate child.

_____

3. They say that his money was inherited from his grandfather.

_____

4. The man is believed to be murdered by one of his close friends.

_____

5. More than half of children in England are reported to have been bullied.

_____

ANSWER

1. It is hoped that the police can find the bank robbers and arrest them soon.
2. It is known that the single actor has more than one illegitimate child.
3. It is said that his money was inherited from his grandfather.
4. It is believed that the man was murdered by one of his close friends.
5. It is reported that more than half of children in England have been bullied.

◆感官動詞的被動語態

在主動語態中，感官動詞後面的受詞，會接原形動詞或現在分詞，但是在被動語態中，感官動詞變成被動語態（be＋V-p.p.）之後，後面的受詞，要接「不定詞」。

> 主動：主詞＋感官動詞＋受詞＋V/V-ing
> 被動：主詞＋be＋感官動詞V-p.p.＋受詞＋to＋V

例：

• We saw the bus driver running the red light.

（我們看到公車司機闖紅燈。）

→ The bus driver was seen to run the red light (by us).

（公車司機被（我們）看到他闖紅燈。）

• Everyone heard the customer complain about her food.

（每個人都聽到那個顧客抱怨她的食物。）

→ The customer was heard to complain about her food.

（那個顧客被聽到她在抱怨自己的食物。）

馬上動手練一練 ❻

將下列句子改為被動句

1. Some students heard Peter laughing at Julie.

_____

2. The audience watched the dolphins perform different tricks.

_____

3. The teacher noticed James dozing off during the class.

_____

4. No one saw him stealing money from a tourist. （寫出兩種）

_____

_____

5. All customers in the restaurant saw the man shouting at his wife.

_____

ANSWER

1. Peter was heard to laugh at Julie by some students.
2. The dolphins were watched to perform different tricks by the audience.
3. James was noticed to doze off during the class.
4. • He was seen to steal money from a tourist by no one.
   • He wasn't seen to steal money from a tourist by anyone.
5. The man was seen to shout at his wife by all customers in the restaurant.

◆使役動詞的被動語態

使役動詞的被動語態，主詞接被動語態（be動詞＋過去分詞）後，接「不定詞」表被指派的動作。

主動：主詞＋使役動詞＋受詞＋V
被動：主詞＋be動詞＋過去分詞（V-p.p.）＋to＋V

例：• Dad made Vincent stay at home for the whole weekend.
（爸爸叫文森特整個週末都待在家裡。）

• Vincent was made to stay at home for the whole weekend.
（文森特被規定整個週末都要待在家裡。）

使役動詞let有「允許」的含義，被動語態不用let，而是要用allow（允許）來表示

例：• Mom won't let me play online games.
（媽媽不會讓我玩線上遊戲的。）
→I won't be allowed to play online games.
（我不會被允許玩線上遊戲的。）

• They didn't let Cinderella go to the party with them.
（她們不讓仙杜瑞拉跟她們一起去參加派對。）
→Cinderella was not allowed to go to the party with them.
（仙杜瑞拉不被允許跟她們一起去參加派對。）

馬上動手練一練 ❼

將下列句子改為被動句

1. The doctor made me drink 1,500 liters of water per day.

_____

2. Mom made Jack clean up his bedroom.

_____

3. I can't let you enter the library without seeing your student ID.

_____

4. The teacher won't let us go until we finish our cleaning tasks.

_____

5. His wife made him quit smoking within a month.

_____

ANSWER

1. I was made to drink 1,500 liters of water per day by the doctor.
2. Jack was made to clean up his bedroom by Mom.
3. You are not allowed to enter the library without showing your student ID.
4. We will not be allowed to go until our cleaning tasks are finished.
5. He was made to quit smoking within a month by his wife.

文法總複習
快來試試自己的實力吧！

A. 選擇正確的動詞語態

1. (　　) I am still doing my homework, but it _____ in less than thirty minutes.
   A. is done
   B. will do
   C. will be done
   D. is doing

2. (　　) My car broke down on my way to work. It _____ in the garage at the moment.
   A. has been fixed
   B. was fixed
   C. will be fixed
   D. is being fixed

3. (　　) The injured person _____ to the hospital immediately.
   A. was sending
   B. will send
   C. sent
   D. was sent

4. (　　) So far, the Guinness Book of World Records _____ into 370 languages and dialects.
   A. is being translating
   B. has been translated
   C. will be translated
   D. had been translated

5. (　　) When I returned to the store, the white dress _____.
   A. had already been sold
   B. will have been sold
   C. is being sold
   D. is selling

6. (　) I'm sorry that I can't take your reservation. All tables in this restaurant _____ tonight.
   A. are booked
   B. will be booked
   C. is booking
   D. has been booked

7. (　) Your application _____ at the moment. The result _____ in two days.
   A. was processed; is being announced
   B. will be processed; had been announced
   C. is being processed; will be announced
   D. has been processed; is announcing

8. (　) Listen! A child _____. We should call the police now.
   A. is being hit　　B. hit　　C. will be hit　　D. is hitting

9. (　) These apples _____ to the market later.
   A. are sending　　B. will be sent　　C. sent　　D. sends

10. (　) The bus driver _____ run the red light.
   A. was seen to　　B. was seeing　　C. saw　　D. see

B. 將主動句改為被動句

1. Pierre and Marie Curie discovered Radium.

   _____

2. We will hire a caregiver to look after our old mother.

   _____

3. The boy is making fun of a girl.

   _____

4. The traffic officer asked the man to show him his driver's license.

   _____

5. They say that Mr. Johnson is the biological father of this child.
   （寫出兩種）

   _____

   _____

6. The old couple found a baby crying at the front door.

   _____

7. Mom saw a mouse eating the bread in our kitchen.

   _____

8. My brother ate my birthday cake yesterday.

   _____

9. A police officer is chasing a robber now.

   _____

10. A teacher is punishing the students now.

    _____

ANSWER

A. 選擇

1. **C** 2. **D** 3. **D** 4. **B** 5. **A**

6. **A** 7. **C** 8. **A** 9. **B** 10. **A**

1. 功課將會被做完，未來式被動will be 過去分詞

2. 現在進行式被動語態，be動詞+being+過去分詞

3. 過去簡單式被動語態，be動詞+過去分詞

4. 現在完成式被動語態，has/have+been+過去分詞

5. 比過去式更早則使用過去完成式，裙子為被買，故使用被動，had been 過去分詞

6. 所有的位子今晚已被預訂，現在簡單式被動語態，be動詞+過去分詞

7. process處理

   申請表正在被處理，現在進行式被動語態，be動詞+being+過去分詞

   結果將會在兩天內宣布，未來被動語態will be 過去分詞

8. 小孩正在被打，現在進行式被動語態

   be動詞+being+過去分詞

9. 蘋果將會被送去市場

   will be 過去分詞

10. 被看到，過去簡單式被動語態，be動詞+過去分詞

B. 將主動句改為被動句

1. Radium was discovered by Pierre and Marie Curie.

2. A caregiver will be hired to look after our old mother.

3. A girl is being made fun of by the boy.

4. The man was asked to show the traffic officer his driver's license.

5. • Mr. Johnson is said to be the biological father of this child.

   • It is said that Mr. Johnson is the biological father of this child.

6. A baby was found to cry at the front door by the old couple.

7. A mouse was seen to eat the bread in our kitchen by Mom.

8. My birthday cake was eaten by my brother yesterday.

9. A robber is being chased by a police officer now.

10. The students are being punished by a teacher now.

NOTE

可視爲副詞片語

常用來表示轉折語氣

└─ to be honest, to be sure, to be short

獨立不定詞

Lesson **8**

動狀詞1 不定詞

當副詞用

修飾前面的動詞

→We went to see her.

修飾前面的形容詞

→They are ready to go.

修飾前面的副詞

→I don't have much to say.

不定詞／不定詞片語

- to＋原形動詞

- 當名詞用

  - 作為受詞
    - 常接不定詞的動詞：mean, decide
    - We need to talk.

  - 作為主詞
    - 強調目的或意願
    - To win the Olympic is every athlete's dream.

  - 作為主詞補語
    - My plan is to have a beach wedding.

  - 作為受詞補語
    - 使役動詞的受詞後面
    - The man begged the doctor to save his life.

- 當形容詞用

  - 關係代名詞作主詞引導的形容詞子句
    - This is the only thing that needs to be done.
    - ＝This is the only thing to be done.

  - 關係代名詞做受詞引導的形容詞子句
    - I have no friends whom I can talk to.
    - ＝I have no friends to talk to.

  - be動詞＋不定詞
    - What am I to say?

Lesson 8　動狀詞1：不定詞

動狀詞是由動詞變化而來，接在句子中的動詞後面，作為準動詞的詞類。動狀詞有三種，即不定詞、動名詞及分詞。動狀詞在句子中的角色，可以是名詞，在句中作主詞（主詞補語）或受詞（受詞補語）用，也可以是形容詞，用來修飾名詞，亦可以是副詞，用來修飾動詞。

三種動狀詞將分三章（Lesson8、Lesson9、Lesson10）詳細介紹，本章就將以「不定詞」為動狀詞拉開序幕！

一・不定詞／不定詞片語

不定詞即「to＋原形動詞」所組成的動狀詞。不定詞在句子中的角色及功能有三種：

◆不定詞／不定詞片語當名詞用

❶ 作為動詞的受詞

例：• We need to talk.
（我們得談談。）

（不定詞作need的受詞）

• They wanted to leave.
（他們想離開了。）

（不定詞作want的受詞）

192

● Mary decided to quit her job as a restaurant waitress.
（瑪麗決定辭去她餐廳服務生的工作。）

（不定詞片語作decide的受詞）

● I can't afford to buy a house in the city center.
（我買不起市中心的房子。）

（不定詞片語作afford的受詞）

　　不定詞可以作為及物動詞或不完全及物動詞的受詞。作及物動詞之受詞時，通常是用來表示意願、目的或意圖。

　　★後面常接不定詞或不定詞片語作為受詞的動詞：

afford 負擔得起	endeavor 努力	prepare 準備
agree 同意，贊成	expect 期待	pretend 假裝
arrange 安排	fail 失敗	promise 承諾；同意
ask 要求	hope 希望	refuse 拒絕
attempt 企圖，嘗試	intend 打算	threaten 威脅
decide 決定	learn 學習	try 試圖
desire 渴望	manage 設法做到	want 想要
deserve 應得	mean 故意	wish 希望
determine決心	offer 提出	

例：● I didn't mean to hurt you.（我不是故意要傷害你的。）

　　● She agreed to meet me at three o'clock this afternoon.
　　（她同意今天下午三點與我碰面。）

　　● He managed to get all his work done by the deadline.
　　（他設法在截止期限之前將所有工作完成。）

　　● Dad promised to quit smoking for the sake of his health.
　　（爸爸承諾會為了健康戒煙。）

◎ deserve這個動詞後面可接名詞或不定詞來表示被動的概念：

---

deserve ＋一般名詞＝應得某物
deserve ＋to＋be＋過去分詞＝「應受到……」

例：• The man deserved <u>the most severe punishment</u>.
　　＝The man deserved <u>to be punished the most severely</u>.
　　（男子應受到最嚴厲的懲罰。）

　　• Jerry deserves <u>a promotion</u>.
　　＝Jerry deserves <u>to be promoted</u>.
　　（傑瑞應得到晉升。）

當不定詞或不定詞片語作為不完全及物動詞的受詞時，則要以it作虛受詞，接受詞補語之後，再接不定詞（真受詞）來完整句意，句型結構為：

主詞＋不完全及物動詞＋it＋受詞補語（名詞／形容詞）＋不定詞

★常用在此類句型的不完全及物動詞有：

• find 發現	• deem 認為
• think 認為	• feel 覺得
• believe 相信	• make 使成為
• consider 認為	

例：• I find it difficult <u>to get used to the changeable weather in England</u>.（我發現要習慣英國善變的天氣很困難。）

　　• Most people believe it worthwhile <u>to invest in space exploration</u>.
　　（大部分的人相信太空探索的投資是值得的。）

- We consider it necessary <u>to reform the existing education system</u>.

（我們認為改革現存的教育制度是有必要的。）

- She makes it a rule <u>to go to the gym every day</u>.

（她將每天上健身房變成了習慣。）

重點筆記

表示否定時，將**not**加在不定詞之前：| **not＋to＋原形動詞** |

例：• She found it challenging not to eat late-night snacks.

（她發現不吃宵夜是很具挑戰性的。）

- I once thought it impossible not to care about what other people think.

（我曾經以為不去在乎他人的想法是不可能的。）

- We deem it important not to force your teenagers to communicate with you.（我們認為不要強迫你的青少年孩子跟你溝通是很重要的。）

馬上動手練一練 ❶

選擇適當的動詞，並做適當的修改，填入空格中

apologize	kill the hostages
ask a woman her weight	ignore the noise
improve the working conditions and rights	

1. I believe it inappropriate _____ in public.

2. He found it impossible _____ from the next door, so he called the police.

3. The kidnapper threatened _____.

4. The authorities promised _____ of migrant workers.

5. I want _____ for all the inconvenience that we may have caused.

ANSWER

1. to ask a woman her weight
2. to ignore the noise
3. to kill the hostages
4. to improve the working conditions and rights
5. to apologize

❷ 作為句子的主詞

不定詞/不定詞片語作主詞時,通常用來強調目的或是未完成的意願。

例:• To win an Oscar Award is every actor's dream.
（贏得一座奧斯卡獎是每一個演員的夢想。）

• To be the president of the United States, you must be at least 35 years old.
（要當美國總統,你必須至少有三十五歲。）

當不定詞/不定詞片語作為句子的主詞時,常因主詞太長,而以虛主詞it代為作句子的句首,將不定詞/不定詞片語（真主詞）則放在句尾,以避免句子頭重腳輕。

句型結構: It＋動詞＋補語＋不定詞/不定詞片語

例：• It takes 21 days to form a new habit.
（要養成一個新習慣需要二十一天的時間。）

• It is cruel to keep animals in cages.
（把動物關在籠子裡是很殘忍的。）

• It has always been my dream to visit the Maldives for my honeymoon.
（去馬爾地夫度蜜月一直都是我的夢想。）

馬上動手練一練 ❷

將提示字以不定詞形式填入空格中，以完成句子

1. (prevent carbon monoxide poisoning)

_____, do not run engines in a closed area.

2. (order catering food online)

My backup plan is _____.

3. (visit the Great Wall of China)

_____ was one of his birthday wishes.

4. (lay off the entire Marketing Department)

It is our final decision _____.

5. (break the Guinness World Record)

His ultimate purpose is _____.

ANSWER

1. To prevent carbon monoxide poisoning
2. to order catering food online
3. To visit the Great Wall of China
4. to lay off the entire Marketing Department
5. to break the Guinness World Record

❸ 作為主詞補語

不定詞／不定詞片語可以接在be動詞後作為主詞的補語

例：• My plan is to have a beach wedding.
（我的計劃是要有個沙灘婚禮。）

• His only wish is to find his biological mother.
（他唯一的心願就是找到他的親生母親。）

• The goal of education is to prepare our children for a successful life.（教育的目的是要讓我們的孩子為成功人生做好準備。）

◎有些句子中be動詞之後的不定詞可省略to，直接接原形動詞作為補語。

例：• All I can do right now is (to) pray for them.
（我現在所能做的就是為他們祈禱。）

• The only thing he did this morning was (to) run errands for his boss.（他今天早上所做的唯一一件事就是幫他老闆跑腿辦事。）

• What we should do is (to) be reduce the use of plastic.
（我們現在應該做的事情就是減少塑膠的使用。）

❹ 作為受詞補語

在有使役動詞意味的動詞後面的受詞，常會接不定詞／不定詞片語作為受詞補語，這類動詞有：

- ask 要求
- advise 建議
- allow 同意
- beg 懇求
- cause 造成
- enable 使得

- expect 期許
- force 強迫
- get 說服，使
- hope 希望
- invite 邀請
- lead 引導

- order 命令
- permit 允許
- persuade 說服
- remind 提醒
- want 希望
- wish 希望

例：
- The man begged the doctor to save his life.
（男子懇求醫生救他一命。）

- We invited Jerry and his family to join us for dinner.
（我們邀請傑瑞和他的家人與我們共進晚餐。）

- Tina reminded me to cancel the reservation for dinner.
（提娜提醒我要取消晚餐的訂位。）

馬上動手練一練 ❸

圈出正確的字

1. All we can do is (wait/waiting/waited) patiently.

2. The customer asked the waiter (return/returning/to return) his dish to the kitchen.

3. We expect our children (pursue/to pursue/pursued) their dreams.

4. The man's last wish (was/will be/has been) to see his youngest daughter before he died.

5. It wasn't my intention (hurting/hurt/to hurt) you.

ANSWER

1. wait   2. to return   3. to pursue   4. was   5. to hurt

◆不定詞／不定詞片語當形容詞用

不定詞／不定詞片語也可作形容詞用，但是與一般形容詞不同的是，不定詞／不定詞片語必須放在名詞後面，也就是以後位修飾的方式來修飾前面的名詞或代名詞。

❶ 作為關係代名詞作主詞所引導的形容詞子句

例：• This is the only thing that needs to be done.
　　=This is the only thing to be done.
（這是唯一要做的事情。）

• The old lady has no family who can take care of her.
=The old lady has no family to take care of her.
（老太太沒有可以照顧她的家人。）

❷ 作為關係代名詞作受詞所引導的形容詞子句

例：• The man is looking for a place which he can stay overnight.
　　=The man is looking a place to stay overnight.
（該男子正在找一個可以留宿一晚的地方。）

• I have no friends whom I can talk to.
= I have no friends to talk to. （我沒有可以聊天的朋友。）

• Let's grab something that we can eat for lunch.
=Let's grab something to eat for lunch.
（我們去找點東西當午餐吃。）

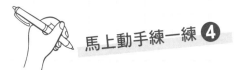

用不定詞改寫句子

1. I don't know what <u>I should say</u>.

_____

2. We can't decide what <u>we should buy</u> Mom for her birthday.

_____

3. Can anyone tell me <u>where I can return</u> the goods?

_____

4. There is nothing <u>that we can eat</u> at the party.

_____

5. There are still a lot of house chores <u>that need to be done</u>.

_____

ANSWER

1. I don't know what to say.
2. We can't decide what to buy Mom for her birthday.
3. Can anyone tell me where to return the goods?
4. There is nothing to eat at the party.
5. There are still a lot of house chores to be done.

❸ 作為be動詞之後的補語

　　不定詞／不定詞片語放在be動詞之後，有以下三種時機及用法：

A. 表示不久的將來確定發生的動作

　　句型結構： | be＋不定詞＝will＋原形動詞＝be going to＋原形動詞 |

例：• I will teach him a lesson.
　＝ I am to teach him a lesson. （我要教訓他一下。）

　• He will propose to his girlfriend on the Valentine's Day.
　＝He is to propose to his girlfriend on the Valentine's Day.
　（他將在情人節那天向女友求婚。）

　• Thousands of college faculty members are going to go on strike tomorrow.
　＝Thousands of college faculty members are to go on strike tomorrow.
　（數以千計的大學教職員明天將舉行罷工。）

B. 表示應當執行的義務

句型結構： be＋不定詞＝should＋原形動詞

例：• What should I say? ＝What am I to say?
　（我該說什麼？）

　• He should tell the truth.＝He is to tell the truth.
　（他應該據實以告。）

◎ 不定詞／不定詞片語作形容詞也可用在被動語態的句子中。

例：• The garden should be watered once a day.
　＝The garden is to be watered once a day.
　（花園一天要澆水一次。）

　• The new policy should be put into practice without delay.
　＝The new policy is to be put into practice without delay.
　（新政策應立刻付諸實行。）

C. 表示完全沒有

句型結構： be＋nowhere＋不定詞被動（to＋be＋過去分詞）

這類句子常用在被動語態中，表示「哪兒都找不到」、「哪兒都看不到」。

例：• It never occurred to me that my cat would go missing, but now he is nowhere to be found.
（我從沒想過我的貓會不見，但是現在到處都找不到牠。）

• We called 110 to report a crimehalf an hour ago, but the police officers are still nowhere to be seen.
（我們半小時前已經打110報警了，到現在仍然連一個警察人影也看不到。）

馬上動手練一練 ❺

依提示填入不定詞，以完成句子

1. I thought my cellphone was in my bedroom, but it's nowhere _____ (find).

2. Normally, the receptionist should be at the reception counter, but today she is nowhere _____ (see).

3. The students _____ (submit) their term papers by the end of this week.

4. I have never babysat toddlers before. What _____ I _____ (do) right now?

5. Now that you are officially an adult, you _____ (take responsibility) for your actions.

ANSWER

1. to be found　　2. to be seen　　3. are to submit
4. am, to do　　5. are to take responsibility

◆不定詞／不定詞片語當副詞用

不定詞／不定詞片語亦可作副詞用，並一律以「後位修飾」的方式來修飾前面的動詞、形容詞或副詞。

❶ 放在動詞後面修飾動詞

例：• These young men volunteered to help.
（這些年輕人自願幫忙。）

• We went to see her. （我們去看她。）

◎ 不定詞修飾動詞時，通常是為了表示動作的目的；用來表示目的的不定詞／不定詞片語，可以與其他同樣表示「目的」的片語交替使用。除了 so as to 之外，不定詞以及表示「目的」的片語都可以移到主詞前，以逗點與主詞隔開。

★其他表示「目的、意圖」的片語：

in order to	so as to	in an attempt to

例：• He wrote a card to give her some comfort.

（他寫了一張卡片安慰她。）

= To give her some comfort, he wrote a card.
= In order to give her some comfort, he wrote a card.
（為了給她一些安慰，他寫了一張卡片。）

• She rushed all the way to the airport to see us off.

（她一路飛奔趕到機場就是為了幫我們送行。）

=To see us off, she rushed all the way to the airport.
= In an attempt to see us off, she rushed all the way to the airport. （為了要幫我們送行，她一路飛奔趕到了機場。）

重點筆記

表示否定目的時，通常以in order not to或so as not to來表示，而不用not＋不定詞

例：（O）We arrived at the airport early so as **not** to miss the flight.
　　（X）We arrived at the airport early not to miss the flight.
（我們很早抵達機場，才不至於錯過航班。）

（O）He studied hard in order **not** to fail the exam.
（X）He studied hard not to fail the exam.
（他努力用功，才不至於考試失敗。）

❷ 放在形容詞後面修飾形容詞

例：• Such a trivial matter is not worthy to be mentioned.

（這樣的小事不值得一提。）

• The soldiers were ready to die on the battlefield for their countries.

（戰士們已準備好為他們的國家戰死沙場。）

❸ 放在副詞後面修飾副詞

例： • If your immune system is strong enough to beat the virus, you won't get sick.

（如果你的免疫系統強壯得足以擊敗病毒，你就不會生病。）

• I don't have much to say. （我沒有太多話想說。）

圈出正確的詞

1. I am pleased (see/to see/seeing) you.

2. Mom will be (surprise/surprising/surprised) to receive this gift.

3. There isn't much (do/to do/done) here. Why don't we go to the museum?

4. George was very disappointed (hearing/heard/to hear) that his parents couldn't attend his college graduation.

5. She drank lots of coffee (in order not to/not to/so as not) doze off at work.

ANSWER
1. to see　2. surprised　3. to do　4. to hear　5. in order not to

二・獨立不定詞

以上介紹的不定詞及不定詞片語，在句子中具有著重要的文法地位。但是有一種不定詞片語，是獨立於文法句型之外，與句子其他部分之間不具文法關係，而是用來作為語氣轉折，用來修飾句子用的「獨立不定詞」。獨立不定詞可視為副詞片語，在英文口語及寫作中是常被利用的轉折詞。

◆常用的獨立不定詞

• to be honest 老實説	• to be short 簡短地説
• to be frank 老實説	• to be brief 簡短地説
• to tell the truth 説實話	• to cut a long story short 長話短説
• to be plain with you 老實跟你説	• to put it mildly 説得婉轉些
• to be sure 誠然	• to put it in another way 換句話説
• to be precise 正確地説	• to cut the matter short 簡言之
• to begin with 首先	• to make matters worse 更糟糕的是
• to sum up 總之	• to crown it all 最棒的是；最慘的是
• to conclude 總之	• to cap it all 最後；加之

例：• To begin with, I would like to welcome all of you to join our team.

（首先，我想要歡迎各位參加我們的團隊。）

• To put it in another way, plastic is the cancer of the ocean.

（換句話説，塑膠是海洋的惡性腫瘤。）

• To make matters worse, my car broke down in the middle of the nowhere.

（更糟糕的是，我的車在一個鳥不生蛋的地方拋錨了。）

馬上動手練一練 ❼

(A) To be precise	(B) To put it mildly	(C) To make matters worse
(D) To be honest	(E) to crown it all	

1. I prefer not to invite Simon to my party. _____, he is the last person I would like to see on my birthday.

2. Rape is one of the most common crimes against women in India. _____, there were 24,923 rape cases across India in 2012.

3. This poor old dog was abandoned by his owner. _____, he was hit by a truck and was seriously injured.

4. _____, the way she dealt with customer complaints was not very appropriate. I believe she needs more training for customer service.

5. It was a fantastic party. We had great hosts, amazing guests, delicious food, and, _____, the best band in town.

ANSWER

1. (D) 2. (A) 3. (C) 4. (B) 5. (E)

Lesson8

文法總複習
快來試試自己的實力吧！

A. 選擇正確的選項

1. (　) I couldn't fix the problem on my own, so I ask John _____.
   A. to help me　　　　　　　　B. helped me
   C. helping me　　　　　　　　D. help me

2. (　) We haven't decided _____ our summer vacation.
   A. which to eat　　　　　　　B. what to say
   C. where to spend　　　　　　D. how to make

3. (　) They persuaded me _____ the fitness club.
   A. to join　　　　　　　　　　B. to joining
   C. joined　　　　　　　　　　D. joining

4. (　) He left home pretty early _____ catch the train.
   A. not to　　　　　　　　　　B. so as to
   C. in order not to　　　　　　D. to not

5. (　) I can't _____ to go on an European cruise vacation with you.
   A. appear　　　　　　　　　　B. attempt
   C. pretend　　　　　　　　　　D. afford

6. (　) _____ is almost every girl's dream.
   A. Marry a prince　　　　　　B. Married a prince
   C. Marrying a prince　　　　　D. Marries a prince

7. (　) Joseph is a great colleague _____.
   A. to work   B. work with
   C. working with   D. to work with

8. (　) She wrote a card _____ cheer her friend up.
   A. in order to   B. not to
   C. so as not to   D. as well as

9. (　) We _____ Jerry and his family to join us for dinner last night.
   A. let   B. invited
   C. wandered   D. recalled

10. (　) My teacher _____ us to keep studying.
    A. persuaded   B. forgave
    C. invited   D. tried

B. 以不定詞結構改寫句子

例："Remember to bring an umbrella with you," Susan reminded Jack.

  →Susan reminded Jack to bring an umbrella with him.

1. "Don't be late for tomorrow's meeting," my boss warned me.

  _____

2. "Get down and put your hands where I can see them," the police officer ordered the man.

  _____

3. "Would you like to go to the movies with me," John asked me.

  _____

4. "Could you give me a hand," Sarah asked Pete.

  _____

5. There is one more thing that we must accomplish before we leave.

_____

6. His dissertation leaves nothing that can be desired. I am happy to give him an "A".

_____

7. We are looking for a nice hotel where we can stay during our trip.

_____

8. I have nothing that I can do here.

_____

9. I don't know what I can eat here.

_____

10. She deserves a promotion.

_____

ANSWER

A. 選擇正確的選項
1. **A**　2. **C**　3. **A**　4. **B**　5. **D**
6. **C**　7. **D**　8. **A**　9. **B**　10. **A**

1. ask 請求／要求+to原形動詞

2. 關係代名詞引導的形容詞子句

3. persuade說服+to原形動詞

4. so as to 為了要

5. afford 負擔

6. 動名詞當主格，marry→marrying

7. 不定詞／不定詞片語也可作形容詞用必須放在名詞後
   to work with 一起工作

8. in order to 為了要

9. invite 邀請

10. persuade 說服

B. 以不定詞結構改寫句子

1. My boss warned me not to be late for tomorrow's meeting.

2. The police officer ordered the man to get down and put his hands where he can see them.

3. John invited me to go to the movies with him.

4. Sarah asked Pete to give her a hand.

5. There is one more thing to accomplish before we leave.

6. His dissertation leaves nothing to be desired. I'm happy to give him an "A".

7. We are looking for a nice hotel to stay during our trip.

8. I have nothing to do here.

9. I don't know what to eat here.

10. She deserves to be promotion.

原形動詞＋ing

Lesson9

動狀詞2
動名詞

當副詞

The book is worth reading.

當補語

Your problem is taking
things too seriously.

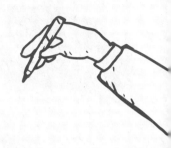

當主詞

- Swimming is fun.
- 使用虛主詞，動名詞要改成不定詞
  - It is fun to swim.

當受詞

在動詞後

- I couldn't help wondering why.
- 只能接動名詞的動詞：avoid, keep, quit

在介系詞後

- How about having lunch together?
- 必須接動名詞的動詞片語：

  dream of, think about, keep from, insist on

Lesson 9

動狀詞2：動名詞

緊接著不定詞，本章將繼續介紹第二種動狀詞：動名詞。動名詞是由原形動詞＋ing（如同現在分詞）而來，顧名思義是由動詞變成名詞，為名詞的相等詞，可在句子中作為主詞、受詞及補語。

動名詞／動名詞片語

動名詞即「原形動詞＋ing」所形成的動狀詞。誠如其名，動名詞為名詞的對等語，具有名詞的性質，其在句子中的功能與名詞一樣，可以作主詞、受詞及補語。

◆動名詞／動名詞片語作句子的主詞

動名詞作主詞時，視為單數名詞，故主詞後面的動詞必須是單數動詞，助動詞亦需使用單數助動詞。此外，如果動名詞是由及物動詞演變成動名詞，後面仍需要受詞。

例：• Swimming is fun.（游泳很好玩。）

• Teaching is learning.（教學相長。）

• Being strong doesn't mean you can't cry.
（堅強不代表你不能哭泣。）

• Making fun of disabled people is discourteous.

（嘲笑殘疾人士是很失禮的行為。）

make fun of為表示「嘲笑」的及物片語動詞，後面必須有受
詞。此例以disabled people（殘疾人士）作為受詞。因此此句
的主詞即「嘲笑殘疾人士」這個行為。

　　以動名詞或動名詞片語作為主詞時，亦可以用it來作虛主詞，
並將真主詞移到句尾。只是移到句尾的動名詞必須改成不定詞片
語。

例：• To some people, planning for future is a waste of time.

　　→ To some people, it is a waste of time （ X ）planning for future .

　　　　　　　　　　　　　　　　　　↓

　　　　　　　　　　　　　　（ O ）to plan for future

（對有些人來說，計劃未來是浪費時間的事。）

• Catching up with friends is my favorite thing to do.

→It is my favorite thing to do （ X ）catching up with friends .

　　　　　　　　　　　　　　　↓

　　　　　　　　　　（ O ）to catch up with friends

（跟朋友小聚是我最喜歡做的事。）

馬上動手練一練 ❶

將提示的動詞改成動名詞形式的主詞，填入空格中完成句子

1. (eat late-night snacks)

_____ is not healthy.

2. (smoke in public places)

_____ should be banned.

3. (nurse)

_____ is a big responsibility, especially with very sick hospital patients.

4. (learn a foreign language well)

_____ takes time and dedication.

5. (sleepwalk)

_____ can be dangerous, as the sleepwalkers might injure themselves while sleepwalking.

ANSWER

1. Eating late-night snacks
2. Smoking in public places
3. Nursing
4. Learning a foreign language well
5. Sleepwalking

◆動名詞╱動名詞片語作句子的受詞

❶ 當動詞的受詞

具有名詞性質的動名詞╱動名詞片語可作為動詞的受詞。

在〈Lesson4動詞〉中，我們已經知道有些動詞後面可以接不定詞與動名詞當受詞，而有些動詞後面通常只接動名詞當受詞。這裡再次將這類動詞做整理：

★ 只能接動名詞為受詞的動詞或片語動詞：

- admit/admit to 承認
- avoid 避免
- consider 考慮
- delay 耽擱
- deny 否認
- dislike 不喜歡
- enjoy 喜歡
- fancy 想像
- feel like 想要

- finish 結束
- give up 放棄
- can't help 忍不住
- imagine 想像
- involve 意味著
- keep 繼續
- keep on 繼續
- mind 介意
- miss 想念

- postpone 推遲
- practice 練習
- put off 延後
- quit 戒除
- risk 冒險
- resist 抗拒
- recommend 推薦
- stand 忍受
- suggest 建議

例：• The retired officer **admitted** <u>disclosing</u> military secrets to the enemy country.
（該退役軍官承認洩露軍機給敵國。）

• He **considered** <u>giving up</u> his high-paying job for a less stressful one.
（他考慮為一個壓力較小的工作放棄他的高薪工作。）

• I **couldn't help** <u>wondering</u> where he got the insider information.
（我忍不住納悶他是從哪裡得到那些內線消息。）

• They **postponed** <u>sending</u> wedding invitations to their friends.
（他們延緩對朋友們寄出婚禮請帖。）

◎表示否定動作時，將not放在受詞動名詞之前： not＋V-ing

例：• He **denied** <u>not paying</u> taxes on time.
（他否認沒有準時繳稅。）

- I can't **stand** <u>not living</u> with my children.
  （我無法忍受不跟孩子住在一起。）

- We **consider** <u>not sending</u> our son to a regular school and start homeschooling.
  （我們考慮不將孩子送到正規學校，開始在家教育。）

　　許多動詞後面接動名詞或不定詞作受詞，兩者所表達的意思並沒有太大差別，如begin, like, hate, prefer等（詳細介紹請見Lesson4動詞）。

例：
- He <u>began searching</u> for a job after graduation.
  ＝He <u>began to search</u> for a job after graduation.
  （畢業後他就開始找工作。）

- I hate working on the weekend.
  ＝I hate to work on the weekend.
  （我討厭在週末工作。）

　　但是有些動詞，後面接動名詞或不定詞作受詞時，兩者所表達的意思完全不相同：

	接動名詞當受詞	接不定詞當受詞
stop	**stop + V-ing** 停下正在做的事	**stop + to V** 停下原本做的事，轉而做另一件事
go on	**go on + V-ing** 繼續原來正在做的事	**go on + to V** 原本正在做某事，改做另一件事
try	**try + V-ing** 試試看做某事，以觀測其效果	**try + to V** 努力做某事，看能不能成功
regret	**regret + V-ing** 對已做過的事感到後悔	**regret + to V** 對正要做的事致歉

remember	remember + V-ing 記得曾經做過的事	remember + to V 記住要去做某事
forget	forget + V-ing 忘記曾經做過的事	forget + to V 忘記要去做某事

例：• The police officer <u>stopped to look</u> at the boy.
（警察停下來看看男孩。）

• The police officer <u>stopped looking</u> at the boy.
（警察不再看著男孩。）

• The old man <u>went on talking</u> about his adventure on the desert island.
（老人繼續說著他在荒島上的經歷。）

• The old man spoke about his mother, and then <u>went on to talk about</u> his wife.
（老人先說到他的母親，接著講起他的妻子。）

• Why don't we <u>try homeschooling</u> our son, and see how it goes?（我們何不試試看自己在家教育兒子，然後看看效果如何？）

• We <u>tried to homeschool</u> our son, but it turned out to be unsuccessful.
（我們試過在家教育兒子，但是結果並不成功。）

• I <u>regret telling</u> you all my secrets.
（我真後悔把我所有的秘密都告訴你。）

• I <u>regret to tell</u> you that your application was rejected.
（很遺憾通知您，您的申請未獲核准。）

- I remember returning the book to the library.
（我記得把書還給圖書館了。）

- I'll remember to return the book to the library.
（我會記得把書還給圖書館的。）

- She forgot borrowing $5,000 from me.
（她忘記跟我借了五千元。）

- She forgot to return the money. （她忘記要還錢了。）

★need接動名詞與不定詞的用法有差異。

need「需要」是另一個需要特別留意用法的動詞。

a. need用來表達主動的概念時，動詞後面接一般名詞或不定詞作受詞

例：• You need a break. （你需要休息。）
- You need to take a break. （你需要休息一下。）

- I need a day off. （我需要一天休假。）
- I need to take a day off. （我需要休一天假。）

b. need用來表達被動的概念時，動詞後面可接不定詞或動名詞

> need＋動名詞＝「需要某事物」
> need＋to be＋過去分詞＝「需要被……」

例：• The Christmas tree needs decorating.
（聖誕樹需要裝飾。）
＝The Christmas tree needs to be decorated.
（聖誕樹需要被裝飾。）

- The apartment needs <u>cleaning</u>.（這間公寓需要打掃。）
＝The apartment needs <u>to be cleaned</u>.
（這間公寓需要被打掃。）

★go這個動詞可以用來表示「進行、從事」某種活動，後面經常接動名詞，表示「進行、從事某種活動」。如：

go	• biking/cycling 騎單車 • bowling 打保齡球 • boating 划船 • boardsailing 風帆衝浪 • bungee jumping 高空彈跳 • camping 露營 • dancing 跳舞 • hiking 健行 • jogging 慢跑	• mountain climbing 爬山 • picnicking 野餐 • sailing 帆船航行 • scuba diving 水肺潛水 • skiing 滑雪 • snorkeling 浮潛 • shopping 逛街購物 • surfing 衝浪 • swimming 游泳

例：• I'll never <u>go bungee jumping</u> because I'm afraid of height.
（我絕不會去高空彈跳，因為我懼高。）

• Grandpa makes it a rule to <u>go jogging</u> every morning.
（爺爺習慣每天早上去慢跑。）

• We <u>went snorkeling</u> nearly every day when we were in Green Island.（我們在綠島的時候幾乎天天去浮潛。）

★動名詞既然具名詞性質，因此也與一般名詞一樣，可以在前面加上定冠詞the、不定形容詞some/any，來描述所做的事，或是在動名詞前面加上代名詞所有格，來表示某人所做的事。

例：• If you do <u>the cooking</u>, I'll do <u>the washing-up</u>.
（如果你做飯，我就負責洗碗。）

- I need to do <u>some grocery shopping</u> this afternoon.
（我今天下午得去買點日常雜貨。）

- As for the toilet, we do <u>the cleaning</u> once a week.
（至於廁所，我們是一星期清潔一次。）

- <u>His not passing the exam</u> really disappointed me.
（他沒有通過考試真的讓我很失望。）

- Do you mind <u>my smoking here</u>?
（你介意我在這裡抽菸嗎？）

馬上動手練一練 ❷

將提示字做適當變化後，填入空格中，以完成句子

1. Could you please stop _____ (scream)? It's just a little cockroach, and it's already dead!

2. I won't consider _____ (change) my job unless I have a better offer.

3. The kitchen tap needs _____ (fix). It has been leaking for two days.

4. Do you mind _____ (I sit) next to you?

5. It is such a beautiful day! Why don't we go _____ (picnic) at the park?

ANSWER

1. screaming   2. changing   3. fixing
4. my sitting   5. picnicking

❷ 當介系詞的受詞

當有動詞放在介系詞（如before, after, about, in, of, on, from 等）之後作受詞時，就要改成動名詞形式。

必須接動名詞作受詞的片語動詞有：

• be fond of 喜愛	• keep from 阻止，避免
• prevent from 阻止	• be interested in 對……感興趣
• dream of 夢想	• be excited about 對……感興奮
• think of 打算	• go about 從事，忙於
• think about 考慮	• insist on 堅持，一定要

例：• Are you interested in <u>going</u> to the movies with me tonight?
（你有意今晚與我一起去看電影嗎？）

• I'm thinking of <u>moving</u> to the countryside.
（我在考慮搬到鄉下一事。）

• How about <u>having</u> lunch together?
（要不要一起吃午餐？）

◎ 注意：to也可以是介系詞，遇到片語動詞的介系詞是to時，可別心不在焉，立刻接上原形動詞。記住：介系詞後面的動詞必須是動名詞才行！

介系詞為to的片語動詞或連接詞：

片語動詞	連接詞
• look forward to 期待 • admit to 承認 • be devoted to 專心致力於 • be/become/get used to 習慣 • be/become accustomed to 　對⋯⋯習以為常 • pay attention to 注意，專心	• in addition to 　除⋯⋯之外 • with regard to 　有關⋯⋯ • when it comes to 　當提到⋯⋯

例：
- We look forward to <u>seeing</u> you again.
（我們期待能再次見到你。）

- He admitted to <u>stealing</u> her money.
（他承認偷了她的錢。）

- I'll never get used to <u>working</u> with a perfectionist like Jenny. （我永遠無法習慣跟一個像珍妮那樣的完美主義者共事。）

- People seldom pay attention to <u>breathing</u>, because it's an unconscious process. （人們很少注意到呼吸這件事，因為它是一個無意識的過程。）

- When it comes to <u>dealing</u> with difficult customers, Lena is an expert. （講到應付難纏的顧客這方面，萊娜可是個高手。）

- In addition to <u>speaking</u> four foreign languages, Tom is also a specialist in network programming. （除了會說四種外語之外，湯姆還是個網路程式設計專家。）

be used to與used to的用法比較

1. be used to

be used to/become used to/get used to都是表示「對某事感到習慣」，受詞為動名詞或是其他名詞相等語。

例：• I am used to getting up early.（我習慣早起。）

• The children have become used to walking 15 miles to school every day.
（孩子們已經習慣每天走十五哩的路去上學。）

• My grandparents are getting used to living in a metropolitan city.
（我的祖父母漸漸習慣生活在大都會裡。）

2. used to

used為use的過去式，used後面接不定詞（to＋V），用來描述「過去習慣或經常做的事」，沒有現在式的用法。

例：• I used to get up early, but now I am a typical night owl.
（我以前經常早起，但現在我是典型的夜貓子。）

• The children used to walk 15 miles to school before the bridge was built.（在橋搭建好之前，孩子們經常要走十五哩的路去上學。）

• My grandparents used to live in the rural village before they moved to the city.
（我的祖父母在搬到都市之前，曾經住在農村裡。）

將提示字做適當變化，填入空格中完成句子

1. (work in the new office)

It won't take you too long to get used to _____.

2. (break up with Jack)

To be honest, I am thinking about _____.

3. (visit the city again soon)

We loved Paris so much. We both look forward to _____.

4. (return the product for a full refund)

The customer insisted on _____.

5. (take me to dinner)

In addition to _____, he also bought me a birthday present.

ANSWER

1. working in the new office
2. breaking up with Jack
3. visiting the city again soon
4. returning the product for a full refund
5. taking me to dinner

◆動名詞／動名詞片語作為補語

動名詞／動名詞片語可以放在be動詞後面，作為主詞補語。

例：• My new year resolution is getting a driver's license.
（我的新年新希望就是考到駕照。）

• Your problem is taking negative comments too seriously.
（你的問題就是太認真看待負面評論。）

• The first thing we need to do is reconstructing the village.
（我們需要做的第一件事就是重建這個村落。）

馬上動手練一練 ❹

將句子中的不定詞改成動名詞重寫句子

1. What you should care about is to pass your finals.

_____

2. His first job was to deliver newspapers.

_____

3. The next thing on my to-do list is to pick up the laundry.

_____

4. All you have to do is to tell the police what you witnessed.

_____

5. My plan is to travel around Europe all by train.

_____

ANSWER

1. What you should care about is passing your finals.
2. His first job was delivering newspapers.
3. The next thing on my to-do list is picking up the laundry.
4. All you have to do is telling the police what you witnessed.
5. My plan is traveling around Europe all by train.

◆動名詞作為副詞

　　動名詞亦可作副詞用，並以「後位修飾」的方式來修飾前面的形容詞。

　　例：• Many friends of mine believe that bitcoin is **worth** investing in.
　　　　（我許多朋友認為比特幣是值得投資的。）

　　　　• I consider it **worthwhile** doing（to do）a master's degree.

　　（我認為取得碩士學位是值得一做的事。）

worth後面可接一般名詞，表示「值得一……」，
worth也可接動名詞，表示「值得……的」。

例：• The book is **worth** a read.
＝The book is **worth** reading.
（這本書值得一讀。）

• The National Gallery is **worth** a visit.
＝The National Gallery is **worth** visiting.
（國家美術館值得參觀。）

圈出正確的詞

1. Is this car worthwhile (to buy/buying/buy)?
2. I highly recommend their boeuf bourguignon. It is definitely worth (to try/a try/a trying).
3. I heard that the museum is worthwhile (visit/to visit/visiting). Shall we go together sometime this week?
4. Well, if you ask me, the film is not worth (to see/seeing/seen). The story is boring and the cast is only so-so.
5. I believe bitcoin is worth (investing/investing in/to invest). Some of my friends have made a big profit already.

ANSWER

1. to buy/buying	2. a try	3. to visit/visiting
4. seeing	5. investing in	

NOTE

動名詞的慣用語

以下為常與動名詞連用的慣用語,建議可以背下句型,以便在聽說讀寫上活用:

1. It is no use＋V-ing

＝It is of no use＋to V　表示「……是無用的」

例:• It is no use crying over spilt milk.
　＝It is of no use to cry over spilt milk.
　(事情已成定局,後悔也沒有用。)

　• It is no use learning without thinking.
　＝It is of no use to learn without thinking.
　(不動腦思考,學了也沒用。)

2. It is a pleasure/honor/privilege ＋V-ing

＝ It is a pleasure/honor/privilege＋to V
　表示「很榮幸能夠……」

例:• It is my pleasure having you as my supervisor.
　＝It is my pleasure to have you as my supervisor.
　(很榮幸能有您擔任我的指導者。)

　• It was a great privilege working with you.
　＝It was a great privilege to work with you.
　(很榮幸能與您共事合作。)

3. There is no reasoning with...

＝It is impossible to reason with　表示與……理論是不可能的

例:• There is no reasoning with such an irrational person.
　＝ It is impossible to reason with such an irrational person.
　(要跟這麼不可理喻的人講理是不可能的。)

4. cannot help/resist/refrain from/stop＋V-ing

表示「忍不住……；無法抑制……」

例：• Hanna <u>cannot help laughing</u> when she heard the joke.
（Hanna聽到笑話時忍不住大笑。）

• The woman <u>couldn't resist frowning</u> when hearing the weird laughs.
（女子聽到那詭異的笑聲忍不住皺眉頭。）

• Please <u>refrain from talking</u> during the show.
（表演期間請忍住不要說話。）

馬上動手練一練 ❻

將提示做適當變化填入空格中，以完成句子

1. It's no use _____(regret) your mistakes. Let bygones be bygones.

2. It's our great pleasure _____(have) you with us.

3. The woman couldn't stop _____(scream) when seeing a rat in her house.

4. Darren is a very selfish person. It is of no use _____(ask) him for help.

5. Stop _____ (try). There is no _____(reason) with a self-opinionated person.

ANSWER

1. regretting   2. to have/having   3. screaming
4. to ask   5. trying, reasoning

文法總複習

快來試試自己的實力吧！

A. 選擇正確的動詞語態

1. (　) Your passport has expired. It needs _____.
   A. renew　　　B. renewed　　　C. renewing　　　D. to renew

2. (　) We need _____ every day in order to improve our skills.
   A. practice　　B. practiced　　C. to practicing　　D. to practice

3. (　) Soon you will be used to _____ pretty soon.
   A. speaking in public　　　　　B. speak in public
   C. spoken in public　　　　　　D. to speak in public

4. (　) Doctors warn that _____ can greatly increase the risk of lung cancer.
   A. smoke　　B. smoking　　C. be smoking　　D. to be smoked

5. (　) The firefighter risked _____ their lives by entering the burning building to save people.
   A. to lose　　　B. lost　　　C. lose　　　D. losing

6. (　) It is no use _____ for your mistakes.
   A. making up excuses　　　　　B. to cover
   C. to apologize　　　　　　　　D. of applying

7. (　) They avoided _____ the accident in front of the victims.
   A. to mention　　　　　　　　　B. mentioned
   C. mentioning　　　　　　　　　D. being mentioned

8. (　) Once she stopped _____ her son to eat carrots, he
　　 _____ to eat them.
　　A. persuading; started　　　　B. making; enjoyed
　　B. to persuade; disliked　　　　D. to tell; tried

9. (　) Stop _____ her because she has regretted what she did.
　　A. to scold　　B. scolding　　C. scold　　　D. scolded

10. (　) How about _____ dinner later? There is a newly-opened
　　restaurant beside the office.
　　A. to have　　B. having　　C. have　　　D. had

B. 以動名詞結構完成句子

1. What do you think about _____ (they/get married)?

2. Thanks for _____(invite) me. I'm looking forward to
　_____(attend) your wedding ceremony.

3. My grandma insisted on _____(we/stay) for dinner with
　her.

4. _____(chop onions) always makes me weep.

5. I would like to apologize for _____(no/show up) to the
　party.

6. Believe me. _____(babysit) three young children at a
　time is no easy task.

7. The biggest challenge of my job is _____ (deal with)
　demanding customers.

8. If you want to stay healthy, you have to avoid _____ (stay
　up) late.

9. It is no use _____ (cry) for lost things.

10. I am thinking of _____ (move) to countryside.

ANSWER

A. 選擇正確的動詞語態
1. **C**   2. **D**   3. **A**   4. **B**   5. **D**
6. **A**   7. **C**   8. **A**   9. **B**   10. **B**

1. 物+need（需要）+ving

2. 人+need（需要）+to v

3. be used to ving習慣於

4. 動名詞當主格

5. risk後面只能加動名詞為受詞的動詞或片語動詞

6. It is no use＋V-ing
   ＝It is of no use＋to V 表示「……是無用的」

7. avoid只能接動名詞為受詞的動詞或片語動詞

8. Once……S+V 一……就……
   Stop+V-ing停止做某事，persuade說服

9. Stop+V-ing停止做某事，scold責罵

10. about介系詞+名詞/V-ing

B. 以動名詞結構完成句子
1. their getting married
2. inviting, attending
3. our staying
4. Chopping onions
5. not showing up
6. Babysitting
7. dealing with
8. staying up
9. crying
10. moving

NOTE

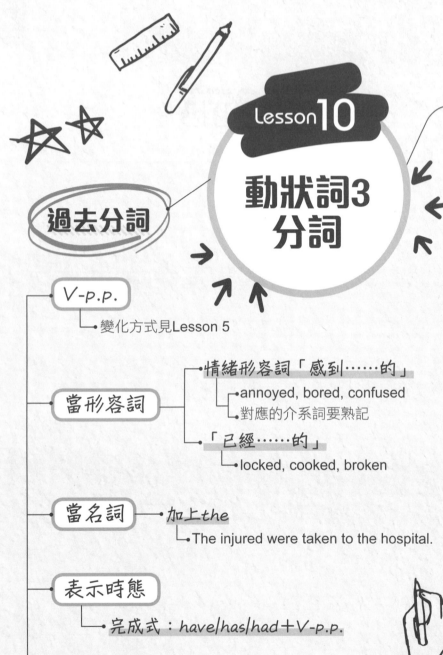

Lesson **10**

動狀詞3 分詞

過去分詞

- **V-p.p.**
  - 變化方式見Lesson 5

- **當形容詞**
  - 情緒形容詞「感到……的」
    - annoyed, bored, confused
    - 對應的介系詞要熟記
  - 「已經……的」
    - locked, cooked, broken

- **當名詞** — 加上the
  - The injured were taken to the hospital.

- **表示時態**
  - 完成式：have/has/had＋V-p.p.

- **被動語態** — be＋V-p.p.

現在分詞

原形動詞＋ing
- 變化方式見Lesson 5

當形容詞
- 情緒形容詞「令人覺得……的」
  - annoying, boring, confusing
- 「……中的」
  - closing, falling, sleeping

當副詞 →It's burning hot today!

表示時態
- 進行式：be＋V-ing
- 完成進行式：have/has/had＋been V-ing

動狀詞3：分詞

分詞也是由動詞演變而來的其中一種動狀詞，有現在分詞與過去分詞之分。兩種分詞都具有形容詞性質，可以用來修飾名詞或代名詞，也可以用來作為補語。

除了具形容詞性質之外，分詞的另一個功能就是搭配be動詞或助動詞形成各種時態或是被動語態。

值得注意的是：現在分詞的形式為「原形動詞＋ing」，與動名詞形式相同，但是在句子中所扮演的角色並不同，只要確實弄清楚兩者各自的用法，分辨上就不會有太大的難度。

一‧現在分詞

現在分詞由原形動詞＋ing演變而來。有關原形動詞變成現在分詞的方式請複習〈Lesson5動詞的時態〉。

◆作形容詞用

❶ 現在分詞作形容詞，可用來描述「使人產生某種感覺」的人或事物，這類形容詞稱為「情緒形容詞」。可以放在名詞或代名詞前做修飾，也可以放在be動詞或連綴動詞後當補語。

例：• The movie is interesting.（這電影很有趣。）

> 動詞interest意指「使有興趣」
> 現在分詞interesting意指「有趣的；讓人感到有趣的」

• Playing with young children all day can be very exhausting.
（跟小孩子玩一整天可能會讓你筋疲力竭。）

> 動詞exhaust意指「使耗盡；使筋疲力竭」
> 現在分詞exhausting意指「令人筋疲力竭的」

★由情緒動詞演變而來的情緒形容詞，常用來形容「令人覺得……的」

原形動詞	現在分詞形容詞
amaze 使驚愕，使驚奇	amazing 驚人的，令人吃驚的
amuse 使歡樂，使發笑	amusing 好笑的，好玩的
annoy 惹惱，使生氣	annoying 使人惱火的，討人厭的
bore 使厭煩	boring 無聊的，令人厭煩的
confuse 使困惑	confusing 使人困惑的
charm 使陶醉，吸引	charming 迷人的，有魅力的
depress 使消沈，使心灰意冷	depressing 令人沮喪的
embarrass 使困窘	embarrassing 令人尷尬的
entertain 招待，使歡樂	entertaining 令人愉快的，有娛樂性的
exhaust 使耗盡，使筋疲力竭	exhausting 令人精疲力竭的

frighten 使驚恐	frightening 令人害怕的
excite 使興奮	exciting 令人興奮的
interest 使感興趣	interesting 令人感到有趣的
relax 使放鬆	relaxing 令人放鬆的
satisfy 使滿意	satisfying 令人滿意的
shock 使震驚	shocking 令人震驚的
stun 使目瞪口呆	stunning 令人目瞪口呆的
surprise 使驚訝	surprising 令人驚訝的
thrill 使激動，使興奮，使毛骨悚然	thrilling 令人激動的
tire 使疲累	tiring 令人疲累的

實例應用：• an embarrassing question 一個很尷尬的問題
　　　　　• a stunning view 一個讓人目瞪口呆的景象
　　　　　• a surprising result 一個讓人驚訝的結果
　　　　　• a frightening experience 一個令人驚恐的經歷
　　　　　• a boring speech 一場無聊的演講
　　　　　• a charming lady 一個有魅力的女士

馬上動手練一練 ❶

將提示字做適當變化填入空格中，以完成句子

1. I had a very _____ (tire) day. All I want to do now is to rest.
2. The news was _____ (shock). I still can't believe it really happened.

3. The noise that you are making is very _____ (annoy).

4. Feeding the dolphins is the most _____ (excite) experience I have had.

5. The man has a _____ (frighten) look, but he is actually very kind.

ANSWER

1. tiring   2. shocking   3. annoying   4. exciting   5. frightening

❷ 現在分詞形容詞，也可以用來表達「進行中」的概念，形容「正在……中的」或「即將……的」人事物

例：• She tried to comfort her crying baby.
（她試著安撫她哭泣中的寶寶。）

動詞cry指「哭泣」
現在分詞 crying意指「正在哭的，哭泣中的」

• Now, I'm going to poach some eggs with boiling water.
（現在，我要來用滾水煮一些蛋。）

動詞boil意指「使沸騰」
現在分詞 boiling意指「正在沸騰的，煮沸的」

★更多表示「進行中」的現在分詞形容詞

原形動詞	現在分詞形容詞
open 打開	opening 即將開啟的

close 關閉	closing 即將關閉的
age 變老	aging 日漸變老的
boil 沸騰	boiling 沸騰的
fall 掉落	falling 正落下的
bleed 流血	bleeding 正在流血的
sleep 睡覺	sleeping 正在睡覺的
retire 退休	retiring 即將退休的

實例應用： • Do not wake a sleeping dog.
（不要叫醒一隻正在睡覺的狗。）

• Listen to the rhythm of the falling rain!
（聽聽那落雨聲的節奏。）

• My aging father found it hard to remember things.
（我日漸年邁的父親發現很難記住事情。）

• The man raised his bleeding arm and cried for help.
（男子抬起他血流不止的手臂呼救。）

★ 現在分詞形容詞也含有「主動」的概念，常與名詞結合，成為慣
用字彙

• a walking stick 拐杖	• a walking advertisement 活廣告
• the living room 客廳	• a living dictionary 活字典
• the waiting list 候補名單	• the waiting room 候診室
• falling star 流星	• falling sickness 癲癇
• opening speech 開幕詞	• opening ceremony 開幕典禮

• <u>cooking</u> oil 食用油	• a <u>cutting</u> board 砧板
• <u>sleeping</u> pill 安眠藥	• <u>drinking</u> water 飲用水

 **重點筆記**

現在分詞形容詞除了作主詞補語之外，亦可作為受詞補語：

例：• I saw the man <u>running the red light</u>.
（我看到男子闖紅燈。）

• She talked to me with her eyes <u>smiling</u>.
（她雙眼帶著笑意地跟我說話。）

◆作副詞用

少數現在分詞可以作為副詞，修飾後面的形容詞。

例：• It is <u>burning</u> hot today! （今天天氣超熱的！）

• Be careful! The soup is <u>boiling</u> hot!
（小心！湯超滾燙的！）

• It's been <u>freezing</u> cold these days.
（最近真的冷到快凍僵了！）

 **馬上動手練一練 ❷**

將提示字做適當變化，填入空格中完成句子

1. I find it _____ (embarrass) to dance in front of my classmates.

2. Watching TV news can be quite _____ (depress).

3. Taking a walk along the river is very _____ (relax).

4. I have something _____ (interest) to share with you guys.

5. Jeff knows everything. He is literally a _____ (walk) dictionary.

◆形成時態

1 現在分詞搭配be動詞，即可形成「進行式」時態：**be＋V-ing**

例：• 現在進行式→I <u>am trying</u> to figure out what <u>is going on</u>.
（我正試著弄清楚現在發生什麼事。）

• 過去進行式→ We <u>were talking</u> about our plan for the weekend when he came in.
（他進來的時候，我們正在討論週末的計劃。）

2 現在分詞搭配助動詞have/has/had及be動詞，即可形成「完成進行式」時態：**have/has/had＋been＋V-ing**

例：• **現在完成進行式**→ Ms. Lin <u>has been waiting for</u> you in the reception room since two o'clock.
（林小姐從兩點開始就一直在會客室等您了。）

• **過去完成進行式**→ The little boy <u>had been crying</u> for two hours when his mom finally showed up.
（小男孩在媽媽終於出現之前已經哭了兩小時了。）

• **未來完成進行式**→We <u>will have been living</u> in this apartment
for exactly one year by tomorrow.
（到了明天，我們就將已經在這房子住滿一年了。）

馬上動手練一練 ❸

依句意將提示字作適當時態修改，填入空格中完成句子

1. Can anyone tell me what ＿＿＿＿＿＿＿ (go on) here?
2. They ＿＿＿＿＿＿＿ (wait) for the bus for half an hour now.
3. We ＿＿＿＿＿＿＿ (fly) to New York this time tomorrow.
4. I ＿＿＿＿＿＿＿ (try/hide) the newspaper when he burst in.
5. Marie ＿＿＿＿＿＿＿ (work) in the company for two years when
she got a better job offer.

ANSWER

1. is going on　　2. have been waiting　　3. will be flying
4. was trying to hide　　5. had been working

二・過去分詞

　　過去分詞為原形動詞變化而來，動詞變化可分為「規則變化」
與「不規則變化」兩種形式，而不規則變化中又有四種不同的變化
形式，請複習〈Lesson5動詞的時態〉，將動詞的三態變化方式再
熟悉一次。

◆作形容詞用

① 過去分詞作形容詞，可用來描述「心中的感覺或想法」，主詞通常是「有感知能力」的「人或動物」等。這類形容詞也屬於「情緒形容詞」。可以放在名詞或代名詞前做修飾，也可以放在be動詞或連綴動詞後當補語。

例：• He looked tired.
（他看起來很累。）

• She tasted the cake, but didn't seem very satisfied.
（她嚐了蛋糕，但是似乎並不非常滿意。）

動詞satisfy意指「使滿意」
過去分詞satisfied意指「感到滿意的」

• I was completely exhausted after a long day at work.
（在工作了漫長的一天之後，我感到徹底地筋疲力竭。）

動詞exhaust意指「使耗盡；使筋疲力竭」
過去分詞 exhausted意指「感到筋疲力竭的」

★ 由情緒動詞演變而來的情緒形容詞，用來形容「感到……」

原形動詞	過去分詞形容詞
amaze 使驚愕，使驚奇	amazed 感到吃驚的
amuse 使歡樂，使發笑	amused 被逗樂的
annoy 惹惱，使生氣	annoyed 感到惱火的

bore 使厭煩	bored 感到無聊的
confuse 使困惑	confused 感到困惑的
depress 使消沈，使心灰意冷	depressed 感到沮喪的
disappoint 使失望	disappointed 感到失望的
embarrass 使困窘	embarrassed 感到尷尬的
entertain 招待，使歡樂	entertained 感到愉快的
exhaust 使耗盡，使筋疲力竭	exhausted 感到精疲力竭的
frighten 使驚恐	frightened 感到害怕的
excite 使興奮	excited 感到興奮的
interest 使感興趣	interested 有興趣的
relax 使放鬆	relaxed 感到放鬆的
shock 使震驚	shocked 感到震驚的
stun 使目瞪口呆	stunned 感到目瞪口呆的
surprise 使驚訝	surprised 感到驚訝的
thrill 使激動，使興奮，使毛骨悚然	thrilled 感到激動的
tire 使疲累	tired 感到疲累的
worry 使擔憂	worried 感到擔憂的

　　這些分詞形容詞的前面經常是be動詞或連綴動詞，後面以介系詞接受詞，形成一個慣用的片語用法。由於與每個情緒形容詞連用的介系詞不盡相同，所以最好將以下片語表記熟，方能正確使用在句子中。

句型結構：　主詞＋{ be動詞 / 連綴動詞 }＋情緒形容詞＋介系詞＋受詞

be interested in 對……感興趣	be terrified at 對……感到害怕
be annoyed by 被……惹怒	be bored with 對……感到無聊
be annoyed at/with 對……感惱火	be confused about 對……感到困惑
be amused by 被……逗樂	be excited about 對……感到興奮
be concerned about 對……關心	be frightened of 對……感到害怕
be disappointed at/in 對……感到失望	be worried about 對……感到擔憂
be satisfied with 對……感到滿意	be tired of 對……感到厭煩
be embarrassed about 對……感到困窘	be scared of 對……感到害怕
be surprised at 對……感到驚訝	be thrilled with 對……感到興奮，激動

例：• They seemed interested in our proposal.
（他們似乎對我們的提案很感興趣。）

• I was so annoyed by the noise from the street.
（我對馬路傳來的噪音感到非常火大。）

• I'm worried about Jack. He hasn't eaten anything today.
（我很擔心傑克。他今天什麼東西都還沒吃。）

- The boys <u>were embarrassed about</u> not winning the game.
（男孩們對於沒有贏得比賽感到很不好意思。）

- The kids <u>felt scared of</u> their father.
（孩子們對他們的父親感到很畏懼。）

重點筆記

過去分詞形容詞除了作主詞補語之外，亦可作為受詞補語。

例：
- I found the man <u>injured</u>.
（我發現男子受傷了。）

- The woman sat there with her legs <u>crossed</u>.
（女子雙腿交叉坐在那兒。）

❷ 過去分詞形容詞，也可以用來表達「已經完成」的概念，形容「已經……的」人事物。

例：
- The <u>retired</u> professor was still devoted to the study of history.
（那位退休的教授仍專心致力於歷史研究。）

動詞retire指「退休」
過去分詞 retired意指「已經退休的」

• Our backyard is now covered with fallen leaves.
（我們的後院現在被落葉給覆蓋了。）

動詞fall意指「落下」
過去分詞 fallen意指「已經落下的」

★ 更多表示「已經……的」的過去分詞形容詞：

原形動詞	過去分詞形容詞
lock 鎖	locked 上鎖的
age 變老	aged 上了年紀的
poach 水煮	poached 水煮的
cook 烹煮	cooked 煮熟的
wound 使受傷	wounded 受傷的
injure 弄傷	injured 受傷的
break 破壞	broken 壞掉的
organize 組織	organized 組織

實例應用：• There is a locked room in this house.
（這房子裡有個上了鎖的房間。）

• I have a poached egg for breakfast every day.
（我每天早餐都吃一顆水煮蛋。）

• My mother may be aged, but she is still healthy and happy.
（我母親也許已經上了年紀，但她仍然健康快樂。）

• The wounded man was sent to the hospital without delay. （受傷的男子立刻被送往醫院。）

★ 過去分詞形容詞同時含有「已經完成」、及「被動」的概念，常
　與名詞結合，成為慣用詞彙。

a haunted house 鬼屋	a broken home 破碎家庭
a grilled fish 烤魚	fried rice 炒飯
dead end 死胡同，困境	dried milk 奶粉
spoken language 口頭語言	written language 書面語言
finished product 成品	arranged marriage 媒妁之言的婚姻
organized crime 集團犯罪	developed country 已開發國家
guided missile 導向飛彈	hidden resources 地下資源

馬上動手練一練 ❹

將提示字做適當變化填入空格中，以完成句子

1. Can you have someone replace the _____ (break) window?

2. I'll make some _____ (fry) noodles for dinner tonight.

3. Be careful with the _____ (boil) soup. You don't want to hurt yourself.

4. The girls didn't dare to visit the _____ (haunt) house.

5. Don't eat chicken unless it is _____ (cook).

ANSWER
1. broken　2. fried　3. boiled　4. haunted　5. cooked

◆作名詞用

少數過去分詞可以在前面加上定冠詞the，變成名詞。

例：• Doctors and nurses rushed to the disaster area to treat the wounded.

（醫生及護理師趕往災區治療傷患。）

• The injured were taken to the hospital.

（傷者被送往醫院。）

◆形成時態

過去分詞搭配助動詞have/has/had，即可形成「完成式」時態：

have/has/had＋V-p.p.

例：• **現在完成式**→I have had lunch already.

（我已經吃過午餐了。）

• **過去完成式**→Josh had cleaned the house before I came home.

（在我回家之前，喬許已經把屋子打掃好了。）

• **未來完成式**→We will have lived in this house for five years by the end of this month.

（到這個月底，我們就將住在這棟房子五年了。）

◆形成語態

過去分詞搭配be動詞，即可形成「被動語態」。

例：• **現在被動** →The mission is <u>completed</u>.
（任務已經完成了。）

• **未來被動** →Paper books <u>will be replaced</u> by e-books one day.
（紙書有一天將會被電子書給取代。）

• **過去被動** →The tickets <u>were</u> all <u>sold out</u>.
（門票全部被賣光了。）

• **完成式被動** →The city <u>has been destroyed</u>.
（這城市已經被毀滅了。）

 馬上動手練一練 ❺

依句意將提示字作適當時態變化，填入空格中以完成句子

1. The dismemberment case ＿＿＿＿＿＿ (report) for days. You can hear the related news whenever you turn on the TV.

2. Because of the war, the once prosperous city ＿＿＿＿＿ (destroy) within an hour.

3. The restaurant ＿＿＿＿＿ (close) for renovation for a month from tomorrow.

4. We_____ (lose) contract with Lily for three months. No one _____ (hear from) her since the day she left home.

5. By the time you return, the office _____ (move) to the city center already.

Lesson 10 **文法總複習**
快來試試自己的實力吧！

A. 根據句意圈出正確的字

1. According to the research, people grew up in a (breaking/broken) home are more vulnerable to mental disabilities.

2. Drinking (polluting/polluted) water can lead to serious diseases and health problems.

3. The house has been (abandoning/abandoned) for decades. No one has ever (been seen/been seeing/seen) the owner since he left for no reason.

4. Hundreds of (injuring/injured) villagers were rushed to the hospital after the (terrifying/terrified) earthquake.

5. I have a (breaking/broken) leg. That's why I need to walk with a (walking/walked) stick.

6. After an (exhausting/exhausted) day, I was too (tiring/tired) to go anywhere except my bedroom.

7. The school building has finally (being repairing/been repaired). The children are all very (exciting/excited) about going back to school tomorrow.

8. Be careful of (fallen/falling) rocks in the mountains.

9. That (haunted/haunting) house looks frightening. Don't go inside.

10. The kids looked (frightened/frightening) after they watched the horror movie.

B.根據句意，選出適當的動詞，將其變成分詞形容詞後填入空格中

confuse	satisfy	bore	scare
embarrass	amuse	interest	
tire	disappoint	annoy	

1. Many customers are _____ in trying out our new products.

2. I'm very _____ in you, as you didn't keep your promise.

3. We were all _____ about the teacher's assignment. None of us have done it correctly.

4. The kids were so _____ by the teacher's silly jokes that they almost laughed their heads off.

5. My supervisor didn't seem _____ with my research proposal. I might need to rewrite it.

6. The actress decided to retire because she was _____ of being in the spotlight.

7. Everyone makes mistakes. There's nothing to be _____ about.

8. You can tell that the children are _____ to death as they keep yawning during the speech.

9. The students are _____ that they act up every day at school.

10. I am _____ about bugs. I cannot help screaming once I see them.

ANSWER

A.根據句意圈出正確的字

1. broken

2. polluted

3. abandoned, seen

4. injured, terrifying

5. broken, walking

6. exhausting, tired

7. been repaired, excited

8. falling

9. haunted

10. frightened

1. broken home破碎家庭

2. polluted water被汙染的水源

3. 再也沒人見過No one has seen see，abandoned被棄置

4. injure跟villagers關係為被動，故使用過去分詞injured

5. break跟leg關係為被動，故使用broken leg

6. exhausting day令人勞累的一日。一日不可能主動感覺勞累，故不能使用exhausted。I was tired人主動感到勞累，故使用tired

7. school building是被修理，故使用repaired。人主動感到興奮，故使用excited

8. falling rocks正在滾落的石頭，fallen rocks已經滾落的石頭

9. haunted house鬼屋

10. look frightened看起來很驚恐。人主動感到驚恐故使用frightened

B.根據句意，選出適當的動詞，將其變成分詞形容詞後填入空格中

1. interested

2. disappointed

3. confused

4. amused

5. satisfied

6. tired

7. embarrassed

8. bored

9. annoyed

10. scared

NOTE

表示位置

- 在……之中：in, inside
- 在……之上：on, above, over
- 在……之下：under, below, beneath
- 在……之前：before, in front of
- 在……之後：after, behind
- 在……之外：outside
- 在……旁：at, by, next to, beside
- 在（兩者）之間：between

Lesson 11

介系詞

表示擁有或穿戴

- 擁有（某物、特質）：with
- 穿戴：in

其他用法

- **at**
  - 從事某種活動：at work
  - 數字相關的表達：at the age of 10
  - 朝某人做某事：yell at him

- **by**
  - 藉由：by riding a bike
  - 被（某人事物）：be V-p.p. by sb./sth.

- **from**
  - 免於：keep sb. from

- **with**
  - 以某物做某事：eat with fork
  - 跟隨、擁有：come with me, with your help

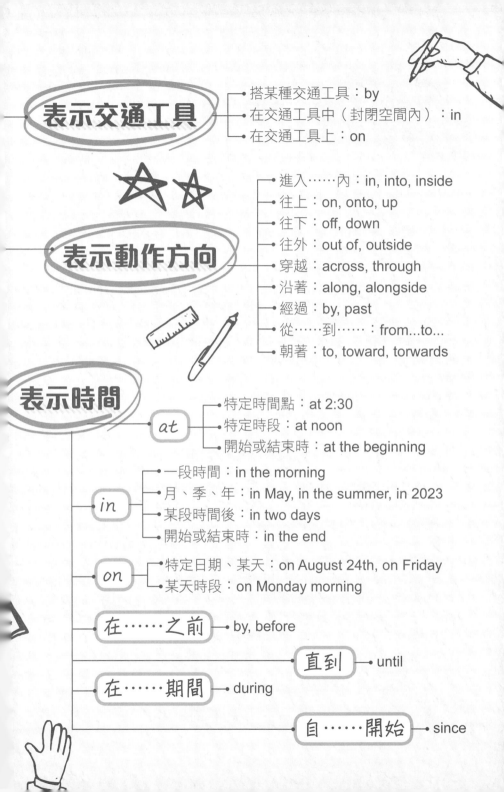

表示交通工具
- 搭某種交通工具：by
- 在交通工具中（封閉空間內）：in
- 在交通工具上：on

表示動作方向
- 進入……內：in, into, inside
- 往上：on, onto, up
- 往下：off, down
- 往外：out of, outside
- 穿越：across, through
- 沿著：along, alongside
- 經過：by, past
- 從……到……：from...to...
- 朝著：to, toward, torwards

表示時間

at
- 特定時間點：at 2:30
- 特定時段：at noon
- 開始或結束時：at the beginning

in
- 一段時間：in the morning
- 月、季、年：in May, in the summer, in 2023
- 某段時間後：in two days
- 開始或結束時：in the end

on
- 特定日期、某天：on August 24th, on Friday
- 某天時段：on Monday morning

在……之前 → by, before

直到 → until

在……期間 → during

自……開始 → since

Lesson 11 介系詞

介系詞在英文句型中，往往起著如「螺絲釘」般的重要功用。介系詞可以是一個單字，如in（表示「在……裡」），也可以是一組字，如on top of（表示「在……之上」）透過介系詞與其他字詞的關係，可以讓我們清楚表達概念、人物、事物、事件等的位置、時間、移動，或相對關係等。

我們經常利用介系詞引導出一個片語，目的是在提供有關主詞或動作更多的必要資訊，不同的介系詞有不同的意義，往往左右著整個片語的含義，因此能正確使用介系詞，在英文句型中是十分重要的。

一・表示位置的介系詞

常用來表示「位置」或「地點」的介系詞有：

表示「在……之中」	in, inside
表示「在……之上」	on指「在某物上面」，與某物有直接接觸 above指「在某物之上」，與某物無直接接觸 over指「在……上面」，有覆蓋的含義 on top of有「在頂端」的含義
表示「在……之下」	under, below, beneath, underneath
表示「在……之前」	before, in front of
表示「在……之後」	after, behind, in back of

表示「在……之外」	outside
表示「在……旁」	at, by, next to, beside,
表示「在……附近」	near, around
表示「在（兩者）之間」	between
表示「在……對面」	opposite

例：
- Tom locked himself **in** the room.（湯姆把自己鎖在房間裡。）
- The courier is waiting **at** the door.（快遞正在門口等著。）
- She put her hands **over** her face.（她把手放在臉上。）
- Do you mind my sitting **next to** you?
（你介意我坐在你旁邊嗎？）
- Please don't park your car **in front of** my garage.
（請勿把車停在我的車庫前。）
- Normally I don't eat anything **between** meals.
（我通常不在兩餐間吃東西。）

 **重點筆記**

★比較**in front of**與**at the front of**
1. 要表示在「在……前面」時，要用before或in front of
2. 要表示「在……前方，位在前面」時，要用at the front of
例：
- I was waiting **at the front of** the queue, and a man suddenly cut **in front of** me.（我本來排在隊伍前，然後一個男子突然插隊到我前面。）
- The teacher stood **at the front of** the classroom and demonstrated how to do the experiment **in front of** the class.（老師站在教室前面，在全班面前示範怎麼做實驗。）

★ 比較in back of與at the back of

1. 要表示在「在……後面」時，要用behind或in back of

2. 要表示「在……後方，位在後面」時，要用at the back of

例：
- A man **at the back of** the bus told the driver that there was dog **in back of** the bus before the driver ran over it. （一個坐在公車後方的男子，在司機碾過一隻狗之前告訴司機車子後面有一隻狗。）

- My seat was **at the back of** the theater, but the worse part is, I was sitting **in back of** a tall and fat man.
（我的座位在戲院的後方，但更糟的是，我坐在一個又高又胖的男子後面。）

馬上動手練一練 ❶

選出適當的介系詞填入空格中

| between | on top of | in front of | behind | over | by |

1. Do you know the woman sitting _____ the window?

2. The little girl was so frightened that she hid _____ her mother.

3. The birds built a nest _____ the tree.

4. There is a river _____ the two villages, so the villagers built a bridge _____ the river.

5. We had to have the car which parked _____ our store towed away.

ANSWER

1. by   2. behind   3. on top of   4. between, over   5. in front of

二．表示方向的介系詞

常用來表示「動作方向」的介系詞有：

表示「進入到……內」	in, into, inside
表示「往……上」	on, onto, up
表示「往……下」	off, down
表示「往……外」	out of, outside
表示「穿越」	across, through
表示「在……之外」	out of, outside
表示「沿著……旁」	along, alongside
表示「圍繞著……，在……週邊」	round, around
表示「經過」	by, past
表示「從……到……」	from ... to ...
表示「朝著……」	to, toward, towards

例：• Before you get **on** the bus, let people get **off** first.
（在你上公車之前，讓人先下車。）

• The cat jumped **up to** the wall and then **onto** the rooftop.
（貓往上跳到牆上，然後又跳上屋頂。）

• They drove **past** their house and headed directly **toward** the hospital. （他們開車經過家門，並直接前往醫院。）

- They ran **along** the streets, climbed **over** the hedges, walked **through** the wood, swam **across** the river, and finally arrived at the finish line. （他們沿著路跑，攀爬過障礙物，穿越樹林，游過河流，然後終於抵達終點線。）

重點筆記

前往home, here/there時，前面不加介系詞to
例：**(O)** I'm going home. （我正要回家。）
　　(X) I'm going to home.

　　(O) Come here. （來這裡。）
　　(X) Come to here.

馬上動手練一練 2

選擇適當的介系詞填入空格中

around	down (X2)	out	over	to
toward	into	from (X2)	outside	across

1. They looked _____ _____ their balcony and saw the car ran _____ the old lady who was trying to walk _____ the street.

2. Tom came _____ Julia, put his hand _____ his pocket and took _____ a ring. He proposed to her. With tears rolling _____ her cheeks, Julia said yes.

3. Please stop your children from running _____ the restaurant. It's very dangerous.

4. How long will it take to go ____ here ____ the nearest post office?

5. If you want to smoke, please go _____.

ANSWER

1. down, from, over, across   2. toward, into, out, down
3. around   4. from, to   5. outside

三、表示時間的介系詞

at	(1) 一天內某指定時間：at three o'clock/at 2:30 (2) 一天內特定時段：at noon/at lunchtime/at night (3) 表示「起／始」：at the beginning/at the end
in	(1) 一天內部分時間：in the morning/afternoon/evening (2) 較長的時間（月、季、年）：in April/in the spring/ in 2018 (3) 表示「起／始」：in the beginning/in the end (4) 表示「在某段時間之後」：in five days/in two weeks
on	(1) 某特定日期：on March 24th/on the first day of January/on Christmas (2) 某天：on Monday/on the weekend (3) 某特定日子的部分時間：on Saturday night
by	表示「在某時間之前」：by Friday/by next week
during	表示「在……期間」：during the weekend
before	表示「在……之前」：before breakfast

after	表示「在……之後」：after sunset
until	表示「直至某時」：until midnight
from... to...	表示「自某時到某時」：from 2 pm to 4 pm/ from Monday to Friday
for	表示「持續一段時間」：for three hours/for ten days
since	表示「自某時間開始」：since last week/ since three hours ago
ahead of	表示「提前」：ahead of time/ahead of schedule

例：• The meeting will be held **on** Monday, August 7, 2023.
（該會議將在2023年八月七日星期一舉行。）

• Please keep your mobile phone in silent mode **during** the concert.
（在音樂會進行期間請將手機保持在靜音模式。）

• The bookstore opens **from** 10 am **to** 8 pm every day.
（書店每天從早上十點開到晚上八點。）

• We will have been married **for** twenty years **by** the end of next month.
（到下個月底時，我們將已經結婚二十年。）

• They might finish the work **ahead of** schedule.
（他們可能會提前完成工作。）

重點筆記

不加介系詞的時間副詞

next, last, this, every, all, each, some, any, one之前不需加介系詞

例： • See you **next week**. （下週見。）

• They will be leaving **this Friday**.
（他們這星期五就要離開了。）

• We go on a vacation in Hawaii **every summer**.
（我們每個夏天都會去夏威夷度假。）

• Let's have dinner together **some time**.
（我們找個時間一起吃晚餐吧。）

• He stayed in his room **all day** long.
（他一整天都待在房間。）

• You are welcome to visit us **any time**.
（任何時間都歡迎你來看我們。）

馬上動手練一練 ❸

填入適當的介系詞，不需加介系詞則在空格內打**"X"**

1. He was so tired that he couldn't help dozing off _____ the meeting.

2. They go to the countryside to visit their grandparents ____ every weekend.

3. My father asked me to come home _____ 10 o'clock.

4. Promise me you will stay with me _____ my parents return.

5. Their first child was born _____ the first day _____ January.

四・表示交通工具的介系詞

by	加名詞，描述使用某種交通工具：by car/by taxi/by subway
in	car/bus/train等交通工具之前有冠詞（a/the）或所有格（my/his），要用in：in my car/in a bus/in the train
on	(1) bike/scooter/motorcycle等交通工具之前有冠詞（a/the）或所有格（my/his），要用on：on my bike/on a scooter/on her motorcycle (2) 表示「步行」：on foot

例：• My father commutes to work **by** MRT every day.
（我父親每天搭捷運通勤上班。）

• If you want to get there faster, go **by** subway instead of taxi. （如果你想快一點到那裡，就搭地下鐵而不要搭計程車。）

• If it's not rainy, I don't mind going **on** foot.
（如果沒有下雨，我不介意走路去。）

重點筆記

注意以下表示交通工具的介系詞用法：
(O) I usually go to school *by car*. （我通常搭車上學。）
(O) I usually go to school *in my dad's car*.
（我通常搭我爸的車上學。）

(X) I usually go to school ~~by my dad's car~~.

(O) We travel around the country **by train**.
（我們搭火車在該國到處旅行。）
= We travel around the country <u>on the train</u>.
(X) We travel around the country ~~by the train~~.

(O) They rushed to the hospital **by taxi**.
（他們搭計程車趕到醫院。）
(O) They rushed to the hospital **in a taxi**.
（他們搭一輛計程車趕到醫院去。）
(X) They rushed to the hospital ~~by a taxi~~.

馬上動手練一練 ❹

在空格中填入介系詞**on, by**或**in**

1. Amy always goes to school ＿＿ her bike.

2. The best way to travel around the city is ＿＿ MRT.

3. It takes about 10 minutes to go to the office ＿＿＿ bus and about 25 minutes ＿＿ foot.

4. I didn't go to work ＿＿ my car because it had broken down.

5. Why don't you go to Kaohsiung ＿＿ the train?

ANSWER

1. on   2. by   3. by, on   4. in   5. on

五‧表示擁有或穿戴的介系詞

◆with 表示「擁有」某物

例：
- My roommate is a sweet girl **with** blond hair and blue eyes. （我室友是個有著金髮碧眼的甜美女孩。）
- She is a famous blogger **with** over one million followers. （她是個擁有超過一百萬個追蹤者的名部落客。）

◆in 表示「穿戴」某衣物或飾品

例：
- It's not appropriate to attend a funeral **in** red. （穿著紅色衣服出席喪禮並不合宜。）
- Who's that woman **in** blue jeans? （穿著藍色牛仔褲的女子是誰？）

馬上動手練一練 ❺

依句意填入 **in**或**with**

1. We are looking for a middle-aged man _____ brown curly hair and a scarf on the right cheek.

2. Tony looked gorgeous _____ the dark blue suit.

3. We need an apartment _____ two bedrooms.

4. Mary is a charming woman _____ a great sense of humor and a beautiful smile.

5. It's not appropriate to go out _____ your pajamas and slippers.

ANSWER
1. with　2. in　3. with　4. with　5. in

六・介系詞的其他用法

◆at 的其他用法

表示「從事某種活動」	• at work（上班、工作） • at school（上學、在學校） • at rest （在休息）
表示以某種與數字有關的方式	• at the age of ten （在十歲的年紀） • at the speed of 30 km/h （以時速三十公里的速度） • at the cost of sth. （以某物為代價） • at the price of $ （以某價格） • at the risk of （以……為賭注）
朝某人做某事	• shout at sb. （對某人吼叫） • laugh/mock at sb. （嘲笑某人） • point at sb. （指著某人） • throw sth. at sb. （將某物朝某人丟）

例：
• Do not talk to me when I'm *at work*.
（我在工作時不要跟我講話。）

• The whiz-kid went to college *at the age of 12*.
（那個天才兒童在十二歲時就上大學了。）

• He would accomplish his dream *at the cost of his life*.
（他以生命為代價來完成他的夢想。）

• Don't you *point at me* with your finger. It's very rude.
（不准你用手指著我。這非常沒禮貌。）

◆by 的其他用法

表示「程度差距」	• younger than sb. by ... years（小某人幾歲） • taller than sb. by ... centimeters（高某人幾公分）
表示「依照」	• charge by the hour（按時計費） • sell by the dozen（論打販售）
表示「藉由某種方式」	• by driving a taxi 藉由開計程車 • by regular exercise 藉由規律運動
表示「抓著身體某部位」或衣物	grab/grasp/hold/catch sb. by the hand（抓著某人的手）；by the collar（抓著衣領）
表示被動語態	be V-p.p. by sb./sth. 被某人或某物……

例： • My mother is younger than my father **by five years**.
（我母親比我父親小五歲。）

• Normally, student workers are paid **by the hour**.
（一般來說，工讀生都是按時支薪。）

• The woman lost thirty kilograms **by regular exercise and healthy diet**.
（女子藉由規律運動及健康飲食減了三十公斤。）

• The man caught the pickpocket **by the arm**.
（男子抓住扒手的手臂。）

• It is believed that the man was murdered **by his roommate**.
（據信該男子是被他的室友給殺害的。）

◆from 的其他用法

表示「分辨兩者差異」	• be different from... （與某人或某物不同） • tell right from wrong（分辨是非）
表示「忍住」做某事	• cannot refrain from doing...（忍不住做某事）
表示「免於」	• keep/prevent sb. from...（阻止某人做某事） • protect sb. from...（保護某人免於） • stop/restrict/retrain/prohibit/forbid sb. from ...（禁止某人做某事）

例：• Teaching children to **tell** right *from* wrong is all parents' responsibility.

（教孩子明辨是非是所有家長的責任。）

• I couldn't **refrain** *from* laughing when I heard the joke.
（當我聽到那笑話時，忍不住大笑。）

• The vaccine can effectively **protect** you *from* serious diseases such as encephalitis.
（這個疫苗可以有效保護你感染如腦炎這類的重大疾病。）

◆with 的其他用法

表示「以某物做某事」	• eat with chopsticks （用筷子吃東西） • handle with care （小心處理）
表示「跟隨」	• come with me（跟我來）
表示「擁有，伴隨著」	• with your help （有你的幫助）
表示「患有疾病」	• come down with ... （罹患某疾病） • be infected with ... （感染某病）

例：• A foreigner as he is, he is good at eating **with** chopsticks.
（他雖然是個外國人，卻很會用筷子吃東西。）

• I want you to stay here **with** your mother.
（我要你跟媽媽一起待在這裡。）

• **With** your support and encouragement, I am no longer afraid of new challenges.
（有了你的支持與鼓勵，我再也不害怕新挑戰。）

• No sooner had he been diagnosed **with** lung cancer than he died.
（他被診斷出罹患肺癌後不久就死了。）

 重點筆記

with的反義詞→ without，表示「沒有」

例：• We can't live **without** air, water and food.
（我們無法沒有空氣、水和食物而活。）

• I wouldn't have done it **without** your help.
（沒有你的幫助，我沒有辦法完成這件事。）

馬上動手練一練 ❻

填入介系詞**at**、**by**、**from**或**with**

1. Don't yell _____ me. It's not my fault.
2. They built a fence around the yard to prevent their dog _____ going out.
3. Twins as they are, Emily and Anna are very different _____ each other.
4. John is taller than me _____ five centimeters.
5. He killed the mosquito _____ a fly swatter.

ANSWER

1. at   2. from   3. from   4. by   5. with

A. 選擇正確的介系詞選項

1. (　) John is always absent-minded when he is _____ work.
   A. from　　　　B. on　　　　C. in　　　　D. at

2. (　) We beat them _____ one point.
   A. with　　　　B. by　　　　C. over　　　　D. on

3. (　) The apartment was sold _____ the price of $10,000,000.
   A. at　　　　B. with　　　　C. for　　　　D. after

4. (　) My sister has learned swimming _____ quite a long time. She is a very good swimmer.
   A. under　　　　B. since　　　　C. for　　　　D. at

5. (　) The meeting is scheduled to be held _____ next Monday morning.
   A. on　　　　B. for　　　　C. X　　　　D. to

6. (　) If he was born _____ 2003, he is older than you _____ six years!
   A. in; by　　　　B. on; for　　　　C. at; with　　　　D. in; about

7. (　) There is a post office right _____ my office.
   A. next　　　　　　　　B. at the front of
   C. across　　　　　　　D. opposite

8. (　) She is a sweet girl ____ black hair.
   A. with　　　　B. in　　　　C. have　　　　D. on

9. (　) She got promotion when she was ＿＿＿ the age of thirty.
   A. in   B. on   C. at   D. with

10. (　) I go to school ＿＿＿ bus every day.
   A. in   B. on   C. by   D. at

B. 選出正確的介系詞填入空格中

in	on	between	from
by	with	past	at

1. There is a bookstore ＿＿＿＿＿ the bank and the restaurant.
2. When will your flight arrive ＿＿＿ London.
3. The bus went ＿＿＿ me without stopping.
4. I am leaving for Spain ＿＿＿ two weeks.
5. I can't drive, so I have to go to work ＿＿＿ my motorcycle.
6. The police are searching for a man ＿＿＿ a scarf on his left face.
7. My father can distinguish a genuine painting ＿＿＿ a replica.
8. The two people who lost hearing communicate with each othe ＿＿＿ means of sign language.
9. She goes to school ＿＿＿ foot.
10. A coffee shop is ＿＿＿ a flower shop and a restaurant.

ANSWER

A. 選擇正確的介系詞選項
1. **D**　2. **B**　3. **A**　4. **C**　5. **C**
6. **A**　7. **B**　8. **A**　9. **C**　10. **C**

1. at work 上班，表示「從事某種活動」+at

2. 差距一分，by用來表示程度差距

3. 和某個數字有關用at

4. 表示「持續一段時間」：for three days/for one month

5. next, last, this, every, all, each, some, any, one之前不需加介系詞

6. 在某年出生使用in，表示差距使用by

7. at the front of位在前方

8. 長在身上的特徵用with

9. 和數字有關用at

10. 乘坐交通工具使用by

B. 選出正確的介系詞填入空格中

1. between

2. at

3. past

4. in

5. on

6. with

7. from

8. by

9. on

10. between

NOTE

形容詞比較級

原級＋er（注意不規則變化）

形容詞最高級

原級＋est（注意不規則變化）

形容詞的比較

最高級的比較句

主詞＋連綴動詞＋the＋
[形容詞最高級
most形容詞原級
least形容詞原級]

最高級是三者以上比較
- in/of/among＋比較對象
- that＋完成式子句
  →This is the best thing that has ever happened to me.

用副詞修飾最高級
- by far, much, really, definitely
- 主詞＋連綴動詞＋副詞＋形容詞最高級＋than…

原級的比較句

- 主詞+連綴動詞+as+形容詞+as+比較對象
- 否定：主詞+連綴動詞+not+as/so+形容詞+as +比較對象

比較級的比較句

- 主詞+連綴動詞+形容詞比較級+than+比較對象
- 否定：
  主詞+連綴動詞+ $\begin{bmatrix} not\ 比較級 \\ less\ 形容詞 \end{bmatrix}$ +than+比較對象
  - This box is not heavier than that one.
  - This box is less heavy than that one.
- 與特定團體的所有人比較

  主詞+連綴動詞+
  比較級+than + $\begin{bmatrix} any\ other單數名詞 \\ all\ the\ others複數名詞 \\ all\ the\ others \\ anyone\ else \end{bmatrix}$ +in⋯

- 與無特定團體的所有人比較

  主詞+連綴動詞+
  形容詞比較級+than + $\begin{bmatrix} any單數名詞 \\ all\ the複數名詞 \end{bmatrix}$ +in⋯

- 越來越⋯⋯
  - be+getting+ $\begin{bmatrix} 形容詞比較級and形容詞比較級more \\ and\ more形容詞原級 \end{bmatrix}$
- 用副詞修飾比較級
  - far, even, a lot, still, a great deal
  - 主詞+連綴動詞+副詞+形容詞比較級+than⋯

形容詞的比較

英文中的形容詞比較句型結構可分為三級。兩者之間互相比較，且程度相同，即為「原級」；兩者之間互相比較，出現程度差別的結果，即為「比較級」；三者或以上之間互相比較，出現其中一者程度較其它兩者更甚的結果，即為「最高級」。

在比較句構中的形容詞，會有比較級與最高級的變化，其變化方式與動詞一樣，有「規則變化」及「不規則變化」之分。

一·比較級與最高級的變化方式

與一般動詞一樣，形容詞也可分為「規則變化」與「不規則變化」。

◆規則變化

	原級	比較級	最高級
(1)單音節形容詞	short strong	加er shorter stronger	加est shortest strongest
(2)字尾為e的 形容詞	nice wise	加r nicer wiser	加st nicest wisest

(3)字尾為子音＋y 的形容詞	lazy early	將y改i，再加er lazier earlier	將y改i，再加est laziest earliest
(4)短母音＋單子音的單音節形容詞	big fat	重複字尾加er bigger fatter	重複字尾加est biggest fattest
(5)兩個音節以上形容詞	famous important	前面加more more famous more important	前面加most most famous most important

◆不規則變化

原級	比較級	最高級
good/well bad/ill many/much little	better worse more less	best worst most least

★ 有些形容詞有兩種不同的比較級和最高級，且代表含義稍有不同：

	比較級	最高級
old 老；舊	older 更老的；更舊的 elder 較年長的；較資深的	oldest eldest
far 遠	farther 更遠的 further 更進一步的	farthest furthest
late 遲；晚	later 較晚的 latter 後者的	latest last

二 · 原級的比較句構

◆ 句型結構：

> 主詞＋連綴動詞＋as＋形容詞＋as＋比較對象

as... as 為表示「與……一樣」的片語用法，介系詞as後面所接的是與主詞相比的比較對象。

例：• My brother is as handsome as Eddie Peng.
　　（我哥哥就跟彭于晏一樣帥。）

　　• Drowsy driving is just as dangerous as drunk driving.
　　（疲勞駕駛就跟酒後駕車一樣危險。）

　　• To some foreigners, stinky tofu smells as terrible as dirty socks. （對有些外國人來說，臭豆腐聞起來就像髒襪子一樣可怕。）

重點筆記

as 為連接詞，後面應該要接與前面的主要子句結構一樣的副詞子句，但是副詞子句中與主要子句相同的述詞可以省略。

例：• Dianna is as creative as Simon (is).
　　（戴安娜跟賽門一樣有創意。）

　　• The meat pie tastes as great as the beef stew (does).
　　（這肉派嚐起來就跟燉牛肉一樣棒。）

◆否定式

原級比較表達否定的方式：

主詞＋連綴動詞＋not＋ $\left\{ \begin{array}{c} \textbf{as} \\ \textbf{so} \end{array} \right\}$ ＋形容詞＋as＋比較對象

例：• I was not as early as Frank (was).
＝I was not so early as Frank (was).
（我沒有法蘭克那麼早來。）

• The ice cream does not taste as good as I expected.
= The ice cream does not taste so good as I expected.
（這冰淇淋沒有我原先期待的那麼好吃。）

重點筆記

so... as 只能用在否定的原級比較結構，不能用在肯定句。

例：（ O ）The storm is as destructive as we predicted.

（ X ）The storm is **so** destructive as we predicted.

（暴風雨一如我們所預測的具破壞性。）

馬上動手練一練 ❶

圈出正確的字，以完成句子

1. Brian is (as/so) hardworking as his brother.

2. She was not (very/so) lucky as you (are/were).

3. French cuisine is not as greasy (as/so) Chinese cuisine.

4. The cake (does/is) not as delicious as it (is/should be).

5. His wife looks as old as his mother (is/does).

三・比較級的比較句構

◆句型結構：

> 主詞＋連綴動詞＋形容詞比較級＋than＋比較對象

例：• Cindy is <u>younger</u> than Peter (is). （辛蒂比彼得年輕。）

• The cake tastes <u>better</u> than it looks.
（這蛋糕吃起來比看起來好。）

• Your idea sounds <u>more practical</u> than mine.
（你的點子聽起來比我的實際。）

重點筆記

就文法上的正確性來說，than後面若是代名詞指稱比較
對象，要接主格（才能跟前面的主詞相對應），但是口
語上多數人很習慣以受格取代之，久而久之也就不以為
錯了。

例：• You are no better than I am.
（你並沒有比我優秀。）
→很多人會習慣用You are no better than me.

• She is younger than he is. （她比他年輕。）

→很多人會覺得She is younger than him. 聽起來比較順耳。

　　一個語言的語法雖然有其規則，但是語言畢竟是「活的」東西，不可能永遠死板地不起變化，因此對這些小小的「文法錯誤」，我們是可以包容的。

◆含介系詞

　　當主要子句中的形容詞需以介系詞接受詞時，than所引導的副詞子句亦必須有對等的句構。重複的述詞可省略，但介系詞絕不可省略。

例：• Mary is more interested in shopping than she is interested in cooking. （瑪麗對逛街比對烹飪有興趣。）

　　→（O）Mary is more interested in shopping than she is in cooking.

　　→（O）Mary is more interested in shopping than in cooking.

> in shopping than in cooking是將「對逛街的興趣」與「對烹飪的興趣」做比較。

　　→（X）Mary is more interested in shopping than cooking.

> cooking前面少了介系詞，就會變成Mary跟cooking這兩者做比較，語意上不合邏輯

- I am more scared of snakes than I am scared of rats.
（比起老鼠我更怕蛇。）
→（**O**）I am more scared of snakes than I am of rats.
→（**O**）I am more scared of snakes than of rats.
→（**X**）I am more scared of snakes than rats.

> rats前面少了介系詞of，就會變成I跟rats做比較，語意上
> 會變成：「我比老鼠更怕蛇。」讓人摸不著頭緒。

 馬上動手練一練❷

在空格中依括號中的提示填入適當的字，以完成句子

1. My brother is _____ (interested) in Lego than he is in Barbie Doll.
2. Ms. Green is _____ (proficient) in Spanish than she is in German.
3. Mom was _____ (angry) with Peter than she was with Matt.
4. The woman is _____ (patient) with her children than she is with her husband.
5. Sometimes we are _____ (nice) to strangers than we are to our parents.

ANSWER
1. more interested　2. more proficient　3. angrier
4. more patient　5. nicer

◆含地方副詞或所有格

　　主詞與比較對象必須是屬性相同的兩者做對比，因此當主要子句的主詞含有介系詞片語，或是所有格時，要特別注意than所引導的副詞子句必須與主詞對等。

　　例：• The students <u>in the back</u> are taller than those <u>in the front</u>.
（後面的學生比前面的高。）

主詞為複數名詞時，than後面的主詞使用代名詞複數those對應；地方副詞in the front則與in the back相對應。

　　（X）~~The students in the back are taller than the front.~~
　　→ 這句比較句構是錯誤的，因為the students in the back
　　　 與the front屬性不相同，一個指「後方的學生」，一個
　　　 指「前方」。「學生」應該要與「學生」做比較，而不
　　　 是「地點」。

　　• Dad's hair looks grayer than Mom's.
　　= Dad's hair looks grayer than that of Mom.
　　（爸爸的頭髮看起來比媽媽的要白一些。）

主詞為Dad's hair（爸爸的頭髮），因此比較對象屬性必須相同。為避免重複相同述詞，因此以所有格Mom's 或that of Mom表示。

　　（X）~~Dad's hair looks grayer than Mom.~~
　　→ 這句比較句構是錯誤的，因為Mom與Dad's hair屬性不
　　　 相同，無法做比較。「爸爸的頭髮」應該要與「媽媽的
　　　 頭髮」做比較，而不是「媽媽」。

馬上動手練一練 ❸

圈出正確的字，以完成下列比較句構

1. The development of South Korea is better than (it/that) of North Korea.

2. Helen's health condition is worse than (her husband/her husband's).

3. Children in the city have more learning resources than (that/those) in the countryside.

4. The educational background of Darren is better than (that/those) of Oliver.

5. The facilities in the Disneyland are as attractive as (these/those) in the Universal Studio.

ANSWER

1. that   2. her husband's   3. those   4. that   5. those

- 比較級的否定式

　　not與less都能用來表示否定比較。less為little的比較級，表示「較不……的」。

$$主詞＋連綴動詞＋\begin{Bmatrix} not＋形容詞比較級 \\ less＋形容詞 \end{Bmatrix}＋than＋比較對象$$

例：• This box is not heavier than that one.
（這個箱子沒有比那個重。）

• My car is less expensive than yours.
（我的車沒有你的那麼貴。）

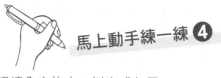

將否定比較級填入空格中，以完成句子

1. Generally, boys are _____(thoughtful) than girls.
2. Lily is _____(happy) than she was.
3. To me, pretty girls are _____(attractive) than smart girls.
4. No one is _____(strong) than my father. （＊小提醒：主詞有no。）
5. This case is _____(urgent) than that one.

ANSWER

1.less thoughtful　　2.not happier　　3.less attractive
4.stronger　　5.less urgent

◆與其他成員比較

❶ 與特定團體內的所有其他成員比較

　　當主詞與所屬團體中的其他成員做比較時，為避免主詞與比較對象的重疊，我們用any other「任何其他的」後面接單數名詞；all the other「所有其他的」後面接複數名詞，以表示主詞與某範圍內的任何一個其他人做比較。

• 句型結構：

主詞＋連綴動詞＋形容詞比較級＋than＋	• any other ＋單數名詞 • all the other ＋複數名詞 • all the others • anyone else	in ～

　　例：• Andrew is more diligent than any other student in his class.

　　　　（安德魯比他班上任何其他學生都要勤勉。）

295

= Andrew is more diligent than all the other students in his class.
（安德魯比他班上所有其他學生都要勤勉。）

= Andrew is more diligent than all the others in his class.
（安德魯比他班上所有其他人都要勤勉。）

= Andrew is more diligent than anyone else in our class.
（安德魯比他班上其他人都要勤勉。）

❷ 與無特定團體的其他成員比較

當主詞與無特定團體的所有其他成員比較時，不須考慮是否與比較對象重疊的問題，因此不需要有表示「其他的」含義的形容詞來描述比較對象。

• 句型結構：

主詞＋連綴動詞＋形容詞比較級＋than＋	any ＋單數名詞 all the＋複數名詞	in ～

例：• Russia is bigger than any country in the world.
（俄羅斯比世界上任何國家都要大。）

= Russia is bigger than all the countries in the world.
（俄羅斯比世界上所有國家都要大。）

• Blue whales are larger than any animal on earth.
（藍鯨比地球上任何動物都大。）

= Blue whales are larger than all animals on earth.
（藍鯨比地球上所有動物都大。）

馬上動手練一練 ❺

圈出正確的字

1. Jimmy is lazier than (anyone/any other) else in his family.

2. The earthquake was deadlier than (all other/all the others) in the past 10 years.

3. Christmas is more popular than (any/all) other holiday in the world.

4. To me, family is more meaningful than all other (thing/things) in my life.

5. Elephants are bigger than (any/all) land animal on earth.

ANSWER

1. anyone   2. all the others   3. any   4. things   5. any

◆其他句型

「get＋形容詞」是用來描述「變成某種狀態」的片語用法。若以「正在進行式」來表示，則可以描述「越來越……」：

• 句型結構：

be＋getting＋	形容詞比較級 and 形容詞比較級
	more and more＋形容詞原級

例：• It's getting hotter and hotter these days.
（最近越來越熱了。）

• The children are getting more and more excited.
（孩子們越來越興奮了。）

◆修飾形容詞比較級的副詞

放在形容詞比較級之前，是用來強調「還要更……」、「甚至更……」、「更……得多了」的副詞：

主詞＋連綴動詞＋$\begin{cases} \text{far} \\ \text{even} \\ \text{a lot} \\ \text{still} \\ \text{a great deal} \end{cases}$＋形容詞比較級＋than ～

例：• My brother is a lot more handsome than Justin Bieber.
（我哥哥比賈斯汀·比伯要帥得多了。）

• The main dish tasted even worse than the starter.
（主餐甚至比開胃菜還要更難吃。）

• This car is far more expensive than my apartment.
（這輛車比我的公寓還要更貴。）

馬上動手練一練 ❻

填入正確的形容詞比較級，以完成句子

1. His health condition is getting worse and _____ (bad).
2. I'm getting more and _____ (confused).
3. This movie is far _____ (interesting) than that one.
4. Don't worry. The situation is getting better and _____ (good).
5. The patient looks a lot _____ (weak) he did a few days ago.

ANSWER

1. worse   2. more confused   3. more interesting   4. better   5. weaker

四‧最高級的比較句構

◆句型結構：

$$主詞＋連綴動詞＋the＋ \begin{cases} 形容詞最高級 \\ most＋形容詞原級 \\ least＋形容詞原級 \end{cases}$$

例：• My father is the tallest (person) in my family.
（我爸爸是我家最高的。）

　　• Lily is the most confident candidate of all.
（莉莉是所有應徵者中最有自信的。）

　　• This handbag is the least expensive (one) in this store.
（這個手提包是這家店最不貴的。）

★　副詞most與least：

most為many/much的最高級，放在形容詞前表示「最……的」；least為little（少的）的最高級，具有否定意味，放在形容詞前表示「最不……的」。

★「the＋形容詞」可以用來作代名詞，故形容詞後面的名詞可省略。

◆比較對象

比較級是用來做兩者之間的比較，可以是「一對一」，也可以是「一對多」。最高級則是用來做三者以上彼此比較的。以下為表示最高級比較對象或比較範圍的副詞片語的方式：

① in/of/among＋比較對象

例：• Gina is the most patient student in our class.
（吉娜是我們班上最有耐心的學生。）

• Among the five applicants, Richard is the most qualified.
（在五個應徵者中，理查是最符合條件的。）

• Undoubtedly, Tom is the best of all.
（毫無疑問地，湯姆是全部人之中最棒的。）

② that＋完成式子句

關係代名詞that在子句中若不是主詞，則可省略不用。

例：• You are the most generous person (that) I've ever met.
（你是我所遇過最慷慨的人。）

• This is the best thing that has ever happened to me.
（這是曾經發生在我身上最好的一件事。）

◆用比較級來表示最高級

將主詞與比較對象以「一對多」的方式做比較，就能用比較級的句構表示最高級：

例：• This is the strongest earthquake over the past decade.
（這是過去十年來最強的一次地震。）

＝This is stronger than any other earthquake over the past decade.
（這次比過去十年來任何一次地震都還要強。）

＝This is stronger than all the other earthquakes over the past decade.
（這次比過去十年來所有其他地震都還要強。）

圈出正確的字，以完成句子

1. (Of/In) all the subjects, chemistry is the most difficult.

2. It was the most destructive tsunami (that/which) has occurred over the past century.

3. This young man is the most qualified (within/among) all the candidates.

4. She is the most absent-minded person (that/whom) I've ever seen.

5. Mark is the most reasonable person of (the two/the three).

ANSWER

1. Of　2. that　3. among　4. that　5. the three

◆不會用在比較級與最高級的形容詞

❶ 有些形容詞本身就有「比較」的含義，因此不使用在as... as 與 than比較句構。這類形容詞有：

superior 較好的，較優越的，較上級的	senior 較年長的，較資深的，位階較高的
inferior 較差的，較次等的，地位較低的	junior 較年幼的，較資淺的，位階較低的

以上形容詞一般要與to連用，後面接比較對象

例：• Men are not superior to women.
　　（男人並沒有比女人優秀。）

• Michael is junior to his wife in the office.
（米歇爾在公司的職位比他妻子要低。）

❷ 有些形容詞本身就有「最……的，極度……的」之含義，可以用在as ... as的比較句構中，但不會在前面加上more或the most等副詞來修飾，因此不會用在than的句構中。此類形容詞，常用的有：

| fabulous 極好的 | excellent 極優的 | perfect 完美的 |
| exceptional 卓越的 | favorite 最喜愛的 | superb 一流的 |

例：（O）No one's life is as perfect as it seems on Facebook.
（沒有人的生活跟臉書上看起來的一樣完美。）

（X）No one's life is more perfect than it seems on Facebook.

（O）She is a superb singer.（她是個一流的歌手。）

（X）She is the most superb singer I've ever known.

◆修飾形容詞最高級的副詞

放在形容詞最高級之前，用來強調「目前為止最……」、「真的是最……」的副詞：

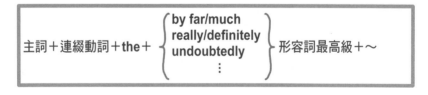

例：• Jennifer is by far the most beautiful girl I've seen.
（珍妮弗是我所見過最美的女孩子。）

- Math is much the most difficult subject of all.
  （數學真的是所有學科中最困難的。）

★ **very** 用來強調「最……」時，放在定冠詞the與形容詞最高級中間，表示「真正的」。

例： • He is the very best actor in Hollywood.
（他是好萊塢最棒的演員。）

圈出正確的字，以完成句子

1. This chapter is by far (more/the most) comprehensible one in this whole book.
2. Sarah is (the very best/very the best) girlfriend that one could every have.
3. This place is (as perfect as/more perfect than) heaven.
4. Chinese New Year is my (more favorite/favorite) holiday of the year.
5. These products are cheaper because they are inferior (than/to) others.

ANSWER

1. the most   2. the very best   3. as perfect as   4. favorite   5. to

A. 選擇正確的選項

1.(　) Your mother looks as young as _____ ten years ago.
 A. she did　　　B. she was　　　C. she　　　D. she could

2.(　) Jenny is _____ her littlest brother by fifteen years.
 A. as old as　B. more old than　C. older than　D. elder to

3.(　) Ron is _____ person I would invite to my party.
 A. the least　　　B. any　　　C. the last　　D. not a

4.(　) This is _____ birthday party that I've ever had in my life.
 A. the better　　　B. the best　　　C. a good　　D. best

5.(　) I am more concerned about his safety than _____.
 A. I am about mine　　　　　B. I am mine
 C. I am about me　　　　　　D. I am

6.(　) Celebrities' lives are not _____ we thought.
 A. more wonderful as　　　　B. as wonderful as
 C. so wonderful　　　　　　　D. more wonderful than

7.(　) David is _____ any other employee in the office.
 A. more senior than　　　　　B. junior than
 C. so senior as　　　　　　　D. senior to

8.(　) Because of the nuclear disaster, Fukushima is more
  destroyed than _____ in Japan.
 A. any other city　B. all other cities　C. other city　D. any cities

9.(　) Math is _____ difficult subject for her.
 A. the most　　　B. most　　　C. more　　　D. the more

10.(　) The main dish tasted ___ worse than the starter.

　　A. very　　　　　B. a lot　　　　C. more　　　　D. a lot of

B. 依提示改寫下列句子

1. Michael is more modest than any other boy in his class. （以most改寫）

　_____

2. The speech is not as informative as I expected. （以less改寫）

　_____

3. I am attractive to Judy. I am more attractive to Amanda. （合併句子）

　_____

4. John has many friends. I have more. （合併句子）

　_____

5. The pineapples in this box are ripe. The pineapples in that box are ripper. （合併句子）

　_____

6. Samantha is the most capable assistant in our company. （以more及all the other改寫）

　_____

7. It was hot yesterday. It is even hotter today.（用than合併句子）

　_____

8. Chinese is difficult. Math is more difficult.（用than合併句子）

　_____

9. Tim is strong. Andy is stronger.（用than合併句子）

　_____

10. The apples are cheap. The peaches are cheaper.（用than合併句子）

　_____

ANSWER

A. 選擇正確的選項

1. **A** 2. **C** 3. **C** 4. **B** 5. **A**
6. **B** 7. **D** 8. **A** 9. **A** 10. **B**

1. look為一般動詞，需找出助動詞。ten years ago 為過去 look→do/does，looked→did

2. old比較級→older

3. the last person I would invite最不想邀請的人

4. the best最好的

5. 我在意他的安全更勝於我的（安全）my safety=mine

6. as...as和……一樣

7. superior/senior/inferior/junior本身就有「比較」的含義，因此不使用在as... as 與than比較句構。

8. 主詞與比較對象以「一對多」的方式做比較，就能用比較級的句構表示最高級：

   This is the strongest earthquake over the past decade.

   （這是過去十年來最強的一次地震。）

   ＝ This is stronger than any other earthquake over the past decade.（這次比過去十年來任何一次地震都還要強。）

9. difficult最高級the most difficult

10. a lot/far/even/a lot/still/a great deal可以用來修飾形容詞比較級的副詞

B. 依提示改寫下列句子

1. Michael is the most modest boy in his class.

2. The speech is less informative than I expected.

3. I am more attractive to Amanda than I am to Judy.

4. I have more friends than John does.

5. The pineapples in that box are ripper than those in this box.

6. Samantha is more capable than all the other assistants in our company.

7. It is even hotter today than it was yesterday.

8. Math is more difficult than Chinese.

9. Andy is stronger than Tim.

10. The peaches are cheaper than the apples.

原級的比較句

- 主詞＋動詞＋as＋副詞＋as＋比較對象
- 否定：主詞＋助動詞＋not＋動詞＋as/ so＋副詞＋as＋比較對象
- as…as慣用句
  - as＋副詞＋as possible
  - as＋副詞＋as one can
  - as soon as
  - as long as

Lesson 13

副詞 的比較

副詞比較級

原級＋er（注意不規則變化）

副詞最高級

原級＋est（注意不規則變化）

比較級的比較句

- 主詞＋動詞＋副詞比較級＋*than*＋比較對象
- 否定：

  主詞＋$\begin{bmatrix}\text{助動詞＋}not\text{＋動詞＋副詞＋比較級}\\ \text{動詞＋}less\text{＋副詞}\end{bmatrix}$

  ＋*than*＋比較對象

  - She does not practice more diligently than I do.
  - She practices less diligently than I do.

- 與同團體其他人比較

  主詞＋動詞＋
  副詞比較級＋than ＋ $\begin{bmatrix}\text{any other單數名詞}\\ \text{all the others複數名詞}\\ \text{all the others}\\ \text{anyone else}\end{bmatrix}$ ＋in⋯

- 與非團體內的人比較

  主詞＋動詞＋
  副詞比較級＋than ＋ $\begin{bmatrix}\text{any單數名詞}\\ \text{all the複數名詞}\end{bmatrix}$ ＋in⋯

- 用副詞修飾比較級
  - far, even, a lot, still, a great deal
  - 主詞＋動詞＋副詞＋副詞比較級＋than...

最高級的比較句

  - 主詞＋動詞＋the＋ $\begin{bmatrix}\text{副詞最高級}\\ \text{most副詞原級}\\ \text{least副詞原級}\end{bmatrix}$

副詞的比較

形容詞是用來修飾名詞或作為主詞補語，而副詞則是用來修飾動詞。副詞的比較句構與形容詞的比較句構非常類似，只是形容詞通常放在名詞前面做修飾，而副詞則通常是放在動詞後面做修飾。

用來修飾動詞的情狀副詞與形容詞一樣，都有「原級」、「比較級」及「最高級」之分，用來描述動作進行狀態的程度。其變化方式亦有「規則變化」及「不規則變化」之分。如果你完全理解形容詞比較句構，那麼副詞的比較句構應該也難不倒你。

一・副詞的變化方式

副詞的變化方式，可分為規則變化與不規則變化兩種：

◆規則變化

	原級	比較級	最高級
(1) 單音節副詞	fast hard loud	加er faster harder louder	加est fastest hardest loudest

(2) 雙音節以上副詞	slowly carefully directly	前面加more more slowly more carefully more directly	前面加most most slowly most carefully most directly

★ **特殊的副詞**

有些副詞的規則變化方式比較特別，要特別留意：

1. early雖然為雙音節副詞，但是其比較級與形容詞一樣，是
   將字尾y改i再加er，而最高級則是將字尾y改i再加est：
   • early→ earlier→ earliest

2. 有兩種變化方式的副詞：
   • friendly→ friendlier/more friendly → friendliest/
     most friendly
   • kindly→ kindlier/more friendly → kindliest/most friendly

3. loud為形容詞與副詞同形，也可以加ly變副詞，意義不變。
   • loud → louder → loudest
   • loudly → more loudly → most loudly

◆不規則變化

原級	比較級	最高級
well	better	best
badly	worse	worst
much	more	most
little	less	least

二・原級的比較句構

◆句型結構

主詞＋動詞＋as＋副詞＋as＋比較對象

as...as 為表示「與……一樣」的片語用法，介系詞as後面所接的是與主詞相比的比較對象。重複的述詞通常可以省略。

例：• She sings as well as you (do).
（她唱得跟你一樣好。）

• Our competitors practice as hard as we (do).
（我們的競爭對手練習得跟我們一樣努力。）

• A cheetah can run as fast as a car (can).
（一隻獵豹可能跑得跟車子一樣快。）

◆否定式

主詞＋助動詞＋not＋動詞＋ { as / so } ＋副詞＋as＋比較對象

例：• A human cannot run as fast as a cheetah.
= A human cannot run so fast as a cheetah.
（人無法跑得跟獵豹一樣快。）

• Vincent does not work as carefully as James.
＝Vincent does not work so carefully as James.
（文森特工作沒有詹姆士細心。）

★注意：so... as 只能用在否定句，不能用在肯定句。

◆as... as 的慣用句

除了與特定比較對象做比較之外，as... as也常接形容詞或副詞子句，表示「盡……地」。

① as＋副詞＋as possible，表示「盡可能地……」

例：• She walked as slowly as possible so that her child could catch up.
（她盡可能地慢慢走，好讓她的孩子跟上。）

② as＋副詞＋as one can，表示「盡量」

例：• He checked his answers as carefully as he could.
（他盡量仔細地檢查答案。）

③ as soon as ~可以表示「盡快」，或接子句表示「一……馬上就」

例：• I want you to come home as soon as possible.
（我希望你盡快回家。）

• Please give me a call you as soon as you arrived.
（請你一到就馬上打電話給我。）

④ as long as ~ 可以「盡量久」。此外也可用在條件句，表示「條件」

例：• You can stay with us as long as you wish.
（你想跟我們一起住多久，就可以住多久。）

• You can buy the watch as long as you can afford it.
（只要你買得起，你就可以買這只手錶。）

馬上動手練一練 ❶

在空格中依提示填入副詞，以完成句子

1. You are going to be late. Please finish your breakfast as _____ (quick) as you can.

2. The doctor examined the patient as _____ (thorough) as possible.

3. He speaks English as _____ (fluent) as a native speaker does.

4. Susan dances as _____ (good) as a professional dancer.

5. The boy sat there as _____ (quiet) as a cat.

ANSWER
1. quickly   2. thoroughly   3. fluently   4. well   5. quietly

三・比較級的比較句構

◆句型結構

> 主詞＋動詞＋副詞比較級＋than＋比較對象

例：• Mom always gets up earlier than I do.
（媽媽總是比我早起。）

• Henry speaks English more fluently than Peter (does).
（哈利英文說得比彼得要流利。）

• She works more patiently than you (do).
（她工作比你有耐心。）

◆主詞與自己比較

當主詞與自己做比較時，可能是跟不同時期的自己做比較，也可能是跟不同動作做比較，要特別注意時態。

例：• Henry speaks English **more fluently than** he did.
（哈利英文說得比以前流利。）
→拿同一個動作的「現在狀態」與「過去狀態」做比較，以助動詞的時態變化做表示，故助動詞did在此處<u>不可省略</u>。

• Henry speaks English **better than** he speaks Japanese.
＝Henry speaks English better than he **does** Japanese.
（哈利英文說得比日文好。）
→ 相同動作可以用助動詞取代，但是不可省略主詞。

（ **X** ）Henry speaks English better than Japanese.
→ 這個句子會讓人誤以為是拿Henry（哈利）與Japanese（日本人）做比較。

❶ 比較級的否定式

not與less都能用來表示否定比較。less為little的比較級，表示「較不……地」。

$$
主詞 + \begin{Bmatrix} 助動詞 + \textbf{not} + 動詞 + 副詞比較級 \\ 動詞 + \textbf{less} + 副詞 \end{Bmatrix} + \textbf{than} + 比較對象
$$

例：• He may be smarter than you, but he does not work harder than you do.
（他也許比你聰明，但他工作並沒有比你努力。）

• I did not drive faster than I should.
（我並沒有開得比我應該開的速度快。）

- She practices less diligently than I (do).
（她練習得沒有我勤。）

- Frank works less enthusiastically than he did.
（法蘭克工作比過去少了點熱忱。）

 **重點筆記**

介系詞as及than後面接的是主格，而非受格。第二個主格後的助動詞可省略。

例：• John arrived as early as I (did).
（約翰回家時間跟我一樣晚。）

- Dogs don't live longer than tortoises (do).
（狗活得沒有烏龜久。）

 馬上動手練一練 ❷

在空格中填入副詞比較級，以完成句子

1. Generally, a child can pick up a second language _____ (easy) than an adult.
2. My father can cook _____ (good) than my mother.
3. Brian prepared his presentation _____ (adequate) than Tom.
4. Peter came home _____ (early) than usual in order to celebrate his mother's birthday.
5. Males don't necessarily work _____ (productive) than females.

ANSWER

1. more easily   2. better   3. more adequately
4. earlier   5. more productively

◆與其他成員比較

➊ 與同團體的其他成員做比較：

主詞＋動詞＋副詞比較級＋than＋	• any other ＋單數名詞 • all the other ＋複數名詞 • all the others • anyone else	in ～

例：• Gary listened more attentively than any other student in the class.

（蓋瑞聽得比班上任何其他學生都要專心。）

＝Gary listened more attentively than all the other students in the class.

（蓋瑞聽得比班上所有其他學生都要專心。）

＝Gary listened more attentively than all the others in his class.

（蓋瑞聽得比班上所有其他人都要專心。）

＝Gary listened more attentively than anyone else in our class.

（蓋瑞聽得比班上任何一個人都要專心。）

➋ 與非團體內的成員做比較：

主詞＋動詞＋副詞比較級＋than＋	any ＋單數名詞 all the＋複數名詞	in ～

例：• A black marlin can swim faster than any fish in the sea.

（黑鎗魚可以游得比海裡任何一隻魚都快。）

＝A black marlin can swim faster than all the fishin the sea.

（黑鎗魚可以游得比海裡所有魚都快。）

• Kadour Ziani can jump higher than any person in the world.
（賈尼可以跳得比世界上任何一個人都要高。）
＝Kadour Ziani can jump higher than all people in the world.
（賈尼可以跳得比世界上所有人都高。）

在空格中填入any other, all the other, any 或all

1. Dr. Huang treats the patients more cautiously than _____ doctor in this hospital.
2. Ms. Peterson teaches more enthusiastically than _____ teachers in the school.
3. A cheetah can run faster than _____ land animal on earth.
4. Gary adapted to the new office faster than _____ newcomer in the office.
5. Lucas Etter can solve a Rubik's Cube faster than _____ people in the world.

ANSWER
1. any other   2. all the other   3. any   4. any other   5. all

◆修飾副詞比較級的副詞

　　放在形容詞比較級之前，是用來強調「還要更……」、「甚至更……」、「更……得多了」的副詞：

$$
主詞＋動詞＋
\begin{cases}
\text{far/even} \\
\text{a lot/still} \\
\text{a great deal}
\end{cases}
＋副詞比較級＋than \sim
$$

例：• The audience shout far louder than they did when the famous singer showed up.

（當那位名歌手出現時，觀眾叫喊得比原本還要更加大聲。）

• She speaks English a lot better than she reads it.
（她英文說得比讀得要好很多。）

• I like baseball, but I like tennis even more.
（我喜歡棒球，但我更加喜歡網球。）

◆不用比較級和最高級的副詞

有些副詞本身就有「最……；極度……」的含義，可以拿來用在as ... as的句構做原級比較，但一般不會使用在比較句或最高級句構中。常見的這類副詞有：

perfectly 完美地　　superbly 一流地　　excellently 極優地

例：（O）• She performed as perfectly as Jane (did).
　　　　　（她表現得跟Jane一樣完美。）

（X）• She performed more perfectly than Jane (did).
　　　（她表現得跟比Jane還要完美。）

（X）• She performed the most perfectly than anyone else (did).
　　　（她表現得比任何一個人都更完美。）

馬上動手練一練 ❹

圈出正確的字，已完成句子

1. He treats influential customers (far/very) more respectfully than he does average customers.
2. Having a large family to support, the man has to work (ever/even) harder than others.
3. She dealt with the problem (a lot/lots) more calmly than her husband did.
4. The young teacher teaches (as excellently as/more excellently than) many senior experienced teachers.
5. The work has been done (more perfectly than/as perfectly as) I expected.

ANSWER

1. far 2. even 3. a lot 4. as excellently as 5. as perfectly as

四・最高級的比較句構

◆句型結構

$$
\text{主詞＋動詞＋(the)＋} \begin{cases} \text{副詞最高級} \\ \text{most＋副詞原級} \\ \text{least＋副詞原級} \end{cases}
$$

例：• Of all the newcomers, James learned the fastest.
（在所有的新人中，詹姆士學得最快。）

- Among the six children, Helen acts the most independently.
  （在六個孩子中，海倫表現得最為獨立。）

- In the office, Kevin works the least efficiently.
  （在公司裡，凱文工作最沒效率。）

❶ 副詞most與least

most放在副詞前表示「最……的」；least具有否定意味，放在形容詞前表示「最不……的」。

❷ 在副詞的最高級比較句構中，定冠詞the可加可不加

形容詞最高級前面一定要有定冠詞the做修飾，以表示「指定」；副詞最高級前面則不一定要有定冠詞。

例：• Of all the nurses, Nancy is the most patient.
（在所有的護士中，南西是最有耐心的。）

- Dr. Cooper is the most prestigious surgeon in this hospital.
（庫柏醫師是這家醫院最有名望
的外科醫生。）

> 形容詞最高級前，
> the不能省略

- Of all the nurses, Nancy treats the patients (the) most
  patiently.
（在所有的護士中，南西是對待病患最有耐心的。）

- Among all the students, Ms. Peterson likes Molly (the)
  most.
（在所有學生中，彼得森女士最喜歡茉莉。）

> 副詞最高級前，the可以省略

❸ 「the＋形容詞」可以用來作代名詞，故形容詞後面的名詞可省略

例：• In the U.S., the gap between the rich and the poor is wider than that in most countries.
（在美國，貧富差異比大部分國家更嚴重。）

◆用比較級表示最高級

與形容詞最高級比較句構一樣，將主詞與比較對象以「一對多」的方式做比較，就能用比較級的句構表示最高級：

例：• Among all the ballerinas on the stage, Isabelle danced the most elegantly.
（在舞台上的所有芭蕾女伶中，伊莎貝拉跳得最優雅。）
= Isabelle danced more elegantly than any other ballerina on the stage. （伊莎貝拉跳得比舞台上任何一個其他的芭蕾女伶都要優雅。）
= Isabelle danced more elegantly than all the other ballerinas on the stage. （伊莎貝拉跳得比舞台上任何一個其他的芭蕾女伶都要優雅。）

• Leo's father died the most miserably of all the victims in the accident. （里歐的父親是這起意外的所有罹難者中死得最慘的。）
= Leo's father died more miserably than any other victim in the accident. （里歐的父親比這場意外中任何一個罹難者死得都要慘。）
= Leo's father died more miserably than all the other victims in the accident. （里歐的父親比這場意外中所有其他罹難者都死得慘。）

馬上動手練一練 5

填入副詞最高級，以完成句子

1. Alex always comes _____ (early) and leaves _____ (late).
2. Of the five employees, Miranda works _____ (absent-minded).
3. Patricia practiced _____ (wholehearted) among all the contestants.
4. Of all the students, Steven calculated _____(careless)
5. Frank apologized to the girl _____(sincere) among the six boys.

ANSWER

1. the earliest/the latest   2. the most absentmindedly
3. the most wholeheartedly 4. the most carelessly
5. the most sincerely

文法總複習

快來試試自己的實力吧！

A. 選擇正確的選項

1. (　) Action always speaks _____ than words.
   A. loud　　　　B. loudly　　　　C. more loud　　　　D. louder

2. (　) He speaks the second language _____ as he does his first language.
   A. as better　　B. so better　　C. well than　　　　D. as well

3. (　) My father drives more prudently _____ in my family.
   A. than anyone else　　　　B. as everyone
   C. than each other　　　　　D. as all the others

4. (　) Cynthia does her homework _____ of all the students.
   A. more careful　　　　B. the most carefully
   C. so careful　　　　　D. more carefully

5. (　) Outgoing people make friends _____ than shy ones.
   A. more easily　　B. easier　　C. as easily　　　D. not so easy

6. (　) To pay off his debt _____, David worked three jobs.
   A. so fast as he can　　　　B. as fast than he can
   C. even faster　　　　　　　D. as faster as possible

7. (　) To pass the college entrance exam, my brother _____ than ever.
   A. studied hard　　　　B. studied harder
   C. more study　　　　　D. harder studied

8. ( ) Among all the girls in my class, I like Julia _____.
   A. well   B. better   C. less   D. most

9. ( ) Tom ran _____ than Lily, so he won the race.
   A. fast   B. faster   C. fastest   D. slow

10. ( ) Annie ate ____ chips than Ben, so she is fatter.
    A. more   B. most   C. less   D. the least

B. 填空（依提示做適當變化）

1. Mary takes care of her dogs more wholeheartedly than _____ her children.

2. We enjoyed bungee jumping more than _____ mountain climbing.

3. No one in the class _____ (well) on English test than Jeff did.

4. Gillian answered the teacher's question _____ (confident) than _____ student in his class.

5. Larry prepared for the interview _____ (adequate) than _____ applicants this time.

6. Anna worried about her mother's health more than _____ her own.

7. We cleaned the house _____ (thorough) as possible.

8. She sings as _____ (good) as you.

9. She cleaned her bedroom as _____ (careful) as she could.

10. Nini always gets up _____ (early) than I do.

ANSWER

A. 選擇正確的選項

1. **D**　2. **D**　3. **A**　4. **B**　5. **A**
6. **C**　7. **B**　8. **D**　9. **B**　10. **A**

1. 比較級的句型結構：
   主詞＋動詞＋副詞比較級＋than＋比較對象
   loud→louder

2. well副詞用來修飾speak。
   主詞＋動詞＋as＋副詞＋as＋比較對象

3. 與同團體的其他成員做比較：
   any other ＋單數名詞

4. carefully修飾do
   副詞最高級themost carefully

5. easily修飾make
   easily比較級more easily

6. even修飾副詞比較級faster

7. hard修飾study
   harder為副詞比較級

8. 最喜歡much 最高級most

9. fast修飾run
   faster為副詞比較級

10. much比較級more 用來修飾eat (ate)

326

B. 填空（依提示做適當變化）

1. she does for

2. we did

3. did better

4. more confidently/any other

5. more adequately/all the other

6. she did about

7. as thoroughly

8. well

9. carefully

10. earlier

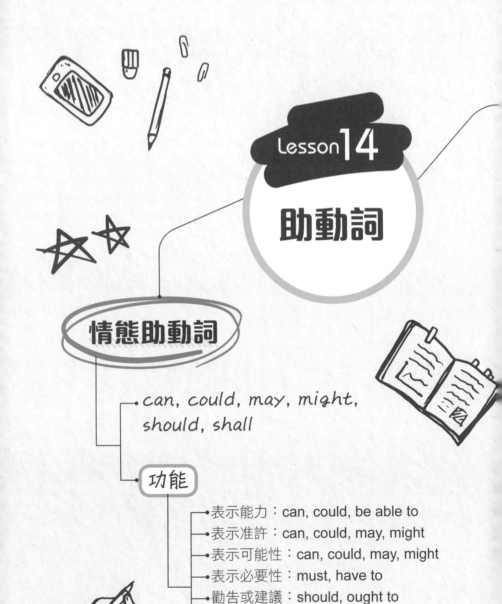

Lesson 14

助動詞

情態助動詞

- can, could, may, might, should, shall

功能

- 表示能力：can, could, be able to
- 表示准許：can, could, may, might
- 表示可能性：can, could, may, might
- 表示必要性：must, have to
- 勸告或建議：should, ought to
- 表示推測：should, must, can
- 表示提議：shall
- 表示承諾或意願：will, would
- 委婉請求：could, would

一般助動詞

be動詞

do/does/did、will/would

功能

- 強調語氣：用在肯定句
- 形成否定句：助動詞＋not＋動詞
- 形成疑問句：助動詞＋主詞＋動詞?
- 形成時態
  - 現在簡單式：do/does＋原形動詞
  - 過去簡單式：did＋原形動詞
  - 未來簡單式：will＋原形動詞
  - 完成式：have/has＋過去分詞
- 表達語態

  被動語態：be動詞＋過去分詞

助動詞的功能在於「幫助動詞」，除了在句子中幫助動詞形成否定及疑問之外，還有表達時態及語態的功能。我們已經認識的助動詞有be動詞、do/does/did、have/has/had以及will/would，這些助動詞稱為一般助動詞，除了可以形成疑問句及否定句之外，還能表達時態及語態。

除此之外，還有一種助動詞，除了同樣可以用來形成否定、疑問、時態，還同時具有表達語氣、情緒、態度等意識的功能，這類助動詞，稱為「情態助動詞」。

一‧一般助動詞

一般助動詞包含be動詞、用在簡單式的do/does/did、用在未來式的will/would，以及用在完成式的have/has/had。前面有助動詞的動詞，無論句子時態為何，一律保持原形。

	第一、二人稱及複數主詞	第三人稱及單數主詞
現在簡單式	do	does
過去簡單式	did	did
現在完成式	have	has
過去完成式	had	had
未來式	will	will

◆一般助動詞用法及功能

① 強調語氣

一般助動詞用在肯定句時，可以強調語氣，表達「的確」、「真的」。

例：• I did quit my job. （我的確是辭去工作了。）

　　• She does sing well. （她真的唱得很好。）

　　• We do like your proposal. （我們真的很喜歡你的提案。）

 馬上動手練一練 ①

在句子中加入助動詞強調確實性

1. They love each other.

_____

2. He proposed to his girlfriend.

_____

3. Maria has two children.

_____

4. We had a great time.

_____

5. I appreciate your support.

_____

ANSWER

1. They do love each other.　　2. He did propose to his girlfriend.
3. Maria does have two children.　4. We did have a great time.
5. I do appreciate your support.

❷ 形成否定句

一般動詞都需要助動詞來形成否定句。

基本句構為： 　**助動詞＋not＋動詞**

{
簡單式：do not = don't; does not= doesn't; did not= didn't
未來式：will not = won't; would not= wouldn't
完成式：have not = haven't; has not = hasn't; had not = hadn't
}

例： • I don't know this guy. （我不認識這個人。）

　　 • She won't come here tomorrow. （她明天不會來。）

　　 • We haven't made our decision yet.
　　 （我們還沒有做出決定。）

be動詞本身就是助動詞，直接在be動詞後面加上not，即可表示否定：

is not = isn't; are not = aren't; was not= wasn't; were not= weren't

（＊am not 一般不用縮寫式來表示）

例： • He isn't my brother. （他不是我的哥哥。）

　　 • They weren't as good as we expected.
　　 （它們不如我們所期待的那麼好。）

重點筆記

1. 助動詞除了跟not縮寫，也可以跟前面的主詞縮寫，如：

• I will = I'll
• we have = we've
• I am = I'm

• she has = she's;
• they had = they'd
• you are = you're; it is = it's

2. ain't可用來表示is not, are not, am not的縮寫，但一般句型中不會使用。

馬上動手練一練 ❷

圈出正確的否定助動詞，以完成句子

1. My boss (don't/didn't) let me leave early.

2. I (don't/doesn't) have problem understanding what he says.

3. We (haven't/don't) seen each other for a long time.

4. They (won't/didn't) be able to join the party with us this Saturday.

5. My mother is a vegetarian. She (hasn't/doesn't) eat any meat.

ANSWER

1. didn't   2.don't   3. haven't   4. won't   5.doesn't

❸ 形成疑問句

一般句子需要助動詞來形成疑問句，將助動詞放在直述句的句首，即成疑問句。

基本句構為：　┃ 助動詞＋主詞＋動詞～？ ┃

例：• Do you and your brother go to the same college?
（你跟你哥哥上同一所大學嗎？）

• Will Jack take the college entrance exam?
（傑克會參加大學入學考試嗎？）

be動詞的句子，形成疑問句時，只要把be動詞移到句首即可。

例：• Are you close to your parents?
（你跟你的父母很親近嗎？）

• Is that what you mean?（你是那個意思嗎？）

- 否定疑問句有兩種表達方式，一般是將助動詞與**not**的縮寫一起移到句首，或是只將否定句的助動詞移到句首，將**not**放在原處。

> 例：• Aren't you going with us? （你不跟我們一起去嗎？）
> ＝Are you not going with us?
>
> • Don't you have any friends here?
> （你在這裡沒有任何朋友嗎？）
> ＝ Do you not have any friends here?
>
> • Haven't you talked to him about it yet?
> （你還沒跟他談過這件事嗎？）
> ＝Have you not talked to him about it yet?

 馬上動手練一練 ❸

將下列句子改為疑問句

1. Your brother is joining us for dinner.

_____

2. That is what you are talking about.

_____

3. Mary hasn't decided whether to accept John's invitation.

_____

4. Frank will not go to college this year.

_____

5. You don't enjoy the meal.

_____

ANSWER

1. Is your brother joining us for dinner?
2. Is that what you are talking about?
3. Hasn't Mary decided whether to accept John's invitation?
4. Will Frank not go to college this year?
5. Don't you enjoy the meal?

④ **表達時態：**不同的助動詞可以幫助句子表達不同時態

①**現在簡單式：do/does 後面接原形動詞**

例：• Some people don't celebrate their birthdays.
（有些人是不慶祝生日的。）

• My dad doesn't like Thai food very much.
（我爸爸不是非常喜歡泰式料理。）

②**過去簡單式：did/would後面接原形動詞**

例：• They didn't get their job done on schedule.
（他們並未如其將工作完成。）

• I did tell you that I would come.
（我的確有告訴過你我會來。）

③**未來簡單式：will後面接原形動詞**

例：• Don't worry. Everything will be fine.
（別擔心。一切都會沒事的。）

• Mom and Dad will come home soon.
（爸爸媽媽馬上就會回家了。）

④**完成式：have/has/did後面接過去分詞**

例：• We have had lunch already. （我們已經吃過午餐了。）

• She hasn't responded to my request yet.
（她還沒有回覆我的請求。）

• Tom's flight had already taken off when she finally
arrived at the airport.
（當她終於到達機場時，湯姆的班機早就起飛了。）

• They will have been waiting for us for more than three hours when we get there. （當我們到那裡時，他們將會已經等我們超過三小時了。）

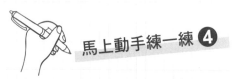

馬上動手練一練 ④

選出正確的助動詞填入空格中，以完成句子

won't	hasn't	doesn't	will have	didn't

1. They lost the game because they _____ practice hard enough.

2. You _____ be late if you go by taxi.

3. She _____ been learning the piano for 10 years next week.

4. My grandma _____ live with us because she is not used to city life.

5. I sent her the invitation, but she _____ responded yet.

ANSWER
1. didn't   2. won't   3. will have   4. doesn't   5. hasn't

⑤ 表達語態

「be動詞＋過去分詞」，用來表達被動語態。

例：• The poor dog was abandoned by his owner.
（這隻可憐的狗狗被它的主人拋棄了。）

- Your order will be delivered to you within 24 hours.
  （您訂購的物品將會在廿四小時之內寄送給您。）

- This mansion has been transformed to a modern shopping center since it was sold to a businessman.
  （這棟大廈自從被賣給一位生意人之後，就被改建成現代化購物中心了。）

馬上動手練一練 ❺

依提示完成下列被動語態的句子

1. It is estimated that over 17 people _____ (kill) in the accident.
2. The village _____ (destroy) by the earthquake in 2013, and _____ (reconstruct) recently.
3. The criminal deserves _____ (punish) severely.
4. We believe that girls should _____ (give) equal education as boys.
5. The patient will _____ (take care of) by professional nurses.

ANSWER

1. were killed   2. was destroyed / has been reconstructed
3. to be punished   4. be given   5. be taken care of

二‧情態助動詞

情態助動詞除了具有一般助動詞的功能之外，還具有表達情緒、態度、口氣等語用功能。情態助動詞在句子中的位置與一般助動詞相同。

◆情態助動詞用法及功能

❶ 表示能力：can/could/be able to

例：‧ She can speak three foreign languages apart from Mandarin and English.
（除了中文及英文之外，她還會說三種外語。）

‧ I'm afraid we cannot make it to the meeting on time.
（我們恐怕無法準時參加會議。）

‧ You won't be able to catch the train if you don't hurry.
（如果你不快一點，你就沒辦法搭上火車。）

❷ 表示准許：can/could/may/might

例：‧ You can't use your cellphone during the class.
（上課期間你不能使用手機。）

‧ You may leave now. （你現在可以離開了。）

重點筆記

★ 表示准許的片語：**be allowed to**

例：‧ We are not allowed to enter the building until 8:00.
（我們在八點之前不得進入大樓。）

‧ Am I allowed to leave now?
（我現在可以離開了嗎？）

❸ 表示可能性：can/could/may/might

例：• You can't be serious. （你不會是當真的吧。）

• He may be right. （他很可能是對的。）

• We haven't got a plan for tomorrow. We might go to the movies.

（我們還沒為明天做計劃。我們很可能會去看電影。）

• **could/may/might＋現在完成式，可以用來表示對過去事實的假設或推測**

例：• I can't find my ticket. I could have lost it on the train.

（我找不到我的車票。我可能把它丟在車上了。）

• James is late. He might have missed the school bus.

（詹姆士遲到了。他很可能錯過了校車。）

馬上動手練一練 ❻

根據語意，選最適當的助動詞填入空格中，以完成句子

might have	cannot	could have	might	may

1. A: What are you going to do tonight?

   B: Not sure yet. We _____ just stay at home and do nothing at all.

2. You _____ enter the library building without your student ID.

3. We _____ won the game if Jack didn't fumble.

4. Those who have done the test _____ leave the classroom.

5. A: I can't find my passport.

   B: You _____ left it in the hotel.

❹ 表示責任或必要性：must/have to

例：• We must protect our environment for future generations.
（我們必須為未來的世世代代保護我們的環境。）

• As parents, you have to be responsible for your young children's safety.
（身為家長，你們必須為年幼孩童的安全負責任。）

• **must表示「必須，一定」，而否定式mustn't則表示「必定不能……」，有「不准許」的含義。**

例：• You mustn't lie to me. （你一定不能對我說謊。）

have to表示「必須；一定」，否定式not have to表示「不必須；不一定要……」。don't have to 也可以用don't need to或needn't（不必須）來表示。

例：• You don't have to feel guilty.
（你不必有罪惡感。）
＝You don't need to feel guilty.
＝You needn't feel guilty.
（need在此作助動詞）

當遇到疑問句詢問「是否必須」時，要留意回答方式。

例：Must I turn off the cellphone?
= Do I have to turn off the cellphone?
（我必須關掉手機嗎？）

• Yes, you must.
＝Yes, you have to.
（是的，你必須。）

• No, you don't have to.
＝No, you don't need to.
（不，你不必須。）

> 這個問句並沒有請求允許的意思，
> 因此不能回答No, you mustn't.（不，你一定不能。）

• Can I go into the meeting room right now?
（我現在可以進會議室嗎？）

• No, you can't.
（不，你不行。）

• No, you mustn't.（不，絕對不行。）

> 這個問句在請求允許，
> 以mustn't回答時有特別強調「必定不可以」的含義。

• **must＋現在完成式，用來表示「對過去或現在事實的推測」**

例：• Jane never called me. She must have forgotten about me.
（珍從未打電話給我。她一定已經忘記我了。）

• Dad didn't answer the phone. He must have been asleep.
（爸爸沒有接電話。他一定已經睡了。）

❺ 表示勸告或建議：should/ought to

should與ought to用來描述責任、義務，或提出勸告或建議。用在疑問句則是向他人詢問建議。

例：• We should spend more time with our children.
（我們應該多花點時間陪孩子。）

• You ought to encourage him to give it a try.
（你應該鼓勵他試試看。）

• You shouldn't talk to your mother like that.
（你不應該那樣跟你母親說話。）

• What should I do now?（我現在應該做什麼？）

• **should＋現在完成式，可以用來表示「應該做卻沒有做的事」**

例：• I should have spent more time with my grandma when she was alive.
（我應該要在我奶奶在世時多陪陪她的。）

• You should have finished your homework before you watched TV.
（你在看電視之前應該要先把作業做完的。）

重點筆記

表示責任或勸告的片語：**had better/be supposed to**

例：• Mothers-in-law had better not interfere in children's private family affairs.
（婆婆媽媽們最好不要干預孩子們的家務事。）

• You are supposed to be at work on time.
（你應該要準時上班。）

⑥ 表示推測：should/must/can

例：• Mom should be at home right now.
（媽媽現在應該在家裡。）

• You must be Amy's brother. （你一定是愛咪的哥哥吧。）

• Where can he be? （他會在哪裡呢？）

• 表示否定推測時，要用can't或shouldn't，不用mustn't（mustn't 意指「不可以」）

例：• The coffee is still warm. The man can't go very far.
（咖啡還溫溫的。那男子不可能走很遠。）

• Mary shouldn't be asleep. She texted me just a few minutes ago.
（瑪麗應該還沒睡。她幾分鐘前才發過訊息給我。）

⑦ 表示提議：shall

例：Shall we go to the beach this weekend?
（我們這週末要去海邊嗎？）

Let's give her a surprise, shall we?
（我們給她個驚喜，要嗎？）

馬上動手練一練 ⑦

圈出正確的助動詞

1. It is already 10 o'clock. The children (must/can) be in bed.

2. I don't see any cake on the table.It (must/must have been) eaten.

3. A: Can I smoke here?　B: No, you (don't have to/mustn't).

4. I can't walk anymore. Let's take a break, (shall/must) we?

5. We've been married for ten years. You (had better know/should have known) that I hate carrots.

ANSWER

1. must　　　2. must have been　　　3. mustn't
4. shall　　　5. should have known

❽ 表示承諾或意願：will/would

例：• I will be there on time. （我會準時到那兒的。）

　　• I would love to do that. （我很樂意那麼做。）

疑問句用來詢問對方意願：

例：• Will you marry me? （你願意嫁給我嗎？）

　　• Sarah is on the line. Would you like to speak to her?
　　（莎拉現在在線上。你想跟她說話嗎？）

 重點筆記

★ 表示意願的片語：be willing to
例：• She's not willing to learn new things.
　　（她不願意學新東西。）

- **would rather＋原形動詞＋than＋原形動詞**：表示「寧願……，也不願……」

  例：• I would rather quit than work for a man who has a bias against women.

  （我寧可辭職也不想為一個對女人有偏見的男人工作。）

  • We would rather lose the game than cheat in the game.
  （我們寧可輸掉比賽，也不願意在比賽中作弊。）

- **would＋現在完成式**：表示「與過去事實不符的假設」

  例：• If Jack had had enough money, he would have bought the car.
  （如果那時傑克有足夠的錢，他就會買那輛車了。）

  • If I had given up my dream, I wouldn't have become a fashion designer.（如果當時我放棄了夢想，我就不會成為一位時裝設計師。）

❾ 表示委婉請求：would/could

will及can可以用來表示要求或請求，用過去式would及could可以讓語氣變得比較委婉客氣。

  例：• Would you do me a favor?
  （你能幫我個忙嗎？）

  • Could you help me book a meeting room on September 12?
  （你可以幫我在九月十二日那天訂一間會議室嗎？）

• 以**would you mind...**提出要求，口氣要比**do you mind...**來得客氣有禮貌

> 句型：Would you mind ＋ { 動名詞（V-ing）
>   if 子句

例：• Would you mind my <u>sitting</u> next to you?
   （你介意我坐你旁邊嗎？）
   ＝Would you mind <u>if I sit next to you</u>?

   • Would you mind <u>opening</u> the door for me?
   （你介意幫我開個門嗎？）

   • Would you mind <u>if I invite my ex-boyfriend to our wedding</u>?
   （你介意我邀請我的前男友來參加我們的婚禮嗎？）

⑩ 表示威嚇：dare

dare做助動詞用時，表示「敢，竟敢」，並且只用於疑問句及否定句。

例：• He dare not to catch the earthworm bare handed.
   （他不敢徒手抓蚯蚓。）

   • How dare you look at my cellphone without my permission?
   （你怎麼敢沒經過我同意就看我手機？）

   • Dare you go into the haunted house with me?
   （你敢跟我進去鬼屋嗎？）

   • No, I dare not.
   （不，我不敢。）

 **重點筆記**

need 與 dare

　　need表「需要」，dare表「敢」，這兩個字都跟do/does及have/has一樣，是動詞，也可以是助動詞。當一般動詞時，要根據主詞及時態做適當變化；當助動詞時，則跟其他助動詞在句子中的用法一樣，可放在句首造疑問句，或是在句子中接原形動詞。

【一般動詞】

　　例：• I need to go home now.
　　　　（我現在需要回家。）

　　　　• Do you need anything from the supermarket?
　　　　（你需要任何超市的東西嗎？）

　　　　• He didn't dare to do a bungee jump.
　　　　（他不敢做高空彈跳。）

　　　　• Do you dare to take up the challenge?
　　　　（你敢接受挑戰嗎？）

【助動詞】

　　例：• A: Need I redo the test?　B: No, you needn't.
　　　　（A：我需要重考嗎？　B：不，你不需要。）

　　　　• A: Dare you eat a live worm?　B: No, I dare not.
　　　　（A：你敢吃活蟲嗎？　B：不，我不敢。）

馬上動手練一練 ❽

圈出正確的助動詞，以完成句子

1. She (dare/dares) not use her father's car without his permission.

2. I'm very confident that I (will/would) win the competition.

3. They would (have cancelled/cancel) the outdoor party if it had rained.

4. Lucy (will have/would have) married Carl if he had had a decent job.

5. He (would/could) rather work fulltime while he studies than take his father's money.

ANSWER

1. dare	2. will	3. have cancelled
4. would have	5. would	

348

Lesson 14 **文法總複習**
快來試試自己的實力吧！

A. 選擇正確的助動詞

1. (　) Jean: Do I have to attend the meeting too?
   Mr. Lee: No, you _____.
   A. don't have 　　 B. needn't 　　 C. couldn't 　　 D. won't

2. (　) I need to use the car this weekend. The repair _____
   be done by Friday.
   A. should have 　　 B. can't 　　 C. will 　　 D. must

3. (　) You _____ have more patience with your children.
   They are so young that they need your love and guidance.
   A. dare 　　 B. should 　　 C. might 　　 D. can

4. (　) It looks like raining. They _____ cancel the outdoor BBQ
   party.
   A. ought 　　 B. need 　　 C. may 　　 D. have

5. (　) The joke was so hilarious that I _____ stop laughing.
   A. couldn't 　　 B. mustn't 　　 C. shouldn't 　　 D. didn't

6. (　) It is just my guess, but your roommate _____ have
   stolen your money.
   A. might 　　 B. would 　　 C. must 　　 D. should

7. (　) A: _____ you please carry this box for me?
   B: Sure thing.
   A. Should 　　 B. Must 　　 C. Would 　　 D. May

8. (　) Cheating is unacceptable. You ＿＿＿＿＿ cheat during the exam.

　　A. dare not　　　B. must not　　　C. need not　　　D. might not

9. (　) You didn't finish your homework yesterday. You ＿＿＿＿ it.

　　A. should have finished　　　　　B. should did

　　C. will do　　　　　　　　　　　D. would have done

10. (　) Dad didn't answer the phone. He must ＿＿＿ slept.

　　A. has　　　　　B. have　　　　　C. did　　　　　D. not

B. 閱讀下列文章，並選入適當的助動詞填入空格中（每字限填一次）

will	don't	should	mustn't
should	can	had better	may

If you have encountered a sleepwalker, you ＿＿1.＿＿ know that it is a very strange state as it features both sleep and waking. While some people believe that we ＿＿2.＿＿ wake a sleepwalker as it ＿＿3.＿＿ cause them to have a heart attack or put them into a coma, sleep experts suggest that it is pretty much harmless. Although you ＿＿4.＿＿ wake them up, you ＿＿5.＿＿ not try to wake them at all, because being woken up in the middle of sleep ＿＿6.＿＿ not be so pleasant for the sleepwalker. What you ＿＿7.＿＿ do is gently lead them back to bed so that they ＿＿8.＿＿ hurt themselves.

ANSWER

A. 選擇正確的助動詞

1. **B**   2. **D**   3. **B**   4. **C**   5. **A**
6. **A**   7. **C**   8. **B**   9. **A**   10. **B**

1. need表「需要」也可以是助動詞，當助動詞時，則跟其他助動詞在句子中的用法一樣，可放在句首造疑問句，或是在句子中接原形動詞

2. must必須

3. should與ought to用來描述責任、義務，或提出勸告或建議
   should have more patience 應該要多些耐心

4. may可能

5. couldn't 無法

6. might have stolen 可能（表推測）已經偷了

7. will及can可以用來表示要求或請求，用過去式would及could可以讓語氣變得比較委婉客氣

8. must not絕對不行

9. should have finished應該要完成，與過去相反表示過去沒完成

10. must have slept一定已經睡著

B. 閱讀下列文章，並選入適當的助動詞填入空格中（每字限填一次）

1. should

2. mustn't

3. may

4. can

5. had better

6. will

7. should

8. don't

NOTE

指示代名詞

this, that,
these, those

代替特定人事物

Lesson **15**

代名詞

不定代名詞

one, a few, each, a little,
some, most, all

代替不特定人事物

疑問代名詞

who	問人
whom	問人
whose	問持有人
what	問事物或職業身分
which	問人事物

人稱代名詞 代替人名或稱謂

- **主格**
  - l, we, you, he, she, it, they
  - 見Lesson 2

- **所有格**
  - my, our, your, his, her, its, their
  - 放在名詞前面，說明「屬於誰」

- **受格**
  - me, us, you, him, her, it, them
  - 動詞或介系詞後的受詞，受詞補語

- **所有格代名詞**
  - mine, ours, yours, his, hers, its, theirs
  - 代替「所有格＋名詞」

- **反身代名詞**
  - myself, ourselves, yourself, yourselves, himself, herself, itself, themselves
  - 主詞跟受詞相同時減少重複

Lesson 15 代名詞

代名詞顧名思義就是「代替名詞」的詞類。代名詞既然代替名詞，便具有名詞的特性，可以在句子中作為主詞、受詞或補語。代名詞除了具有名詞特性之外，有些代名詞也同時具有形容詞特性，可以放在名詞前面修飾或說明。

作為主詞的代名詞，在本書的〈Lesson2名詞作為主詞〉已經做過詳解，這一篇將繼續介紹人稱代名詞受格、反身代名詞、指示代名詞、不定代名詞及疑問代名詞在句子中的用法。

一・人稱代名詞

人稱代名詞可用來代替人名或稱謂，不僅有單複數的區別，並有主格、所有格、受格、所有格代名詞及反身代名詞等五種形式：

		主格	所有格	受格	所有格代名詞	反身代名詞
第一人稱	單數	I	my	me	mine	myself
	複數	we	our	us	ours	ourselves
第二人稱	單數	you	your	you	yours	yourself
	複數	you	your	you	yours	yourselves
第三人稱	單數	he	his	him	his	himself
		she	her	her	hers	herself
		it	its	it	its	itself
	複數	they	their	them	theirs	themselves

◆主格

人稱代名詞主格可作為句子的主詞，若需複習請見〈Lesson2 名詞作為主詞〉。

例：• **I** will be a college student in three months.
（三個月後我將成為一個大學生。）

• **They** were not invited to the ceremony.
（他們並未受邀參加典禮。）

• **It** is good to be home.（回到家真好。）

◆所有格

人稱代名詞所有格為形容詞，放在名詞前面做修飾，以說明「屬於誰」。

例：• I can't find **my** sister. （我找不到我的姐姐。）

• That is not **your** money. （那不是你的錢。）

重點筆記

所有格後面可接own，以強調某物只屬於某人，並非公共用品或向別人借來的：「one's own＋名詞」＝屬於某人自己的某物。

例：• I wish I could have **my own bedroom** some day.
（我希望有一天我能擁有屬於自己的房間。）

• You will have **your own office** if you're promoted to the executive management.
（如果你被晉升至主管階層，你就會有你自己的辦公室。）

◆受格

人稱代名詞受格在句子中有三種用法：

❶ 可作為動詞的受詞

> 例：• I don't <u>know</u> **him**. （我不認識他。）
>
> • Have you ever <u>loved</u> **me**? （你有曾經愛過我嗎？）

❷ 可作為受詞的補語

> 例：• I thought <u>that</u> was **her**. （我還以為那個人是她。）
>
> • We hope <u>it</u>'s not **you**. （我們希望那個人不是你。）

❸ 可作為介系詞的受詞

> 例：• She mistook the man <u>for</u> **him**. （她誤認那個男子是他。）
>
> • He never really cared <u>about</u> **us**. （他從未真正關心過我們。）

★ it除了可以做虛主詞之外（複習請見〈Lesson2名詞作為主詞〉），也可以做虛受詞：

①取代不定詞片語作為虛受詞

it作為虛受詞的句型：

主詞＋
{
find
think
consider
believe
...
}
＋it＋形容詞＋不定詞片語

例：• I find **it** interesting <u>to watch fish swim</u>.

（我發現看魚兒游泳很有意思。）

• We believe **it** necessary <u>to exercise regularly</u>.

（我們相信規律地運動是有必要的。）

②it用來強調

a. 強調主詞
• **It** was <u>your behavior</u> that embarrassed me.
（是你的行為讓我感到丟臉。）

b. 強調受詞
• **It** is <u>your respect</u> that I need. （我需要的是你的尊重。）

c.強調時間或地點
• **It** is <u>at 7 o'clock</u> that the concert will start.
（音樂會開始的時間是七點。）

• **It** is <u>in the City Hall</u> that the ceremony will be held.
（舉行典禮的地方是市政廳。）

d. 強調原因
• **It** is <u>because the alarm clock didn't go off</u> that I was late.
（我會遲到是因為鬧鐘沒有響。）

馬上動手練一練 ❶

圈出正確的代名詞

1. (It/This/There) is your apology that I want to hear.
2. Mom asked (I/my/me) to run errands for (she/her/hers).
3. I find (it/this/its) impossible to get the job done by the deadline.
4. This is how I do it. You can do it (your/you/yours) own way.
5. Jane and Leo are leaving for home tomorrow. Let's go see (they/their/them) off at the airport.

ANSWER

1. It   2. me, her   3. it   4. your   5. them

◆所有格代名詞

所有代名詞為代替「所有格＋名詞」的代名詞，當前面出現過某個名詞時，為了避免重複，後面再提到同樣的名詞搭配不同所有格時，就會使用「所有代名詞」來代替。

例：• Jamie didn't have an umbrella, so I let her use **mine**.
（潔米沒有雨傘，所以我讓她用我的。）

> 句子前面已經提到umbrella，後面不再重複相同名詞，故以mine取代my umbrella

• This is my money, not **yours**. （這是我的錢，不是你的。）

◎ 所有格代名詞經常與表示「屬於」的介系詞of連用，表示「某人的⋯⋯」。名詞前可加數詞、不定冠詞或指示形容詞，但不可加定冠詞the。

$$\left\{\begin{array}{l}\text{數詞（two/a few/some/most）}\\\text{不定冠詞（a/an）}\\\text{指示形容詞（this/these）}\end{array}\right\} +of+\text{所有格代名詞}$$

例：• I met **a friend of yours** in the supermarket today.
（我今天在超市遇到你的一個朋友。）

• She had to sell **a few handbags of hers** for cash.
（她必須出售她的幾個手提包，以換取現金。）

• It is said that **many books of his** were actually written by his wife.
（據說他的許多本書其實都是由他妻子操刀寫的。）

 馬上動手練一練 2

在空格內填入正確的所有格代名詞

1. Josie is one of her friends.＝Josie is a friend of _____.

2. Most of my clothes are old-fashioned.

＝ Most clothes of _____ are old-fashioned.

3. I've got my luggage, but Steven hasn't got _____ (his luggage).

4. Our apartment is a lot smaller than _____ (their apartment).

5. It is our pleasure. = The pleasure is _____.

ANSWER

1. hers   2. mine   3. his   4. theirs   5. ours

◆反身代名詞

當主詞與受詞指的是同一人或同一件事時，受詞要使用反身代名詞。

例：• You should treat **yourself** better.
（你應該要對你自己好一點。）

• He is not strong enough to protect **himself**.
（他沒有強壯到可以保護自己。）

• Their problem is that they lack confidence in **themselves**.
（他們的問題在於他們對自己缺少信心。）

反身代名詞可以用來表示強調：

1. 放在主詞後面強調主詞

例：• She **herself** did it.＝She did it **herself**.
（是她自己做的。）

• He **himself** revealed the secret.
＝He revealed the secret **himself**.
（是他自己洩露這個秘密的。）

2. 放在受詞後面強調受詞

例：• Can I talk to your manager **himself**?
（我可以跟你們經理本人說話嗎？）

• Why don't we ask Jennifer **herself** about her opinion?
（我們何不問珍妮弗本人有關她的意見？）

馬上動手練一練 3

填入正確的反身代名詞

1. Jane _____ told me that she was pregnant.

2. Don't worry. Your mom and I can take care of _____.

3. I _____ prefer Thai cuisine to Mexican cuisine.

4. All you need to do is to have more confidence in _____.

5. My children are still too young to look after _____.

ANSWER

1. herself 2. ourselves 3. myself 4. yourself 5. themselves

二‧指示代名詞

指示代名詞是用來代替「特定人事物」的代名詞，也可以做指示形容詞，修飾後面的名詞。表示單數的指示代名詞有this與that，表示複數的指示代名詞則有these與those。

◆作主詞用

例：• **That** is my idea.（那是我的點子。）

• **Those** are made of quality leather, so they are more expensive.

（這些是以優良皮革製成的，所以比較貴。）

◆作受詞用

例：• Let's talk about **this** later. （我們晚點再談這件事。）

• What do you want **these** for? （你要這些做什麼？）

◆作形容詞用

例：• I would like to return **this** shirt. （我想退這件襯衫。）

• **These** items are all defective.
（這些商品都是有瑕疵的。）

三‧不定代名詞

不定代名詞為用來代替「不特定人事物」的代名詞，也可以做不定形容詞，修飾後面的名詞。

常用的不定代名詞有：

one	一個	a few	幾個
each	每一個	a little	一點
both	兩個	another	另一個
either	兩者其一	the other	（兩個中的）另一個
neither	兩者皆無	each other	（兩者的）彼此
any	任何、若干	one another	（三者以上的）互相，彼此
some	一些	anything	什麼事（東西），任何事（東西）
many	許多	nothing	無事，無物

more	更多	anywhere	任何地方
most	大部分	somewhere	某處
all	所有	someone	某人
none	沒有	anyone	任何人

◆作主詞用

例：• I have two brothers. **One** is married, and **the other** is still single.

（我有兩個哥哥。一個結婚了，另一個依然單身。）

• They adopted two girls. **Both** were from China.
（他們領養了兩個女孩。兩個都來自中國。）

• She had many friends, but **none** of them were willing to offer help when she was in need. （她曾有很多朋友，但沒有一個願意在她有需要的時候提供幫助。）

• **Nothing** is better than spending time with family.
（沒有什麼事會比跟家人一起共度時光要好。）

◆作受詞用

例：• The soup tastes really good. Would you like **some**?
（這湯喝起來真美味。你想不想喝一些？）

• All she wanted was money. Unfortunately, I didn't have **any**. （她想要就是錢。遺憾的是，我一丁點兒都沒有。）

• This is **all** I can give. （這已經是全部我所能給予的。）

• I don't want to hear **anything** about my ex-boyfriend.
（我不想聽到有關我前男友的任何事。）

◆作形容詞用

例：• I have **a few** questions for you. （我有幾個問題要問你。）
　　• Can I bring **some** friends with me?
　　（我可以帶一些朋友跟我一起嗎？）

1. 只能做受詞用的不定代名詞，有each other, one another, somewhere等。這些不定代名詞不能用來做主詞或形容詞。

   (O) • The girls will take care of <u>each other</u>.
   　　（女孩子們會彼此照顧的。）

   (X) • ~~Each other~~ will take care of them.

   (O) • They help <u>one another</u> overcome the difficulties.
   　　（他們幫助彼此克服困難。）

   (X) • ~~One another~~ help themselves overcome the difficulties.

2. one用來代替已經出現過的單數可數名詞，若為複數可數名詞My new car is much則以ones表示。

   例：• My new car is much economical than <u>my old one</u>.
   　　（我的新車比舊的那一輛經濟多了。）

   　　• These dresses are more stylish than <u>the ones</u> in your wardrobe.
   　　（這些洋裝比你衣櫃裡的那些時髦多了。）

★ 不定代名詞的慣用語

A. one by one 一個一個地，逐一

例：• We will beat our competitors **one by one**.
（我們會一個一個地擊敗我們的對手。）

B. one after another （三者以上）一個接一個地；相繼地

例：• The infected died **one after another**.
（受感染者相繼死亡。）

C. one after the other （兩者）相繼地

例：• He stretched his legs **one after the other**.
（他相繼地伸展左右腳。）

D. one ... the other ... （用於特定兩者）一個……，另一個……

例：• I have two bachelor's degrees. **One** is in Business Administration, and **the other** is in Computer Engineering.
（我有兩個大學學位。一個是商業管理，一個是電腦工程。）

E. one ... another ... the other （用於特定三者）一個……，另一個……，還有一個……

例：• She has three brothers. **One** is a computer programmer, **another** is a physician, and **the other** is a school teacher.
（她有三個哥哥。一個是電腦程式設計師，一個是內科醫師，另一個是學校老師。）

F. one ... another （用於非特定兩者）

例：• Everyone has different tastes. **One** may have a sweet tooth, while **another** may prefer savory foods.
（每個人都喜歡的東西都不一樣。有人可能嗜吃甜食，而有人可能比較喜歡吃鹹食。）

馬上動手練一練 ❹

選用不定代名詞填入空格中

one	both	another	the other

1. Tina has three very outstanding brothers. _____ is a professional photographer, _____ is a brilliant actor, and _____ is a Michelin star chef.

2. We own two real properties. _____ are in the United States. _____ is in Los Angeles, and _____ is in New York.

3. Oh, sorry. I haven't decided what to order yet. Can I have _____ five minutes to look at the menu?

4. The students got off the bus _____ after _____.

5. Let's solve the problems _____ by _____.

ANSWER

1. One, another, the other   2. Both, One, the other
3. another   4. one, another   5. one, one

四·疑問代名詞

疑問代名詞是用來詢問「人、事物、時、地、方法、原因」的代名詞,不分單複數,經常放在句首,作為疑問詞。

who	問「人」
whom	問「人」
whose	問「持有人」
what	問「事、物」或「職業、身份」
which	問「人、事、物」

◆作主詞用

例：• **Who** knows the answer?（誰知道答案？）

• **What** is behind the sofa?（什麼東西在沙發後面？）

◆作主詞補語

例：• **Whose** is this?（這個是誰的？）

• **What** is your name?（你的名字是什麼？）

◆作形容詞用

例：• **What** time is it now?（現在幾點？）

• **Which** subject is your favorite?（你最喜歡哪一個學科？）

• **Whose** watch is this?（這是誰的錶？）

◆作動詞的受詞

例：• **Whom** do you love most?（你最愛誰？）

• **Which** would you choose?（你會選哪一個？）

◆作介系詞的受詞

例：• **Whom** are you looking for?（你們在找誰？）

• **What** is this for?（這是用來做什麼的？）

馬上動手練一練 ❺

填入正確的疑問代名詞

1. A: _____ date is today?

   B: It's July 12.

2. A: _____ are you talking about?

   B: We're talking about Jasmine, my sister.

3. A: _____ told you to wait here?

   B: Mark did.

4. A: _____ do you prefer, the red one or the blue one?

   B: The blue one.

5. A: _____ is that?

   B: That's Amy's.

ANSWER

1. What   2. Whom   3. Who   4. Which   5. Whose

Lesson 15 文法總複習
快來試試自己的實力吧！

A. 選擇正確的選項

1. (　) Generally, graduates have to rely on _____ to navigate through underemployment problem.
   - A. them
   - B. they
   - C. themselves
   - D. theirs

2. (　) Peter and Joseph were so close that they never hide any secrets from _____.
   - A. each other
   - B. one another
   - C. one after another
   - D. themselves

3. (　) The mayor answered the reporters' questions _____.
   - A. one and other
   - B. one after other
   - C. each other
   - D. one by one

4. (　) My cellphone is out of battery. Do you mind if I use _____ to make an urgent call to my mother?
   - A. your
   - B. yours
   - C. their
   - D. mine

5. (　) I made a lot of chocolate muffins. You can take _____ home with you if you want.
   - A. some
   - B. something
   - C. a little
   - D. neither

6. (　) Mr. and Mrs. White have two sons, but _____ lives with them.
   A. neither   B. both
   C. either   D. none

7. (　) I would like to have an apartment of _____, but I can't afford one at present.
   A. mine own   B. me
   C. my own   D. myself

8. (　) I haven't heard _____ from Jeremy since he was transferred to New York.
   A. each other   B. anything
   C. what   D. nothing

9. (　) She mistook the man for _____.
   A. him   B. he
   C. this   D. them

10. (　) The soup tastes really good. Would you like _____?
    A. any   B. some
    C. it   D. them

B. 圈出下列句子錯誤之處，並在空格中填入正確的字

_____ 1. I have Sarah's cellphone number, but she doesn't have my.

_____ 2. You have to wash yours own dirty clothes. I won't wash them for you.

_____ 3. Thanks for inviting me to the party. I enjoyed its very much.

_____ 4. I need to find an ATM to withdraw some money. I don't have some on me.

_____ 5. We find this impossible to make it on time.

_____ 6. I wonder if the twins can take care of them when we're not home.

_____ 7. It's a top secret. Don't tell someone about it.

_____ 8. I think my book is in somehow else.

_____ 9. You should treat your better.

_____ 10. She needs money now, but she doesn't have all.

ANSWER

A. 選擇正確的選項
1. **C**　2. **A**　3. **D**　4. **B**　5. **A**
6. **A**　7. **C**　8. **B**　9. **A**　10. **B**

1. 當主詞與受詞指的是同一人或同一件事時，受詞要使用反身代名詞。
   He is not strong enough to protect himself.
   （他沒有強壯到可以保護自己。）

2. each other 彼此

3. one by one 一個接著一個

4. yours=your cellphone

5. some 一些用於問句及肯定句

6. neither 兩者皆不

7. of my own 屬於我自己的

8. anything 任何事情

9. 人稱代名詞受格 he→him

10. some 作受詞，一些

B. 圈出下列句子錯誤之處，並在空格中填入正確的字

1. <u>mine</u> I have Sarah's cellphone number, but she doesn't have my.

2. <u>your</u> You have to wash yours own dirty clothes. I won't wash them for you.

3. <u>it</u> Thanks for inviting me to the party. I enjoyed its very much.

4. <u>any</u> I need to find an ATM to withdraw some money. I don't have some on me.

5. <u>it</u> We find this impossible to make it on time.

6. <u>themselves</u> I wonder if the twins can take care of them when we're not home.

7. <u>anyone</u> It's a top secret. Don't tell someone about it.

8. <u>somewhere</u> I think my book is in somehow else.

9. <u>yourself</u> You should treat your better.

10. <u>any</u> She needs money now, but she doesn't have all.

Lesson 16

頻率副詞 與 程度副詞

頻率副詞

- always, usually, often, sometimes, seldom, never
- 放在一般動詞前、be動詞或助動詞之後
- 可以放在句首句尾的頻率副詞
  - sometimes, usually, normally, generally, frequently
- 否定意味的頻率副詞
  - seldom, hardly, rarely, barely, never
- 複合頻率副詞
  - all the time, once a day, from time to time, every now and then, every day

程度副詞

very, pretty, completely, too, a little, such, nearly, quite, rarely, not at all

- 可以放在句尾的程度副詞
  - at all, completely
- 相關句型
  - too...to...
  - ...enough to...
  - so...that...
- 表示可能性的程度副詞

  impossibly, maybe, perhaps, possibly, probably, definitely

  - 修飾動詞或形容詞
  - 否定句中放在not前
  - maybe和perhaps放句首

Lesson 16　頻率副詞與程度副詞

之前我們認識了主要用來修飾動詞的情態副詞，這一章我們要介紹用來描述動作或事件發生的頻繁程度的頻率副詞，以及用來修飾動詞、形容詞或其他副詞，顯示其強度或程度的程度副詞。

頻率副詞的位置通常是be動詞或助動詞之後，及物動詞與不及物動詞之前。而程度副詞則通常是放在欲修飾的字詞之前，以不同的程度副詞來呈現不同的語氣，使所修飾的形容詞、副詞或動詞表現得更強烈或更微弱。但是這些副詞在句子中的位置並非固定，有些副詞的位置比其他副詞具有彈性，在本篇章中都會逐一詳述。

一・頻率副詞

頻率副詞為用來修飾動詞，說明某個動作、某個狀況或事件發生的「頻率」或「次數」的副詞。

◆常用頻率副詞

最常用的頻率副詞有六個，其所描述的頻率依序為：

> always（總是）＞usually（通常）＞often（時常）＞
> sometimes（偶爾）＞seldom（很少）＞never（從未）

① 頻率副詞放在【一般動詞之前】：

例：• We **always** separate our garbage for recycling.

（我們總是為了回收再利而用將垃圾分類。）

• He **seldom** leaves things to the last minutes.

（他很少將事情留到最後一刻才做。）

② 頻率副詞放在【be動詞或助動詞之後】：

例：• Patrick is **always** there for me when I need him.

（當我需要派翠克時，他總是在我身邊。）

• We don't **usually** travel abroad.

（我們並不經常出國旅遊。）

③ 其他表示頻率的副詞：

generally 通常地	normally 按慣例地	constantly 固定地
repeatedly 反覆地	regularly 定期地	frequently 頻繁地
rarely 很少地	hardly 幾乎不	barely 幾乎沒有

例：• The teacher **repeatedly** reminded the students the importance of honesty.

（老師反覆地提醒學生誠實的重要性。）

• Fiona has changed so much that I can **hardly** recognize her.（費歐娜改變太多了，以致于我幾乎認不出她來。）

④ 有些頻率副詞可以放在句首或句尾

sometimes 有時	usually 通常	normally 一般	often 時常
generally 一般	frequently 頻繁	occasionally 偶爾	oftentimes 經常

例：• **Generally**, students who failed the exam have to take a makeup test. （通常，沒有通過考試的學生需要補考。）

• We don't visit our grandparents very **often**.
（我們並非很常去探望我們的祖父母。）

❺ 含有否定意味的頻率副詞

seldom 很少	hardly 幾乎不	rarely 幾乎不
barely 幾乎不	scarcely 幾乎不	never 從不

含有「否定意味」的頻率副詞，不能與no或not使用在同一個句子中。

例：• It **never** occurred to me that Jack is a real prince.
（我從沒想過傑克會是一個真正的王子。）

• This box is so heavy that I can **hardly** carry it.
（這個箱子太重了，我幾乎搬不動。）

馬上動手練一練 ❶

將頻率副詞加入句子中

1. I don't cook dinner for my family. (always)

_____

2. Sam doesn't go to the staff cafeteria for lunch. (usually)

_____

3. We do grocery shopping on the weekend. (sometimes)

_____

4. They let their children use iPads in the house. (never)

_____

5. Mary is late for work. (often)

_____

ANSWER

1. I don't always cook dinner for my family.
2. Sam doesn't usually go to the staff cafeteria for lunch.
3. We do grocery shopping on the weekend sometimes.
4. They never let their children use iPads in the house.
5. Mary is often late for work.

◆複合頻率副詞

有些頻率副詞是由多字組成，這些複合頻率副詞通常置於句首或句尾。常用的複合頻率副詞有：

all the time 總是	once a day 一天一次
from time to time 有時候	twice a week 一週兩次
now and then 有時候	three times a week 一週兩次
every now and then 有時候	daily 一天一次
now and again 有時候	weekly 一週一次
once in a while 偶爾	monthly 一個月一次
every so often 偶爾	seasonally 一季一次
on occasion 偶爾	annually/yearly 一年一次
at times 偶爾	every day 每天
again and again 屢次地，再三地	once every other day 兩天一次

例：• **Again and again**, the newcomer makes the same mistakes.
（那個新人一而再、再而三地犯相同的錯誤。）

- **Every now and then**, I will take a few days off and visit the countryside.
（偶爾，我會休幾天假到鄉下走走。）

- The elevator of our office building gets out of order **from time to time**.
（我們公司大樓的電梯三不五時就會故障。）

- The medical periodical publishes **monthly**.
（這本醫學期刊一季出版一次。）

 馬上動手練一練 ❷

將頻率副詞加入句子

1. I visit my parents. (once a month)

_____

2. They take their children to the zoo. (from time to time)

_____

3. We re-edit our catalogue. (every season)

_____

4. The car needs preventive maintenance. (periodically)

_____

5. The mother reminded her son to call her. (over and over)

_____

ANSWER

1. I visit my parents once a month.
2. They take their children to the zoo from time to time.
3. We re-edit our catalogue every season.
4. The car needs preventive maintenance periodically.
5. Over and over, the mother reminded her son to call her.

二・程度副詞

◆常見的程度副詞

very 非常	pretty 頗	completely 完全
too 太	fairly 非常	a little 一點
so 如此	just 剛剛	kind of 一點
such 如此	nearly 幾乎	hardly 幾乎不
quite 相當	almost 幾乎	rarely 幾乎不
rather 相當	totally 完全	not at all 一點也不

　　同樣是表示「非常；相當」的副詞，其修飾程度上的差異，如：

very＞rather/pretty＞quite＞fairly

　　例：・It is **very** tasty.（這個非常美味。）＞It is **pretty** tasty.（這個相當美味。）＞It is **quite** tasty.（這個頗為美味。）＞It is **fairly** tasty.（這個蠻美味的。）

　　由句子中的副詞，就可以分辨出美味程度的差別。

◆程度副詞可以用來修飾動詞、形容詞或其他副詞

① 修飾動詞

①放在一般動詞前

例：• She **quite** <u>enjoyed</u> the movie.
（她相當喜歡這部電影。）

• I **rather** <u>like</u> hanging out with Frank.
（我很喜歡跟法蘭克一起玩。）

• He **kind of** <u>worried</u> about his wife's health condition.
（他有點擔心他妻子的健康狀況。）

---

②若有be動詞或助動詞，程度副詞放在be動詞或助動詞與一般動詞之間

例：• The situation <u>is</u> **totally** <u>getting</u> out of control.
（情況完全失控了。）

• This dress is too small that I <u>can</u> **hardly** <u>fit</u> in.
（這件洋裝太小了，我幾乎穿不進去。）

---

③有些程度副詞也可以放在句尾

例：• I don't agree with you **at all**.
（我一點也不同意你說的。）

• She trusted the man **completely**.
（她完全地信任那個男人。）

馬上動手練一練 ❸

將程度副詞加入句子中

1. I like Jeremy's idea. (not at all)

_____

2. My parents are concerned about my performance at school. (rather)

_____

3. When traveling in France, she understood what people said. (scarcely)

_____

4. She discarded the clothes that were new. (almost)

_____

5. I understand what you mean, but I don't agree with you. (totally/ completely)

_____

ANSWER

1. I don't like Jeremy's idea at all.
2. My parents are rather concerned about my performance at school.
3. When traveling in France, she scarcely understood what people said.
4. She discarded the clothes that were almost new.
5. I totally understand what you mean, but I don't completely agree with you.

❷ 修飾形容詞

①放在形容詞之前

例：• The football game last night was **extremely** exciting.
（昨天晚上的足球賽超級刺激。）

• Your plan sounds **pretty** unrealistic.
（你的計劃聽起來頗為不切實際。）

• I'm **too** exhausted to cook dinner tonight. Let's just eat instant noodles.
（我今晚太累了沒辦法做晚飯。我們就吃泡麵吧。）

 **重點筆記**

有些程度副詞可以用來修飾**比較級形容詞**，如much, so much, even, a lot, far等。

例：• Indian curry tastes **much** spicier than Japanese curry.
（印度咖哩吃起來比日本咖哩辣多了。）

• You look **a lot** slenderer in this dress than you did in the previous one.
（你穿這件洋裝看起來比先前那一件苗條得多了。）

②放在形容詞之後

enough 放在形容詞後面做後位修飾的程度副詞。

例：• My brother is not old **enough** to drink alcohol.
（我的弟弟年紀不夠大，不能飲酒。）

• If you are lucky **enough**, you may even win a round-trip ticket to Bangkok.（如果你夠幸運的話，你甚至可能贏得一張到曼谷的來回機票。）

 **馬上動手練一練 ❹**

圈出正確的程度副詞，以完成句子

1. We weren't lucky (too/enough/extremely) to see the aurora.
2. This is a (rather/enough/a little) wonderful opportunity to improve your English speaking skills.
3. The children were (enough/quite/too) excited to get to sleep.
4. Your idea sounds (enough/a little/such) (too/rather/much) idealistic to me.

5. You need to be tall (enough/totally/kind of) to join the basketball team.

ANSWER

1. enough 2. rather 3. too 4. a little, too 5. enough

❸ 修飾副詞

①放在副詞之前

例：• The newcomer learns **rather** <u>fast</u>. I am very surprised.
（那個新人學得相當快。我很驚訝。）

　　• Take a break, will you? You are working **too** <u>hard</u>.
（休息一下，好嗎？你工作得太努力了。）

 重點筆記

有些副詞可以用來修飾**比較級副詞**，如far, much, even, a lot等。

例：• I can do it **much** <u>better</u> than he does.
（我可以做得甚至比他還要更好。）

　　• A cheetah can run **a lot** <u>faster</u> than a kangaroo.
（獵豹可以跑得比袋鼠快得多了。）

②放在副詞之後

enough 放在副詞後面做後位修飾的程度副詞。

例：• We got eliminated because we didn't practice <u>hard</u> **enough**.（我們會被淘汰是因為我們練習得不夠努力。）

- The exhibition wasn't organized <u>well</u> **enough**. We can do better next time.

（展覽規劃得不夠完善。我們下次可以做得更好。）

圈出正確的程度副詞，以完成句子

1. They finished their tasks (far/farther/more) faster than we expected.

2. It surprised everyone that the girl could dance (ever/even/enough) better than her mother.

3. You can never do well (too/enough/so) to fulfill his requirements.

4. We missed the train because we didn't leave the house early (totally/much/enough).

5. My brother speaks Spanish (enough/too/so much) better than he does English.

ANSWER
1. far　2. even　3. enough　4. enough　5. so much

◆比較quite/rather/pretty的用法

❶ 修飾形容詞時

rather與pretty的意思差不多，但是pretty多用於口語，或其他較不拘形式的場合。rather, pretty, quite 都有「相當」的含義，但rather的口氣比quite更強烈，含有「比預期的多」之意。

例：• I didn't have much expectation about the show, but it was **rather** good.

（我沒有對這表演有太多期待，但它非常的棒。）

• The show is **quite** good. You can watch it if you have time.

（這表演蠻好的。如果你有時間的話可以去看。）

❷ 修飾名詞時

quite放在a/an之前，pretty放在a之後

例：• Henry is **quite an** interesting person.

＝Henry is **a pretty** interesting person.

（哈利是個相當有趣的人。）

• It is **quite a** tough task.

＝It is **a pretty** tough task.

（這是份相當困難的任務。）

❸ 修飾動詞時

quite與rather修飾動詞的用法相同，可以放在動詞前，或是be動詞及助動詞後。pretty較常用來修飾形容詞及副詞，很少用來修飾動詞。

例：• I **quite** enjoyed the concert.

（我相當享受這場音樂會。）

• He **rather** likes traveling alone.

（他相當喜歡單獨旅行。）

• I didn't **quite** understand what he said.

（我不是很了解他所說的。）

• It is **rather** hot today.
（今天相當熱。）

圈出最適合的程度副詞，以完成句子

1. He (rather/pretty) loves spending time with himself.
2. He solved the difficult math question (pretty/rather) fast. Even the math teacher was surprised.
3. The man was (quite/rather) dead when he was sent to the hospital.
4. Their favorite singer didn't show up, so they were (rather/pretty) disappointed.
5. I (pretty/quite) enjoyed staying in this hotel.

ANSWER

1. rather   2. pretty   3. quite   4. pretty   5. quite

◆程度副詞的相關句型

❶ too＋形容詞／副詞＋to＋原形動詞：表示「太……以致於不能……」

例：• The math question was **too complicated** for me **to solve**.
（這數學題對我來說太複雜，無法解開。）

• He was **too shy to ask questions**.
（他太害羞了，以致於不敢問任何問題。）

- The girl performed **too well to be neglected**.
（那女孩表演得太棒了，讓人無法忽視。）
- Peter worked **too carelessly to fulfill** his supervisor's requirements.
（彼得事情做得太粗心，以致於無法符合他主管的要求。）

❷ 形容詞／副詞＋enough＋to＋原形動詞：表示「夠……以致於能……」

例：
- This apartment is **big enough to accommodate** twelve people. （這間公寓夠大，能夠讓十二個人住。）

- His performance was not **good enough to make** him stay in the competition.
（他的表現並沒有好到可以讓他繼續留在比賽裡。）

- You didn't perform **well enough to catch** the audience's attention.（你表現得不夠好，無法抓住觀眾的注意力。）

- The teacher had to speak **loud enough to let** everyone hear him. （老師必須說得夠大聲，才能讓所有人聽到他的聲音。）

❸ so＋形容詞／副詞＋that子句：表示「如此／太……，以致於……」

例：
- Victor was **so charming that** almost every girl wanted to be friends with him. （維克多太有魅力了，以致於幾乎每個女生都想跟他做朋友。）

- The party was **so much fun that** we all had a wonderful time. （派對太有趣了，所以我們全都玩得很開心。）

- The customer acted **so rudely that** he was asked to leave the restaurant.
（該顧客行為非常無禮，所以被請出餐廳。）
- Mark learned **so slowly that** he was fired within the probation period. （馬克學得太慢了，所以在試用期間就被開除了。）

◆so與such的用法

so與such都表示「如此地」，但是用法卻不太一樣。

❶ so多用來修飾形容詞

例：• The mistake you made was **so** silly.
（你所犯下的錯誤非常愚蠢。）

• Don't be **so** selfish. （別那麼自私。）

so修飾名詞時，還是要先接形容詞，再接名詞，但這種用法比較少出現。

例：• She is **so** beautiful a girl. （她是如此美麗的一個女孩。）

❷ such多用來修飾名詞

such修飾名詞時，要不要與形容詞配合使用都可以。

例：• You are **such** an idiot. （你真是個傻瓜。）

• You made **such** a silly mistake.
（你犯下如此愚蠢的錯誤。）

❸ 兩者比較

表示「很多」時，so要配合many或much，而such要配合a lot (of)。

例： • There are **so many** things to see in the museum.

＝There are **such a lot of things** to see in the museum.

（博物館裡有好多東西可以看。）

• I have **so much** to do today.

＝ I have **such a lot** to do today.

（我今天有好多事要做。）

馬上動手練一練 ❼

圈出正確的程度副詞，以完成句子

1. There was (so much/so many) food to eat at the party.

2. We didn't know that Jeff's twin sister was (so/such) a pretty girl.

3. The amusement park is (so/such) fun. I will definitely visit it again.

4. The MIS department gave us (so/such) much technical assistance in this project.

5. Don't be (so/such) mean to your sister. She only wants to help.

ANSWER

1. so much　　2. such　　3. so　　4. so　　5. so

◆用來描述對事情肯定程度的程度副詞

possibly 也許，可能	obviously 顯然
probably 可能	definitely 絕對
maybe 可能	undoubtedly 無疑

perhaps 可能	unquestionably 毫無疑問
positively 肯定	impossibly 不可能

❶ 這類可能性副詞可以用來修飾動詞或形容詞

例：• **Maybe** you have left your passport in the hotel.
（你可能把護照留在飯店裡了。）

• Susan **obviously** has a crush on Tim.
（蘇珊顯然迷上提姆了。）

• He's **probably** dead. （他可能死了。）

• This purse is **impossibly** expensive.
（這個錢包貴得讓人難以相信。）

❷ 可能性的副詞在否定句中，會放在否定詞not之前

例：• I **probably won't** visit the Nature History Museum this time.
（我這次可能不會去參觀自然歷史博物館。）

• Mom is **obviously not** very satisfied with my choice.
（媽媽顯然對我的選擇不是非常滿意。）

❸ maybe與perhaps要放在句首

例：• **Maybe** your mom was right about that.
（也許你媽媽對那件事看法是對的。）

• **Perhaps** you should ask him in person.
（也許你應該當面問他。）

在句子中加入程度副詞

1. Jennifer is at Sarah's house at the moment. (probably)

_____

2. You should take a day off and have a good rest. (definitely)

_____

3. Smartphones have become necessities in our lives. (undoubtedly)

_____

4. Our reservation has been cancelled. (perhaps)

_____

5. Mom won't have time to attend my graduation ceremony. (maybe)

_____

ANSWER

1. Jennifer is probably at Sarah's house at the moment.
2. You should definitely take a day off and have a good rest.
3. Smartphones have undoubtedly become necessities in our lives.
4. Perhaps our reservation has been cancelled.
5. Maybe Mom won't have time to attend my graduation ceremony.

A. 選擇適當的副詞

1. (　) She _____ lost her mind.
   A. too　　　　　　　B. totally　　　C. enough　　　D. such

2. (　) I don't _____ understand your question. Could you explain it more specifically?
   A. pretty　　　　　　B. absolutely　　C. quite　　　　D. too

3. (　) The man was _____ seriously injured that he _____ died.
   A. so; nearly　　　　　　　　　B. too; probably
   C. such; almost　　　　　　　　D. a lot; rather

4. (　) Jean's work performance is _____ enough to be promoted.
   A. well　　　　　　　B. better　　　C. good　　　　D. best

5. (　) The man looks _____ familiar to me, but I just don't remember who he is.
   A. such　　　　　　　B. so　　　　C. too　　　　D. obviously

6. (　) That was _____ a rude question that she didn't care to answer it.
   A. frequently　　　　B. too　　　　C. never　　　　D. such

7. (　) Josh works out in the gym _____ a week.
   A. usually　　　　　B. seldom　　　C. twice　　　D. sometimes

8. (　) The applicant has _____ an amazing education background. We are all very impressed.

   A. quite   B. pretty   C. so   D. rather

9. (　) I love the show so much. It is _____ good.

   A. a little   B. quite   C. better   D. enough

10. (　) The kids are _____ naughty and I am so irritated now.

   A. a bit   B. much   C. extremely   D. to

B. 將最適當的副詞填入空格中

1. The woman was _____ devastated that she _____ passed out on the street.

2. The news was ____ good to be true. I could _____ believe it happened!

3. Why don't you just take a guess? _____ you'll get it right.

4. The doctor suggested that he should exercise _____, but he only go to the gym _____ in a while.

5. Reducing the use of plastic is_____ impractical to some people, but it is not a problem to me _____.

6. I'm still _____uncertain about transferring to the branch office.

7. I'll definitely take Mr. Lin's class. He teaches _____ better than the other professor.

8. I am _____ tired to cook tonight. Let's go out to eat.

9. You are not old _____ to drive the car.

10. Lena is _____ pretty _____ I cannot take off my eyes off her.

ANSWER

A. 選擇適當的副詞

1. **B**　2. **C**　3. **A**　4. **C**　5. **B**

6. **D**　7. **C**　8. **A**　9. **B**　10. **C**

1. totally完全地，修飾lost

2. quite副詞，用來修飾understand

3. so+副詞／形容詞that...太……以致於……

4. 形容詞／副詞+enough+to+原形動詞：表示「夠……以致於能……」
   This apartment is big enough to accommodate twelve people. (這間公寓夠大，能夠讓十二個人住。)

5. so+形容詞，如此……

6. such+名詞片語，such a rude question如此無禮的問題

7. twice=two times 兩次

8. quite修飾名詞放在a/an之前
   Henry is quite an interesting person.
   (哈利是個相當有趣的人。)

9. quite修飾形容詞，相當地好quite good

10. extremely=very 非常地，修飾naughty

B. 將最適當的副詞填入空格中

1. so, almost

2. too, hardly

3. Maybe

4. regularly, once

5. probably, at all

6. a bit

7. far

8. too

9. enough

10. so, that

Lesson 17

連接詞與子句

從屬連接詞

- 引導副詞子句修飾主句
- 句型
  - 主句＋從屬連接詞＋從屬子句
  - 從屬連接詞＋從屬子句，主句
- 表示時間
  - as, when, while, before, after, as soon as, until, whenever, since
- 表示因果
  - because, as, since, as a result, therefore
- 表示目的
  - so that, in order that, in case
- 表示矛盾
  - although, though, even though, while
- 表示條件
  - if, as long as, unless, once

對等連接詞

- 連接前後對等的兩個單字、片語或子句
  - *and*： 連接同性質或語義的字、片語或子句
  - *but*： 連接語意相反或矛盾的字、片語或子句
  - *or*：
    - 提供兩種選擇
    - 否定句中表示「也不」
    - 警告意味，「否則」
  - *yet*： 連接語意相反或矛盾的字、片語或子句
  - *so*： 連接表示結果的子句
  - *for*： 連接表示原因的句子
  - *nor*： 否定句＋nor，「既不……也不……」

相關連接詞

- 連接兩個同詞性的字或片語
  - *both...and...*： 兩者都；既……且……
  - *not only...but also...*： 不但……而且……
  - *either...or...*： 不是……就是……
  - *neither...nor...*： 既不……也不……
  - *whether...or...*： 無論……或……

連接詞與子句

連接詞是用來連接句子中的字、片語或子句,使句子能夠傳達更完整的意思。連接詞依其功能及用法分為「對等連接詞」、「從屬連接詞」及「相關連接詞」等三種。

本章節將介紹其二:「對等連接詞」用來連接句子中彼此對等的字、片語或子句,其前後的字、片語或子句,在詞性、時態或架構上都必須對等:如「字對字」、「片語對片語」、「句對句」,「動名詞對動名詞」、「不定詞對不定詞」、「形容詞對形容詞」等。

而「相關連接詞」則是用來連接兩個相關的字、片語或子句。連接詞前後的字、片語或子句無論是詞性、時態或架構通常是一致的,如「動名詞對動名詞、「不定詞對不定詞」、「形容詞對形容詞」等。

一‧對等連接詞

對等連接詞有以下七個:

and(和）	or（或）	but（但是）	yet（但）
so（所以）	for（因為）	nor（也不）	

對等連接詞可以在句子中直接連接兩個詞性相同的字詞或片語,或是以逗號與獨立句子隔開。

◆and：
→連接同性質或語義的字、片語或子句

例：• Jennifer **and** Sarah are Steven's sisters.

（珍妮弗和莎拉是史蒂文的妹妹。）

連接兩個名詞

• The production process is time-consuming **and** labor-intensive.
（這生產過程非常費時且耗人力）

連接兩個性質相似的形容詞

• He is interested in collecting stamps **and** reading comic books.
（他對集郵和看漫畫書有興趣。）

連接兩個動名詞片語

• All you have to do is (to) drink plenty of water **and** (to) get enough sleep.
（你所需要做的事情，就是喝很多的水 以及有足夠的睡眠。）

連接兩個不定詞片語

重點筆記

連接獨立子句時，需要逗號與句子相隔。

例：• Turn right at the intersection, **and** you shall find the subway entrance.
（在十字路口右轉，然後你應該就會看到地鐵入口了。）

• Show her your ticket, **and** she will take you to your seat. （把你的票拿給她看，她就會帶你到你的座位。）

◆but：
→連接語義相反或矛盾的字、片語或子句

例：• The renovation is time-consuming but worthwhile.
（翻修費時卻值得。）

• This is a very creative but not-so-practical plan.
（這是個非常有創意卻不太可行的計劃。）

• She exercises hard but doesn't lose much weight.
（她運動得很努力但是沒減掉太多體重。）

• I can give you my advice, but you are responsible for your own choice.
（我可以給你我的建議，但是你要為自己的選擇負責。）

◆or：
→連接兩個詞性、性質相同的字、片語或句子，提供兩種不同的選擇

例：• Would you like porridge or cereal for breakfast?
（你早餐想吃粥還是麥片？）

• We can take the kids with us, or we can leave them to the babysitter.
（我們可以帶孩子一起去，或是把他們交給保姆。）

❶ or還可用在否定句，表示「也不」

例：• The child never cried or laughed.
（那孩子從來不哭也不笑。）

❷ or也可用來連接有「警告」含義的句子，表示「否則」

例：• Don't be late again, or you will get fired.
（別再遲到，否則你將會被開除。）

- Go to bed early, **or** <u>you'll oversleep yourself tomorrow</u>.
（早點睡，否則你明天會睡過頭。）

馬上動手練一練 ❶

在空格中填入**and, but**或**or**，以完成句子

1. He was very tired, ＿＿ he refused to take a break.

2. We can hold the party in the house, ＿＿ we can hold it in the yard.

3. Show your boarding pass to the flight attendants, ＿＿ they will take you to your seat.

4. Make sure you arrive at the restaurant by 6 p.m., ＿＿ your reservation shall be cancelled.

5. Keep your promise ＿＿ take the kids to the zoo.

ANSWER

1. but　2. or　3. and　4. or　5. and

◆yet：
→ 與but用法一樣，都是連接語義相反或矛盾的字、片語或子句

例：• The journey was <u>exhausting</u> **yet** <u>unforgettable</u>.
（這段旅程令人筋疲力竭卻永誌難忘。）

• Working full-time when studying is challenging, **yet** <u>he managed to survive</u>.
（唸書時全職工作非常有挑戰性，但他設法應付過去了。）

◆so：
→ 連接表示「結果」的子句，用來表示因果關係

例：• The salary wasn't good enough, **so** he didn't accept the job offer.

（薪水不夠好，所以他沒有接受那個工作機會。）

• He doesn't meet our requirements, **so** we won't consider hiring him.

（他不符合我們的條件要求，所以我們不考慮僱用他。）

◆for：
→ 連接表示「原因」的子句，用來提供「理由」

例：• I won't be able to go to Jane's party, **for** I have a prior commitment that day.

（我不會去珍的派對，因為那天我已經先答應別人了。）

• We hire a nanny to look after they baby, **for** both of us have to work. （我們請了一位保姆來照顧寶寶，因為我們兩個都必須工作。）

◆nor：
→ 使用有否定語義的句子中，配合前面有否定語義的字、片語或句子（如no, not, never等），連接具相同詞性的字或片語，以表示「既不……也不……」

例：• This product is **not** economical **nor** eco-friendly.

（這個產品既不經濟，亦不環保。）

• Andy has **no** income **nor** any savings.

（安迪既沒有收入也沒有任何存款。）

選出適當的連接詞填入空格中

so	yet	nor	for

1. He has lived in the U.S for more than fifteen years, ___ he can speak very good English.

2. Walk as fast as you can, ___ you can arrive at school in time.

3. The chicken is nerther seasoned ___ cooked.

4. All the restaurants are closed, ___ it is a national holiday today.

5. I don't agree with you, ___ I will defend your right to say it.

ANSWER

1. so　2. so　3. nor　4. for　5. yet

二·相關連接詞

相關連接詞是用來連接兩個同詞性的字或片語，常用的相關連接詞有以下五個：

both... and...（兩者都）	either... or...（兩者之一）
not only ... but also... （不僅……而且……）	neither... nor... （兩者都不）
whether... or (not)（無論是否）	

連接詞與子句

◆both... and... （兩者都，既……且……）

例：
- **Both** Harvard **and** Stanford have sent me admission offer letters.

（哈佛與史丹福都寄給我入學許可信。）

- The news of her sudden death made us **both** astonished **and** grieved.

（她突然過世的消息讓我們感到既震驚又哀傷。）

◆not only... but also... （不但……而且……）

例：
- The man was diagnosed with **not only** pneumonia **but also** bronchitis.

（這個人被診斷出不僅罹患肺炎還有支氣管炎。）

- Leo is **not only** a good boss, **but also** a great friend.

（里歐不僅是個好上司，也是個很棒的朋友。）

- We **not only** tried bungee jumping **but also** experienced windsurfing.

（我們不但嘗試了高空彈跳，還體驗了風帆衝浪。）

 重點筆記

★當連接兩個主詞時，動詞或助動詞隨but also後的主詞變化。

- **Not only** Rachel **but also** Sophie *was* invited to our wedding.

（不僅瑞秋，蘇菲也受邀參加我們的婚禮。）

- **Not only** he **but also** I *don't* know the answer.

（不僅他，就連我也不知道答案。）

馬上動手練一練 ❸

在空格中填入**not only... but also...**或是**both... and...**

1. Peter _____ helped me move, _____ cleaned the apartment for me.

2. _____ English _____ Math are my favorite subjects.

3. _____ Mom _____ Dad was infected with Dengue fever.

4. You can't take _____ the piano class _____ the painting class. You have to choose one.

5. _____ plastics _____ Styrofoam causes serious environmental issues.

ANSWER

1. not only, but also   2. Both, and
3. Not only, but also   4. both, and
5. Not only, but also

◆either... or...（不是……就是……；……或……），表示「兩者其中之一」

例：• We will settle the payment **either** this afternoon **or** tomorrow morning.
（我們不是今天下午就是明天早上就會將款項繳清。）

• You can **either** drive yourself **or** take a taxi.
（你可以自己開車，或是搭計程車。）

◆neither ... nor ... （既不⋯⋯也不⋯⋯；⋯⋯和⋯⋯都不），表示「兩者皆非」

例：• Emma is interested in **neither** reading **nor** painting.
（艾瑪對閱讀和畫畫都沒有興趣。）

• The wealthy man was **neither** generous **nor** kindhearted.
（那富有的男人既不慷慨也不善良。）

重點筆記

1. 當either... or...連接兩個主詞時，動詞或助動詞隨or後的主詞做變化。

例：• **Either** Mike **or** his twin brother was a fashion model before.
（麥克或他雙胞胎兄弟其中一個以前是時裝模特兒。）

2. 當neither... nor...連接兩個主詞時，動詞或助動詞隨nor後的主詞做變化。

例：• **Neither** fame **nor** gain is important to me.
（名與利對我說都不重要。）

馬上動手練一練 ❹

在空格中填入**either... or...** 或**neither... nor...**

1. We need someone to look after Jamie. _____ you _____ Jack has to stay at home.

2. My mother is a vegetarian. She eats _____ meat _____ seafood.

3. Miranda is not adequate to the job. She should _____ be fired _____ be transferred to another department.

4. His speech was _____ inspiring _____ informative. It was totally a waste of my time.

5. I'm not sure when exactly the meeting will be held this afternoon. It's _____ at 2 p.m. _____ at 3 p.m.

ANSWER

1. Either, or   2. neither, nor   3. either, or
4. neither, nor   5. either, or

◆whether... or...（無論……或……）

whether... or後面可接兩種副詞，以表示不同狀況，或是whether＋子句，並與or not連用，表示正反兩面的狀況。

例：• **Whether** by skills **or** by luck, the team won the champion.
（無論是靠技巧還是考運氣，該隊贏得了冠軍。）

• I will marry you, **whether** you are rich **or** not.
（無論你是否富有，我都會嫁給你。）

馬上動手練一練 ❺

從以下句子中找出「**whether**」和「**or**」應放置的位子並填入，以完成句子（提示：whether可能出現在句首，也可能出現在句中）

1. I will not change my mind you agree with me not.

2. By car by bus, they will go to school on time.

3. The meeting will be held on time, he is coming not.

4. You're doing it by yourself, you're going to have someone to help you, the job needs to be done by the deadline.

5. My father is always working, on the weekdays on the weekend.

ANSWER

1. I will not change my mind whether you agree with me or not.
2. Whether by car or by bus, they will go to school on time.
3. The meeting will be held on time, whether he is coming or not.
4. Whether you're doing it by yourself, or you're going to have someone to help you, the job needs to be done by the deadline.
5. My father is always working, whether on the weekdays or on the weekend.

三·從屬連接詞

從屬連接詞是用來引導出一個副詞子句，以修飾意思表達不夠完整的主句，為主句做補充説明，如描述「時間」、「原因」或「條件」等。

從屬連接詞是用來補充有關「時間」、「原因」、「目的」、「條件」或「矛盾」等訊息，使主句意思更為完整的連接詞。

基本句型為：

> 主句＋從屬連接詞＋從屬子句
> ＝從屬連接詞＋從屬子句，主句

從屬連接詞放在句中時，不需逗號。放在句首引導出副詞子句時，要以逗號與主句相隔。

例：• Everyone was terrified **when** the volcano erupted.
　　＝**When** the volcano erupted, everyone was terrified.
　　（當火山爆發時，所有人都嚇壞了。）

◆表示時間

as （當……）	after （在……後）
when （當……時）	before （在……前）
while （當……時）	until/till （直到）
as soon as （一……就……）	whenever （每當……）
once （一……立刻……）	since （自從）

❶ as, when, while 用來描述兩個同時發生的動作或事件

例：• We saw James **as** we were walking across the street.
（我們正在過馬路時看到了詹姆士。）

• The phone rang **when** she was changing the baby's diaper. （當她正在幫寶寶換尿布時，電話響了。）

• They usually have lunch **while** they are having a meeting.
（他們經常在開會的時候吃午餐。）

重點筆記

1. 動作持續時間較長的句子通常以when, while, as＋正在進行式表示

例：• The earthquake occurred **when** I was taking a shower.

　　發生時間短暫　　　　　　　動作持續時間較長

（地震發生時，我正在洗澡。）

2. 描述兩個同時發生的短暫動作，通常會用as，或是just as來表示

例：• The bus door closed **(just) as** I got onto the bus.

　　前後兩個瞬間動作幾乎同時發生

（公車門在我上公車時剛好關上。）

3. while通常用來引導描述持續動作的句子，而不用來引導描述瞬間動作的句子

例：（O）It suddenly started to rain **while** we were having a picnic.　　野餐是持續動作，可以用while引導

（當我們正在野餐時，突然下起雨來。）

（X）A beautiful woman walked out ~~while~~ the elevator door opened.　　門打開是瞬間動作，不用while引導

（當電梯門打開時，一位美麗的女子走了出來。）

❷ before, after, as soon as 用來描述發生順序不同的兩個動作，或某動作或事件緊接著另一個動作或事件發生

例：• We had already had lunch **before** we came here.

（我們在來這兒之前，已經吃過午餐了。）

• **After** we had been stuck in traffic for two hours, we were finally home.

（在馬路上塞車兩個小時之後，我們終於回到家了。）

a. as soon as 是用來引導「瞬間動作」副詞子句的連接詞，表示「當……立刻；一……馬上就……」。

例：All people in the building evacuated **as soon as** the fire alarm went off.

（大樓裡所有的人一聽到火災警報器響起，就立刻疏散。）

b. once表示「一旦，當……時」，可取代as soon as用來引導瞬間動作副詞子句。

例：• The man admitted killing the woman **once** the police took out the evidence.

（警方一拿出證據，男子就立刻承認殺害了女子。）

❸ until/till 表示「直到」，用來描述「動作停止」的時間

a. ... until...：表示「直到某時間為止」。

例：• We will wait **until** you are ready.

（我們會一直等到你準備好為止。）

b. not ... until ...：表示「直到某時間之前都不能……」。

例：• I won't say anything **until** my lawyer arrived.

（直到我的律師到來之前，我什麼都不會說。）

★ not until可以放在句首引導倒裝句

例：• I **wasn't** allowed to enter the hall **until** I showed them the invitation.

= **Not until** I showed them the invitation **was** I allowed to enter the hall.

（直到我出示邀請函，他們才讓我進入禮堂。）

• I **won't** stop trying **until** I succeed.
= **Not until** I succeed **will** I stop trying.

（直到我成功之前，我都不會停止嘗試。）

❹ whenever表示「無論何時、每當」，用來引導描述當某情況出現時，便發生某動作的副詞子句

例：• I play the piano **whenever** I feel depressed.

（當我感到沮喪時，我就會彈鋼琴。）

• Consult with your supervisor **whenever** you have problems with writing your dissertation.（無論何時，當你寫論文出現問題，就去請教你的指導教授。）

❺ since表示「從某動作發生後一直到現在」，通常接在完成式句子後面，引導過去式副詞子句，提供更多時間資訊

例：• We have lost contact **since** we graduated.

（自從畢業之後，我們就失聯了。）

• This village has changed so much **since** I left in 1998.

（這個村莊自從我在1998年離開之後到現在，變了好多。）

圈出適當的連接詞，以完成句子

1. Don't take any action (since/until) you receive further instructions.
2. Press this button (unless/whenever) there's an emergency.
3. We made a reservation at that restaurant (as soon as/while) he recommended it.
4. The postman came (while/until) I was vacuuming the living room.
5. (Once/Unless) he was left alone, he started to look for food.

ANSWER

1. until　2. whenever　3. as soon as　4. while　5. Once

◆表示因果

表示「原因」	because, because of, as, since
表示「後果」	as a result, therefore, so/such... that

❶ 表示原因

because/as/since 後面接子句，because of後面接名詞。

例：• We had Japanese food today **as** the Chinese restaurant was closed.
（我們今天吃日本料理，因為中國餐廳沒開。）

• We'd better make a reservation **because** it is a very popular restaurant.
（我們最好先訂位，因為這是一家很受歡迎的餐廳。）

- All flights have been cancelled **because of** the storm.
（因為暴風雨的關係，所有航班都已經被取消了。）

Since有「既然，由於」的含義，用來引導表示「原因」或「事實狀況」的副詞子句。

例：· **Since** the Chinese restaurant is closed today, let's eat Japanese food instead.
（既然中國餐廳今天沒開，我們就改吃日本料理吧。）

· **Since** I'm already late, I'll take the morning off.
（既然我都已經遲到了，我上午就休假好了。）

❷ 表示結果

so 通常放句中，as a result及therefore通常放句首。

例：· The elevator is out of order, **so** we have to take the stairs.
（電梯故障了，所以我們得爬樓梯。）

· She lost her ticket. **As a result**, she had to buy another ticket.
（她弄丟了車票。因此，她必須補票。）

· He failed the course. **Therefore,** he had to retake it next semester. （他這堂課沒過。因此，他下學期得重修一次。）

so/such... that可以用來描述事情的後果。

例：· The twins look **so** alike **that** none of us can tell them apart.
（這對雙胞胎看起來太相像了，所以我們之中沒有人可以分得出他們來。）

- He's **such** an easygoing person **that** everyone likes to work with him. （他實在是個很隨和的人，因此每個人都喜歡跟他共事。）

馬上動手練一練 ❼

選出正確的連接詞填入空格中

so	since	therefore	because	because of

1. Max gets along with everyone _____ he has a very pleasant personality.

2. Susie was promoted to the director of the branch office _____ her outstanding leadership.

3. Neither of us can cook, _____ we always eat outside.

4. _____ they are on sale, I want to buy a dozen of them.

5. They didn't arrive at the restaurant by 6:10 p.m. _____, their reservation was cancelled.

ANSWER

1. because 2. because of 3. so 4. Since 5. Therefore

重點筆記

1. 表示因與果之關係的連接詞不能同時使用在同個句子中。

例：（Ｘ）Because it's very late, so we need to go home.

> 連接詞的功能是引導子句，修飾主詞。但是這個句子有兩個子句，卻沒有主句，是不符合語法的句子。

2. 表示原因的從屬子句可以放在句首，表示結果的從屬子句則不可。

例：（Ｏ）Because I want to keep fit, I need regular exercise.
（因為我想保持健康，我需要規律的運動。）

（Ｘ）~~So I need regular exercise~~, I want to keep fit.

> so引導表結果的子句，不可放句首。

◆表示目的

so that （如此一來）	in order that （為了，以便）	in case 以便

① so that

so that 可以同時表示「目的」及「結果」。

例：• She walked as quietly as possible **so that** <u>she wouldn't wake anyone</u>.
（她盡可能走得很小聲，如此一來才不會吵醒任何人。）

• Write it down **so that** <u>you won't forget</u>.
（把它寫下來，這樣你才不會忘記。）

❷ in order that

in order that 的用法與 so that 一樣。so that 引導的副詞子句不能放句首，但是 in order that 引導的副詞子句可以放句首。

例：• She worked three part-time jobs **in order that** she could pay off the debts as soon as possible.

= **In order that** she could pay off the debts as soon as possible,she worked three part-time jobs.

（為了能夠盡快還清負債，她兼了三份差。）

so that 子句不能放句首

(X) S̶o̶ ̶t̶h̶a̶t̶ ̶s̶h̶e̶ ̶c̶o̶u̶l̶d̶ ̶p̶a̶i̶d̶ ̶o̶f̶f̶ ̶t̶h̶e̶ ̶d̶e̶b̶t̶s̶ ̶a̶s̶ ̶s̶o̶o̶n̶ ̶a̶s̶ ̶p̶o̶s̶s̶i̶b̶l̶e̶, she worked three part-time jobs.

 重點筆記

★ **so that/in order that** 與 **so as to/in order to**的用法比較
so that/in order that與 so as to/in order to皆為表示「目的」的連接詞，so that/in order that接子句，so as to/in order to 接原形動詞。

例：• We should make a reservation in advance **so that** <u>we won't have to wait</u>.
（我們應該要事先預約，如此一來我們就不必等。）

= We should make a reservation in advance **so as to** <u>avoid waiting</u>. （我們應該要事先預約，以避免等候。）

• We must use a GPS **in order that** we don't get lost in the middle of nowhere.

= We must use a GPS **in order not to** get lost in the middle of nowhere.（我們必須使用衛星定位系統，如此一來我們才不會在荒郊野外迷路。）

❸ in case

in case是用來描述「作為預防」或以「為某種情況做好準備」為目的的連接詞，後面接「現在簡單式」取代未來式，描述「未來可能發生之事」。

in case後面接子句，in case of後面接名詞

例：• We should bring an umbrella with us **in case** <u>it rains</u>.
（我們應該帶把傘，以備下雨時可以用。）

• Make a shopping list **in case** <u>you forget anything</u>.
（列一張購物清單，以免你忘記任何東西。）

• We need to have a fire extinguisher in the house **in case of** <u>fire</u>.
（我們得在家裡放一個滅火器，以免失火時需要用。）

若是描述過去為了預防某事發生所做的準備，則in case後面接簡單過去式。

例：• They arrived the station early **in case** <u>they missed the train</u>.（他們很早就到車站了，以免錯過火車。）

馬上動手練一練 ❽

選出正確的連接詞填入空格中

in case	in case of	so that	so as to	in order that

1. We'd better reserve a room now _____ the hotel is all booked up during summer vacation.
2. I spoke as loud as I could _____ everyone in the hall could hear me clearly.

3. _____ he can catch up with his classmates, John has to spend three hours studying every day.

4. Dad built a fence _____ keep our dog from running out.

5. Use the hammer to break through the windows _____ emergency.

ANSWER

1. in case　2. so that　3. In order that　4. so as to　5. in case of

◆表示矛盾

although（雖然；即使）	though（雖然）
even though（縱使；儘管）	while（儘管；雖然）

例：
- **Although** he has learned swimming for two months, he still can't swim.
  （雖然他已經學游泳學了兩個月，他仍然不會游泳。）

- Mary lives a pretty simple life **though** she is very wealthy.
  （瑪麗雖然富有，卻過著相當簡樸的生活。）

- We are still not used to the changeable weather **even though** we have lived here for six years.
  （即使我們已經在這裡住了六年，我們依然不習慣這善變的天氣。）

- **While** the salary was not as good as he expected, he accepted the job offer.
  （儘管薪水不如預期，他還是接受了這個工作。）

表示「矛盾」及表示「但是」的連接詞不能同時使用在同個句子中。

例：(X) <u>Although</u> he had already set off earlier, <u>but</u> he was still late for work.

> 這個句子有兩個由連接詞引導的副詞子句，卻沒有主句，故句法不正確。

2. 表示「矛盾」的從屬子句可以放在句首，表示「但是」的從屬子句則不可。

例：（○）Although he was already full, he kept eating.
（雖然他已經飽了，他還是繼續吃著。）
（X）<u>But</u> he kept eating, he was already full.

> but引導的副詞子句不可放在句首。

馬上動手練一練 ❾

圈出正確的連接詞，以完成句子

1. (But/Although) they have five children, they don't live with any of them.

2. She has slept for twelve hours, (but/even though) she still feels tired.

3. Gary insisted on going to work (but/even though) it was extremely stormy.

4. (While/But) everyone suggested that he should choose the Harvard, Michael decided to go to the Yale.

5. He kept on working (though/but) he was already exhausted.

ANSWER

1. Although　　　2. but　　　3. even though
4. While　　　　5. though

◆表示條件

if（如果）	as long as （只要）
unless（除非）	once （一旦）

　　引導「條件句」的連接詞，用來表示「在某種情況存在」的條件下，才會發生主句所描述的動作或事件。

❶ if

例：• The global warming will get only worse **if** we don't cut carbon emissions. （如果我們不減少碳排放量，全球暖化的問題只會變得更嚴重。）

• Mom will be very angry **if** she finds us not writing our homework.
（媽媽如果發現我們沒有在寫功課，將會非常生氣。）

❷ as long as/once

例：• You can purchase alcohol **as long as** you are 18 years old.
= You can purchase alcohol **once** you are 18 years old.
（只要你十八歲，就可以買酒精類飲料。）

❸ unless

unless當主句中有not，才會用unless引導表示「條件」的副詞子句，表示「除非……」，否則主句不可能成立。

例：• **Unless** it stops raining, I will **not** go out.
（除非停止下雨，否則我不會出門。）

• I will **never** talk to you again **unless** you apologize for what just said. （除非你為你剛剛說的話道歉，否則我不會再跟你說話。）

引導表示「除非」的條件句的連接詞，除了unless還有only if/only when（只有當……時）。
unless要修飾的主句中，要有否定含義的字，如no, not等；only if/when要修飾的主句則不需要有否定含義的字。

例：• You will **not** get better **unless** you get enough rest.
（除非你有足夠的休息，否則你不會好轉。）

• You will get better **only if/only when** you get enough rest.（只有當你得到足夠休息時，你才有可能好轉。）

or及**otherwise**指「否則，要不然」，引導一個「可能結果」的副詞子句，通常有「威脅警告」的含義。要注意的是，unless與or/otherwise不能同時使用在同一個句子中。

例：• You need to apologize to her, **or/otherwise** she will not forgive you.
（你必須向她道歉，否則她不會原諒你。）

(X) <u>Unless</u> you apologize to her, <u>or</u> she will not forgive you.

> 一個句子不能有兩個副詞子句，卻沒有主句

★unless引導的副詞子句可以放句首，or/otherwise引導「可能結果」的副詞子句則不可放句首。

例：• Unless you have my permission, you can't use my cellphone.
（除非你有我的同意，否則不能用我的手機。）

(X) ~~Otherwise you can't use my cellphone~~, you need to have my permission.

> otherwise引導的副詞子句，不能放句首。

◎以現在式取代未來式的副詞子句

由**when, before, after, until, if, unless, as soon as**引導的附屬子句，涉及「未來才會發生的動作」，由於這是屬於「無法控制的未來」，因此以現在簡單式取代未來式。

例：• We always go camping **when** we <u>have</u> a long weekend.
（每當有連假時，我們總是會去露營。）

• Please call me **as soon as** he <u>arrives</u>.
（他一到，就請打給我。）

• Let's finish the cleaning **before** Mom <u>comes</u> back.
（我們在媽媽回來之前，把打掃完成吧。）

描述過去發生的事情時，用過去簡單式。

例：• He didn't go to sleep **until** his mom <u>asked</u> him to.
（一直到他媽媽叫他去睡覺，他才去。）

馬上動手練一練 ❿

圈出正確的連接詞，以完成句子

1. You will get well soon (as long as/as soon as) you follow the doctor's advice.

2. Mr. Chen won't let you take a leave (once/unless) you find someone to cover your shift.

3. My father said that I could drive his car (once/unless) I got a driver's license.

4. Don't try my patience; (as long as/otherwise), it will wear out very soon.

5. (As long as/Otherwise) it is within our budget, you can decide whether to buy it or not.

ANSWER

1. as long as
2. unless
3. once
4. otherwise
5. As long as

Lesson 17 文法總複習

快來試試自己的實力吧！

A. 選擇題

1. (   ) Not only Uncle Jack but also Aunt Lily _____ coming for dinner.
   A. are   B. is   C. were   D. be

2. (   ) Leave me alone, _____ I'll call the police.
   A. for   B. and   C. or   D. but

3. (   ) Jack's father is an American and his mother is a Chinese, so both Mandarin and English _____ Jack's first languages.
   A. are   B. is   C. have been   D. is

4. (   ) Neither Paul nor Jeff _____ an alibi for the night when the woman was killed.
   A. have   B. having   C. had had   D. has

5. (   ) There's only one opening in the bank. _____ Nina or Lisa will be employed.
   A. Either   B. Neither   C. Both   D. Not only

6. (   ) His face turned red _____ anger.
   A. because   B. otherwise   C. because of   D. in case of

7. (   ) _____ she could look after her mother 24/7, she quit her full-time job.
   A. So that   B. In order that C. So as   D. In order to

8. (　) _____ Mom and Dad don't like shopping, we'll just go sightseeing.

   A. Since　　B. So　　　　C. Therefore　　　D. In order that

9. (　) I got poor grades _____ I didn't study at all.

   A. that　　　B. because　　C. so　　　　　　D. in order to

10. (　) This project is not practical _____ time- saving.

   A. nor　　　B. or　　　　C. and　　　　　　D. but

B. 配合題

(a) not only (b) and (c) but (d) nor (e) either (f) both (g) but also	1. Neither Jack ___ Sam volunteered to help, so I asked ___ of them to. 2. You never lose. You ___ win or learn. 3. I am really full right now. I had ___ a bowl of beef noodles ___ ten dumplings for lunch. 4. The speech is boring ___ informative. 5. Steven has double majors in college. He majors in Computer Engineering ___ Electrical Engineering

ANSWER

A. 選擇題

1. **B**　2. **C**　3. **A**　4. **D**　5. **A**

6. **C**　7. **B**　8. **A**　9. **B**　10. **A**

1. 最靠近的主詞為Aunt Lily，故使用is

2. or在此表達否則

3. Both... and...（兩者都，既……且……）
   Both Harvard and Stanford have sent me admission offer letters.
   （哈佛與史丹福都寄給我入學許可信。）

4. 最靠近的主格為Jeff故使用has

5. Either...or...（不是……就是……；……或……），表示「兩者其中之一」不是Nina就是Lisa會被錄取

6. because of 由於／因為＋名詞

7. In order that＋子句（為了要……）

8. Since因為＋子句

9. because因為＋子句
   我考試沒考好因為我完全沒讀書

10. not...nor兩者皆否，既不實際又不省時

B. 配合題

1. (d)　(f)

2. (e)

3. (a)　(g)

4. (c)

5. (b)

原來如此 系列 E267

零基礎自學王：文法心智圖快速學、輕鬆記！
詞類句型、多元題目，速成英語文法體系！

圖像結合文字，一張圖總結文法重點，最實用的致勝17堂課！

作　　者	蔡文宜
社　　長	王毓芳
顧　　問	曾文旭
編輯統籌	耿文國、黃璽宇
主　　編	吳靜宜
執行主編	潘妍潔
執行編輯	吳芸蓁、吳欣蓉
美術編輯	王桂芳、張嘉容
封面設計	盧穎作
法律顧問	北辰著作權事務所　蕭雄淋律師、幸秋妙律師

初　　版	2023年11月
出　　版	捷徑文化出版事業有限公司
電　　話	（02）2752-5618
傳　　真	（02）2752-5619

定　　價	新台幣380元／港幣127元
產品內容	1書

總 經 銷	采舍國際有限公司
地　　址	235新北市中和區中山路二段366巷10號3樓
電　　話	（02）8245-8786
傳　　真	（02）8245-8718

港澳地區經銷商	和平圖書有限公司
地　　址	香港柴灣嘉業街12號百樂門大廈17樓
電　　話	（852）2804-6687
傳　　真	（852）2804-6409

▶本書部分圖片由 Shutterstock、freepik 圖庫提供。

捷徑Book站

國家圖書館出版品預行編目資料

零基礎自學王：文法心智圖快速學、輕鬆記！
詞類句型、多元題目，速成英語文法體系！ /
蔡文宜著. -- 初版. -- 臺北市：捷徑文化出版事業
有限公司, 2023.11
　面； 公分. （原來如此：E267）
ISBN 978-626-7116-44-9(平裝)
1.CST: 英語　2.CST: 語法
805.16　　　　　　　　　　　112015509